SHARON MILLER IS INVISIBLE

Susan Pajewski

ISBN-13: 9781738290802

Publisher: Purple Mushroom Publishing, Calgary, Canada

This book is dedicated to the memory of my beloved parents Tobe and Issak Pajewski.

CONTENTS

CHAPTER 1

Sharon was sitting at the airport boarding gate with her husband, daughter, and large pregnant stomach when the unexpected happened. There he was, standing a short distance away, the man whom she had loved more than life itself. She blinked in surprise. Surely, it could not be him. He didn't even live in Montreal. What was he doing here?

She watched him waiting in line for his coffee and studied his face. A little grey had crept into the curly black hair but otherwise he looked the same. He was as handsome as ever. It had been five years since she had last seen him. The relationship had ended badly. Would he notice her? Should she go up to him and say hello?

As she wondered, she reflected on her own life. Her husband was not the person she had wanted. She fiercely loved her daughter and her soon-to-be child and realized with sadness that she would never leave him. They had made a deal that bound them together forever. Sometimes she felt she had made a deal with the devil. She rubbed at her sore wrist and noticed it was still a bit bruised.

Sharon glanced at her husband beside her. He sat and read the paper. He looked as sexy as the day she met him. People would believe that Sharon was lucky to have him. He doted on his family. His career was thriving. They had a beautiful home. They were on their way to a wonderful winter holiday in Florida. The people who envied Sharon did not know the real story.

She wondered again if she should say hello to her former lover and decided against it. Instead, she stood and watched him pick up his coffee and walk away into the distance. She wanted to scream, wanted to follow him, wanted to say, “I made a mistake. I love you. I want you back,” but she didn’t. She sat silently and felt a tear run down her face.

CHAPTER 2

Sharon was running as quickly as she could. Trees formed a thick canopy around her and branches scratched her face and her lungs hurt but she had to get to her destination. She could see her sister Mimi standing at the edge of the cliff. Mimi seemed calm but Sharon was not fooled, even for an instant. She knew that Mimi was going to fall.

She yelled, "Mimi be careful!" over and over but Mimi did not seem to hear her.

Sharon stood alone looking at the beautiful scenery, not realizing that she was in danger. As quickly as Sharon ran, she could not get closer to her beloved sister. She saw Mimi standing and smiling, her chestnut hair blowing in the breeze, her slim frame relaxed and innocent. Before she could get to Mimi, a strange man came and stood next to her and hugged her passionately. Then the unthinkable happened. He pushed Mimi off the cliff. Sharon saw her sister's look of shock and started screaming.

She woke in a pool of fear and sweat. In the bed beside hers, Mimi was sleeping soundly, snoring quietly. Sharon was too shaken to sleep. She walked to the kitchen to drink some water and calm down. She found half a chocolate fudge cake in the fridge and sliced herself a huge piece and sat eating and wondering why she always soothed herself with food. Still feeling stressed, she then ate another piece. She always ate too much. This is why she was so heavy and Mimi was so slim.

This was not the first time she had had this dream. It was never exactly the same. Mimi was always in danger. Sharon would always try to rescue her and the same man would always kill her.

Sharon did not tell this dream to anyone. She knew that they would all think she was crazy. She knew she was crazy but she loved her sister so much and couldn't seem to save her no matter what she did.

At age 13, Sharon knew two things to be true. The first was that she could not stop eating. The second was that she would never measure up to her sister Mimi who was smart and beautiful while Sharon was a fat mess of anxiety and blubber. This was made worse by their mother's constant criticism which would send Sharon straight to the fridge.

"Why are you eating a third helping?" her mother would always say.

"No man will ever want you if you're fat," she would add.

Sharon already believed that no one would ever want her. The boys fawned over her sister and didn't know that she existed. She was basically invisible to everyone except Mimi and her parents.

Sharon Miller grew up so embedded in her sister's shadow that she almost ceased to exist. She would watch Mimi receive phone calls all the time while no one phoned her.

Her mother would yell, "Mimi phone call for you," whenever the phone rang.

Her mother would yell, "Mimi your swimming lesson starts at two."

Her mother would yell, "What is wrong with you Mimi?" whenever Mimi did not appease her.

So Sharon listened to her mother yelling for Mimi and noticed that Sylvia never yelled for her.

She would sneak food, leave the house whenever she wanted and lead an unsupervised life. This had its perks but she longed to be noticed by her mother. The only time her mother noticed her was when she ate too much at dinner.

She and Mimi did everything together. They shopped, watched

television, did each other's hair and laughed at private jokes that only the two of them understood. Their favourites were their "knock, knock" jokes.

Sharon would say, "Knock, knock."

Mimi, "Who's there?"

Sharon, "Tank you."

Mimi, "You're welcome."

This was one of many of these jokes that made them laugh every day. The girls were equals when they were together but Sharon felt that her sister was so much better than she was.

Sharon watched Mimi from a place in the background as Mimi excelled at everything. She didn't mind. Mimi was still her best friend.

Their mother Sylvia was a bitter and hostile woman. She was always telling both girls about how they could do better than she did.

She would say, "Don't marry a man like your father, so you won't be miserable like I am."

Both Sharon and Mimi were shocked that their mother could say such horrible things about their father who hugged them every day and called them both "His sweetheart."

Sharon was afraid of her mother. Sylvia's rages could be triggered by anything. When Mimi did not get an A in math, Sylvia stated to yell at her.

"How is the hell did you get a B in math? This spoils your perfect record in school."

Mimi turned red and walked away in tears. Sharon wanted to beat her mother senseless.

Sharon would hear her mother saying horrible things to her father every day. One time, her parents were sitting in the den arguing. Sharon stood listening.

"I hate you Martin!"

"Why?"

"You forgot to reserve tickets for the play."

"That is hardly a reason to hate me."

"You disappoint me every day."

"Maybe you expect too much."

She was appalled and went to the kitchen to find food. She often hid when Mimi was not at home. She never felt safe. She thought her mother was crazy and she was terrified of her rage. She especially hated it when her mother picked on her father which was every moment of every day. Why had these two ill fitted people ever married?

CHAPTER 3

Sharon and Mimi grew into attractive and accomplished young women. Mimi was small boned and slim with long red silky hair. It was turning more to chestnut as she got older. Sharon towered over Mimi. She was very attractive in her own way but entirely differently from her sister. She was large boned with wide hips and large breasts. Her hair was a curly dark brown wild mop and her eyes were a golden shade of hazel. Her figure was full but she was not fat by any means. Their closeness remained as strong as ever. As adolescents, they still did everything together. They would take the bus to school together and come home together. Each had separate friends but none as close as their sister.

Sharon's grades were fine but not on par with her sister's. Sharon was used to being less smart than Mimi and it didn't bother either of them. The only person affected was their mother.

Sharon hated that Sylvia took everything that the girls did as an expression of their disdain for her. When her grades fell short, Sylvia believed that Sharon was doing this just to annoy her mother. When Mimi dyed her hair purple, Sylvia was again sure that this was a personal affront.

"They are just trying new things," Martin told her.

"Don't you remember what you were like when you were their age?"

"When I was their age, I did everything my mother told me to do," she remarked with a sad look on her face.

"Didn't you want to have more freedom?" Martin asked her.

"I never really thought of it," was her answer.

She was remembering how her mother had adored Martin and

so wanted her to marry him. Sylvia didn't have any doubts herself at the time. If only she knew then what she now realized. With a sigh, Sylvia came to the conclusion that she would have married Martin anyway.

Both girls preferred their father to their mother. He had an easygoing, forgiving manner. He called them both "my little sweethearts" which made Sylvia cringe.

Sylvia believed that Martin was way too permissive with the girls. When they asked him for something, his stock answer was, "Sure, why not?" How would they ever learn responsibility with an attitude like this from their father?

Their different parenting styles caused a major bone of contention in their marriage. Sylvia believed that the children needed strict limits. Martin believed that these were his two children and that he had the means to help them enjoy their lives. Why should he deny them anything?

"Don't be such a miser," Martin would say to Sylvia when the girls wanted something expensive.

"We have the money."

"Martin, how will the girls ever learn to have a work ethic if you give them everything?" she would ask him every time.

His answer was always the same.

"The girls will learn soon enough that it is hard to be an adult. Let them enjoy their childhood."

Martin liked to spend money on himself and every family member. He worked hard as an emergency room doctor and his experiences at work had taught him that life could be very short.

Sylvia had grown up in a family where money was preserved as much as possible. Both her parents were Holocaust survivors and they were always frightened. There was always the lingering fear that they might have to pack up and leave at a moment's notice. Money was good to have for these types of emergencies. She grew up with the belief that money should be hoarded. Her own mother had been very demanding.

During her childhood, Sylvia dreamed of a man that would free her from her crazy household. She dreamed of a future where she could buy whatever she wanted and did not have to justify it to anyone. She had this with Martin but she was still miserable.

"You will never be satisfied." Martin often told her.

She feared he was correct. Sylvia felt she could do better but didn't know how. She hated that Martin was so smugly satisfied with his life and blamed him for the fact that she was not.

She was rich in material wealth but poor in spirit and love. Her husband and daughters never quite measured up to her invisible standards.

The closest was Mimi, who was named after Sylvia's grandmother. She would be the shining star that brought the family out of the dark, or at least that was what Sylvia hoped. This is why Sylvia was harder on Mimi than on anyone else.

If Mimi came home with a B grade instead of an A, Sylvia would ask her,

"What is wrong with you?"

If Mimi stumbled at her piano recital, Sylvia would ask,

"What is wrong with you?"

When Mimi was having a bad day for any reason, her mother would ask,

"What is wrong with you?"

It became a family joke between the other three. They would walk around asking each other, "What is wrong with you?" They would make up interesting responses to the question.

Sharon would say, "I have the plague."

Her father would answer, "I have just the medicine for that."

Then all three would break into laughter.

Sylvia would listen to them and grind her teeth. Her whole

family was against her and she was all alone. She fought to keep the tears from forming in her eyes.

Both daughters were exceptional. They both received good grades and were really no trouble at all. They were sailing through their teenage years with hardly a wrinkle. This in itself worried Sylvia. Little did she know, everything was about to change in an instant.

CHAPTER 4. SHARON

I will never forget the day my sister Mimi and I met David Michaels. We were in high school. I was in the 10th grade and Mimi in the 11th. I was waiting at the entrance of our school for her. It was a freezing day in early December. I stood shivering in the chill and staring out at the blanket of snow on the streets wondering yet again whether winter would ever end. I was relieved that I had worn my really warm down parka and fuzzy paisley toque. Still, I was getting rather impatient as I awaited my sister. We always walked home together. Mimi was usually quite punctual so I was quite concerned when 15 minutes passed and she was still not there. Had something happened to her?

As usual, I was waiting at the school entrance for her. Impatiently, because it was a cold day in December and the chilly air bit through my gloved hands. Where in the world was she? Just as I was about to go inside, to wait in the heat of the hallway, she came bounding out the front doors, laughing.

"I'm coming, I'm coming," she called and looked behind her.

And there he was, though I didn't know it at the time, the man who would change my life—her life—our lives—forever. Curly brown hair, tall frame, sincere face. Oh my God, he was gorgeous. He stared at Mimi with a slight blush on his cheeks, eyes only for her.

"This is my sister Sharon," Mimi said, breathless.

She was breathless. And she, too, was pink-cheeked, flushed with —. Wait. Were they already in love?

"This is David Michaels. He's new in Montreal: he just moved here from Toronto."

"Welcome to Montreal," I said, then almost kicked myself for how lame it sounded.

"He's walking home with us," Mimi added.

But he didn't walk home with us. He walked home with Mimi. And she walked home with him. I trudged behind them, kicking at the ice formed at the edges of the piles of snow. I was miserable.

Mom wasn't home, thank goodness; she'd get mad at Mimi. I don't know why she cared so much about every little thing Mimi did and she wasn't going to like this. I didn't like it one bit either.

I'd lost my sister; I knew it already. I could see what the future was going to bring with this boy's intrusion. And not only had I lost her but I'd lost her to *this boy*. This boy that I already knew I wanted…for myself. How could I have fallen in love with him so quickly?

When we got home, Mimi invited him in for a snack. The three of us sat and watched "All my Children" on TV and gobbled down huge amounts of potato chips.

It was clear to me that I did not have a chance with him. Mimi and David were already a couple. I found out that he was an only child. His father was a professor who had recently started to do research at McGill University.

I was so relieved that our mother was not at home so she could not interrogate him. I knew this relationship between Mimi and David would be major and I dreaded my mother ever finding out about it. She had to find out soon and then she would be jealous. No one was allowed to come between her and her baby girl. She didn't want to share her precious hope for the future with anyone.

I wondered if my mother would ruin this relationship for Mimi. I somehow knew that she would try. My mother was scary. She was so possessive of Mimi. It was as if she owned her and her actions. As long as mom approved of something, it would be fine. However, mom would not approve of David. I knew it even then when we were all young and immature. This was going to be a major disaster. Our family was already a disaster. We didn't need any more drama.

CHAPTER 5

Sharon was right. It was a disaster.

Sylvia hated David from the moment she met him. There was something about him that got on her nerves. He had a sly smile and an easy manner that made him impossible to trust. He was smug. He was confident and smart and that posed a real threat to her. If she had been honest with herself, she would have admitted that her disdain for David had nothing l to do with him. She hated David because she knew as sure as anything that he would take Mimi away from her.

Somewhere deep inside she must have known this but she would never realize it consciously. So instead she made her daughter's life and relationship as difficult as possible. Even though Sylvia had no real reason for disapproving of David, she would still come up with snide remarks meant to undermine the relationship.

She would comment when he was late.

"He must have found someone else. You can't trust him, Mimi."

Mimi would reply, "Mind your own business mother."

Then she would storm out of the room.

Sharon observed this and marvelled at the way Mimi fought back. Sharon noticed that the bond between Mimi and David was growing stronger with every passing day. She watched him kiss Mimi and wished that it could be her instead. She imagined the taste of his lips on her skin. She imagined him kissing her all over. She watched him kissing Mimi and imagined that it was her he was kissing.

Sharon was so jealous of the relationship between Mimi and

David. She pretended that her teddy bear was David and smothered it with kisses. When she saw Mimi and David being affectionate she would go into a spiral of depression and start to eat everything in the fridge. She would overdo her eating until she felt sick.

After eating way too much she went to bed and fell into an uneasy sleep.

Sharon got out of bed slowly. She was tired and achy and wondered why. She had slept 12 hours the night before but she had had that dream again. Mimi was about to be eaten by a lion in this one and she could not help her. These dreams always left her feeling ill. Maybe that was it.

She saw her parents chatting in their bedroom.

Their bedroom door was open. Her mother was standing naked handing her father a cup of coffee. Sharon noticed how slim and fit her mother was and again felt upset about her own body. She was just too fat. Both other women in the family were slim but she was just a mass of fat.

Her mother was handing her father a coffee.

As they sipped their coffee, Sylvia started tentatively.

“Do you know that Mimi got accepted to every university she applied to?” This was a rhetorical question. Of course, he knew.

Sylvia continued, “She wants to go to McGill because it’s close to home. Don’t you think we should urge her to consider other options?” She knew very well that Mimi was keen on McGill University because David was already there.

“What’s wrong with McGill?” Martin asked her. “We both went there. It’s still considered one of the best in Canada.”

“There’s nothing wrong with it but maybe there is somewhere better for her. The University of British Columbia has an excellent science program.”

“Are you sure you want her to have better schooling or to be further away from David?”

Her cheeks burned crimson red. Martin could always see right through her.

"Well, it did cross my mind that a bit of distance would do them good. She is only seventeen years old. She is too young to be so serious about a boy."

"I think she should go to whatever university she wants," Martin replied and walked to the closet to get his bathrobe.

He left the room before she could say another word.

Sharon quietly tiptoed away. She knew her mother was trying to get her father to agree so Mimi and David would be apart. The family sat and ate their breakfast together. Her parents did not say a word to each other. Everyone was used to these strained silences between them. On Sundays, Martin made pancakes for everyone. Mimi and Sharon sat and chatted while they downed huge portions of fluffy pancakes drowning in maple syrup and topped with whipped cream.

"Great pancakes, dad," Mimi told him.

"Anything for my two princesses," he said.

He truly felt that way. He adored them both.

Sharon and Mimi started to giggle.

Sharon noticed that Sylvia and Martin sat in silence as they often did. It was difficult for her to feel comfortable when there was so much animosity between them.

Martin asked over breakfast, "One of the doctors offered me tickets to the Ice Capades next week. Who would like to go with me?"

"I would, dad!" Mimi yelled.

"Me too, me too," Sharon added.

"How about you Sylvia?"

She did not respond. She was still angry about their last conversation and she thought that he indulged the girls too much.

Later that morning, she told him, “You are spoiling our daughters. They will become self-indulgent little princesses who never grow up. You are not respecting me by doing this.”

“My daughters are the best thing in my life. I will give them what ever they want that will make them happy. Surely you must understand that feeling deprived will not make them any better.”

Sylvia knew he was referring to her and her impoverished childhood. Certainly being deprived had not done her any good. Maybe he had a point. She just wasn't going to give him the satisfaction of admitting it.

CHAPTER 6

Sharon and Mimi were enjoying the sweltering, humid summer in Montreal. They sat in their bikinis on lounge chairs in their lavish backyard filled with blooming flowers and decided that they were in a resort. Each one applied baby oil to the other and they took out their sun reflectors to be sure they would get a suntan.

Sharon valued this time that they had alone. Mimi spent so much of her time with David that the closeness between the sisters was beginning to change. They still loved being together but Mimi found little time for her sister these days. Mimi would be starting university in the fall. She was a math wizard and would be majoring in math. She wanted to teach high school math. She had received a scholarship and the future was looking bright. Sharon was a bit jealous. Mimi had everything going for her – an amazing boyfriend and a scholarship to university while she was still in high school all alone.

"Some champagne dahhling?" Mimi asked her.

She held a frosted pitcher of ice tea in her hand.

"Don't mind if I do."

Mimi poured the ice tea into Sharon's glass.

"Let's go shopping later," Sharon said. This was a suggestion that she knew her sister would love.

"Sorry, but I promised David I would get together with him. We are going out for ice cream. Would you like to join us?"

"No, thanks. I think I will stay here in the backyard."

Sharon was tired of feeling like the third wheel in this

relationship. She didn't want to be dragged along out of pity yet again.

"I think I want to finish reading this book." She didn't really care about the book but this was as good an excuse as any.

"Okay suit yourself. I am going for a shower. Tell mom that I went out with David when she comes home."

"Okay."

Sharon sat alone in the lush backyard feeling sorry for herself. She was losing her sister to David. She felt miserable about this and even worse about her feelings for him. Whenever she saw him, she wondered how such a perfect person could even exist. He was so loving and caring to Mimi. Sharon wanted that love from him and it saddened her soul. She would never try to steal him from Mimi. She decided that she needed to find someone of her own. It would have to be someone as perfect as David. She reasoned that if one perfect man existed, there must be others. Come to think of it, her father was almost perfect. He put up with her crazy neurotic mother with patience and love. Surely, there was one more perfect soul for her to love out there somewhere. Maybe she could find him. She was only 15 years old. There was lots of time for love. Right now she would finish that book and then go raid the fridge. There was a large tub of chocolate ice cream in the freezer. That was bound to make her feel better.

She heard her parents' raised voices before she even walked into the house.

Inside the large palatial air-conditioned house they lived in, Sylvia and Martin were having yet another heated argument. They sat in their kitchen fighting yet again about Mimi.

"She should be dating other people. She is way too young to be so seriously involved with one boy."

"Sylvia, leave this alone. It is none of our business."

"I am afraid she will get herself into a difficult situation."

"What situation is that? Are you afraid that she will become pregnant and have to marry him the way you had to marry me?"

"No, I believe that she needs to concentrate on university and finding a career." Sylvia had always regretted the fact that she had dropped out of university when she got married.

Unbeknownst to them, Sharon was standing beside the kitchen listening to their entire conversation. She stood there stunned and rooted to the spot. Her parents had never mentioned that they had to get married. So, precious Mimi might have been a bastard, she thought. She now understood why two such mismatched people had gotten together but why did they stay together? Divorce was easily available in 1979 and her parents were miserable.

The question in her mind was whether she should tell Mimi. Would it serve a purpose or simply make her sister feel bad? She completely forgot about the tub of ice cream waiting for her in the freezer. She quietly walked up the stairs to her bedroom and plopped down on her bed, forgetting that she was covered with baby oil and would make a mess. She was processing a huge secret that had smacked her in the face. What should she do with it? She realized very quickly that telling Mimi would cause sadness and shame to everyone involved. She decided to keep this secret until the day she died.

CHAPTER 7

Sharon was feeling concerned about her mother. She could see that Sylvia was having one of her difficult days. On these days, her mother hardly seemed able to get out of bed. No one could even talk to her.

As Sharon made lunch, she could see that Sylvia was in trouble. It was already noon and she was still moping around the house in her bathrobe. Martin was out of town at a conference.

"The summer will soon be over and all of our flowers will wither and die," her mom told her.

"I feel as if I am going to wither and die too."

Sharon didn't know what to say. Her mother always loved to make lunch and now she was sitting at the table wearing a ratty bathrobe and talking about withering and death. Sylvia put on the air of a confident woman but inside she was still a frightened little girl.

"Would you like a grilled cheese sandwich?" Sharon didn't know what else to say. Her 16-year-old mind was not equipped to deal with this type of statement.

"My mother is telling me that I am in trouble. She is saying that I should do better."

Sharon was confused. Grandma Fredelle had died many years ago. How was she speaking to her mother?

"Your sister is in trouble and I can't help her. You are smart and level-headed and Mimi is reckless. She is involved with the wrong man."

These words left Sharon so stunned that she almost burnt her sandwich. She took it out of the hot frying pan just in the nick of time. She was so stunned that her mother had said something kind about her.

She watched as her mother opened the French doors that led to their backyard deck and found a comfortable lawn chair to stretch out on. She hoped that the sun on her face would warm her and cheer her up. Her mother always felt more relaxed in the sun.

Always one who cared about her appearance, Sylvia was shocked that she did not even give a damn that she was still in her bathrobe and her hair was uncombed. She knew that if she stayed like this, her daughters would stay far away from her. She was so tired of pleading with Mimi not to make a mistake. She was so tired of Martin not being on her side in this issue. Come to think of it, she was exhausted. As the sun warmed her face, she fell into a deep dreamless slumber.

CHAPTER 8

September continued hot and muggy in Montreal. The sun was still relentless, the heat stifling. Sharon felt as if she could fry eggs on the sidewalk. The drops of perspiration ran down her face as she stood by the door and said goodbye to Mimi. Today was Mimi's first day of university. She and Sharon had discussed it in detail. Mimi had decided that she would get a degree in education and teach high school mathematics.

Mimi told Sharon earlier that day,

"This is the beginning of a new phase in my life. I am not quite an adult but well on my way. I am hoping that soon I can move out of our parents' house into a small apartment in the student ghetto area."

"I know mom would disapprove. I can hear her saying, 'Why do you need to move out? You have everything you need at home,' " Sharon said with a chuckle but they both thought it was not very funny.

Sharon knew that her mother would go nuts when she found out that Mimi was planning to move. Maybe she could move to the Arctic so she wouldn't hear her mother screaming.

Mimi continued, "If I managed to move out, I could finally spend some time with David without mom interfering all the time. I am so tired of the constant arguing. I can't understand why mom is so unhappy about this relationship."

Sharon remembered the conversation that she had overheard. Sylvia was afraid that Mimi would wind up in the same position as she was: pregnant and married to the wrong person.

Sharon looked at Mimi with love and sadness. Mimi was full of the idealism that was so prevalent in the very young. She had the belief in happily ever after. She truly felt that she would eventually marry David and live in a state of bliss forever. They would have a beautiful home and wonderful children. Their lives would be blessed in every way. She was too young and naive to know the expression: people make plans and God laughs. If she did, she might not feel so secure and hopeful. She might instead start screaming.

CHAPTER 9

Another fall and winter passed. The spring was stunning that year. The maple trees glowed with new buds. The buds sparkled in the bright sunshine. The air was mild and the sun was warm and gentle. Mimi was loving both university and David and still dreaming of moving out on her own. Sharon was deciding which universities to apply to for the following year. The problem was that she really didn't know what she wanted to do. No profession called to her. Should she take a year off and travel? She knew her mother would have a fit if she did that. Sylvia and Martin were still not seeing eye to eye on most things. Life went on as usual. However, a huge change was on its way.

On March 21, the first day of spring, and also Mimi's 19th birthday, Mimi and David announced that they were getting married. They were all sitting at the grand dining room table in Sylvia and Martin's home. Sylvia, an excellent cook, had gone out of her way to make a delicious birthday dinner. It was a family tradition to have birthday dinners at home. David and Mimi were sitting at the dining room table having dinner with Sylvia, Martin, and Sharon. They had just finished a Waldorf salad and they were about to have some prime rib which smelled like garlic and rosemary.

Mimi couldn't wait any longer.

She blurted out, "David and I are engaged. We are getting married after I finish school."

"We need to wait until I finish university and David finishes medical school. We will get married in two years."

"How will you support yourselves?" was the first question Sylvia asked them. Martin sat at the massive oak dining table and wondered the same thing.

"I will have a job by then," Mimi answered, "and David will be finished medical school."

"We will get by just fine," David responded.

"Why don't you live here until you finish medical school?" the ever generous Martin blurted out.

As soon as he finished saying it, he knew that he had made a huge mistake. Sylvia glared at him with daggers in her eyes. Mimi and David looked downright embarrassed by this offer.

"No, thank you," David said, "You are very kind but we have to make our own way."

The topic was closed for now but it hung over everyone's heads like a black cloud during the entire meal.

After they finished their chocolate fudge birthday cake and coffee, Mimi and David quickly excused themselves and went out for a walk.

Sharon, knowing a fight was brewing, said she had some homework to do and quickly left the table. It was going to be seconds until Sylvia attacked and she didn't want to be there for the carnage.

"What the hell did you think you were doing telling them that they could live here?" Sylvia shrieked at Martin.

"She is our daughter. If she and her husband need help, we can give it to them. I am happy to support them until they finish school. We can certainly afford it. Why are you so upset?"

"This was not an offer for you to make without consulting me. This is my house too. Besides, you know I can't stand that boy."

Sharon turned on some rock music full blast but it still did not drown out her mother's screechy voice.

David was 22 but Sylvia still thought of him as that boy. It was bad enough that Mimi was marrying that boy but she wouldn't have them living in her house. Martin was insane if he thought she would put up with it.

“He is a fine young man. He treats our daughter very well. There is no reason for you to hate him. He has done you no harm.”

“Don’t you dare tell me who I can like or hate you smug bastard,” she added and stormed out of the room leaving him angry and confused.

Sharon sat upstairs on her bed and listened to the argument between her parents. She had heard it so many times before and it made her quite weary. What really rankled her was the fact that everything was about her sister. Mimi was expected to do well in school. Mimi was expected to marry well. What about her? Was anything expected of her? Both her parents had made such a fuss about the fact that Mimi had been accepted into so many universities. No one had even asked Sharon what university she was applying to. She had all of these acceptance letters and neither parent even knew about them. When Sharon brought home a boy, her parents were friendly and vague. It was as if it just didn’t matter. Sharon felt like she didn’t exist to her family except in Mimi’s shadow. Even Mimi had deserted her. University and David had taken her place. For the first time in her life, she felt all alone. For the first time in her life, she felt truly invisible.

After her parents left the kitchen, she sneaked in and cut herself some leftover roast and a slice of lemon meringue pie. She knew she was eating because of stress but she didn’t care. Being the one who didn’t matter to anyone was difficult. If she had to eat to soothe herself, so be it.

CHAPTER 10. SHARON

I think my mother is losing her mind. She has always been a bit crazy but it is so much worse since Mimi and David got engaged. It is like she is on a personal quest to make everyone's life as miserable as her own.

She has always picked on my poor dad but lately she is horrible. He can't say or do anything without her exploding at him like he is a monster. She is lucky to have him but she doesn't think so. What other man would put up with her crap? He has been taking extra shifts in the emergency room lately. I think he is trying to stay out of the house as much as possible.

She is even worse to Mimi. She criticizes everything that Mimi does and keeps telling her not to marry David. She is rude to David. She hung up on him the other day when he phoned. I think that she has a convoluted idea that she can still break them up. If you ask me, she will just wind up alienating them. After they are married, they will never come over again. I really feel for them but what can I do? Mother never listens to anyone. She should really see a psychiatrist but if you told her this she would probably kill you.

As for me, I guess that I am the lucky one. Mom pretty well ignores me like she has always done. I don't mind because I can get away with whatever I want to do. There are no consequences for me.

Last week, I sneaked out of the house to go to a party where everyone was smoking pot. I came home late and stoned and she didn't even notice. The smell of marijuana was still in the hallways the next day but mom is in such a funk about Mimi that she did not notice the smell. This is strange because she usually has a nose like a bloodhound.

I am looking forward to the summer. I can come and go as I please and stay out as long as I like. My friends are having lots of parties and pot is always on the menu. This summer my two goals are to get tanned and get stoned as often as possible. I may even get myself a boyfriend. Paul Green who I met at a recent party has been asking me out and I just may say yes.

My feelings for David kept getting in the way. Every time I meet someone, I mentally compare him to David and he always falls short. Well, Paul is nothing like David in looks or personality. He is short and dark and intense, and I am beginning to like that look. I was worried that my mother might ruin the summer but I may just have a good time after all. It sometimes pays to be invisible.

Mom has done something so crazy that I think Mimi will never speak to her again. Mom's childhood friend Linda was in town from London, England with her son Robert who is 21 and her daughter Monica who is 18. Mom went out for lunch with them and decided to invite them over for brunch the following Sunday.

Before brunch, mom talked a lot about them, about what a wonderful family they were. She especially talked about Robert and what a wonderful son he was to his mother. Mimi and I sat at the table with mom wondering what this was leading to. Mom always has an agenda.

Well, we couldn't believe it when mom said, "Mimi. Robert is just the type of man for you. He is sweet, kind, and intelligent. He is so much better than that good for nothing David."

At that point, we both stared at each other in shock. Mom was trying to set up Mimi, who was very much in love and engaged to be married to David, with someone else.

Mimi turned bright crimson and looked like she was going to ignite.

"What the hell is wrong with you? You are completely crazy. I am engaged. Why are you trying to introduce me to someone else?" she screamed so loud that people in another city could hear her.

She stormed out of the room and has not spoken to mom since. I can't say I blame her. She was absent from the lavish brunch my mom threw for them.

I looked at the spread of bagels, smoked salmon and cream cheese, and the various salads and canapés on the table. And I indulged. I chatted with Robert who was nice enough but not even close to being as good as David.

Two weeks have passed and Mimi has still not spoken a word to mom. I wonder how long this will go on. Mom has made Mimi's favourite foods and tried as much as she can to be friendly but Mimi just storms out of the room. If it wasn't so pathetic, it would be funny.

Don't get me wrong. My family is about as screwed up as it gets. My mother is definitely a candidate for the mental ward. She has no boundaries as far as Mimi is concerned. She feels that she should do whatever is necessary to protect Mimi. I am afraid she will lock Mimi in her room on her wedding day to try to keep her from getting married. She has gone too far in her latest endeavour.

I heard my dad yelling at her the other night. He was telling her in no uncertain terms,

"Leave Mimi alone or we will lose her. Leave her alone!"

I doubt that she was listening to a word he said.

I heard my mom respond, "We have already lost her to that horrible boy."

"What do I need to do to get you to stop interfering?"

"She is our child, Martin. Don't you love her?"

"Because I love her, I trust her to make her own decisions."

Their voices trailed off and I couldn't hear them anymore.

Mom has crossed the line this time and she will not be able to come back so easily. What was she thinking? Boy oh boy, I wish our family life was a little less exciting.

CHAPTER 11

Sharon was surprised that Mimi was holding a grudge for such a long time. She and Mimi often fought and forgave each other almost immediately. She had even confessed to Mimi that she was in love with David.

One day over ice cream with chocolate syrup on top, she told Mimi, "I have a major crush on David."

Mimi shrugged and said, "Don't we all." That was the end of that conversation.

Mimi could not forgive her mother for what she had done. She could not even look at her mother anymore. She felt revulsion bordering on nausea whenever Sylvia was in the room. Mimi felt that this was a turning point in her life. Before, she had put up with her mother's lack of boundaries but she could not do so anymore.

She decided she was moving out of the house into her own apartment. She had not finished university yet but it didn't matter at this point. It was impossible to stay at home.

"Please don't go," Sharon begged her, "or mom will have only me to pick on."

"I think you should reconsider," her father told her and added, "I fully understand how you feel. I will help you out financially if you need it."

Mimi noticed he was looking a little grey around the edges. She wondered how he was enduring his life sentence with her mother. She thought that her father should be nominated for sainthood simply for being as patient as he was with Sylvia.

Martin told Sylvia, "Mimi is moving out. See what you've done now."

"She will be back. She has no money," was Sylvia's only reply but she really didn't feel so confident.

Sylvia was feeling shattered since Mimi had stopped talking to her. She thought it was temporary but it had lasted two months already. Now Mimi was going to leave and she might never see her again. This was enough to send Sylvia into a panic state. She cried all the time. She lost her appetite and picked on Martin even more than usual. She knew that she was in a downward spiral but did not have a clue as to what to do about it.

Sharon and Martin both noticed this. They were afraid to say anything to her. Eventually Sharon convinced her father to talk to her mother. She herself was terrified to do so.

Sylvia's depression was worse than her wrath. She became so still that she was almost catatonic. "You need to see someone and get some counselling," Martin said to her one evening. They were sitting at the table with Sharon. Sylvia had made a lovely roast chicken with scalloped potatoes and lemon green beans but she was hardly touching her food. Martin had noticed that she was getting rail thin lately. She had red swollen eyes and she wore an old faded T-shirt and sweat pants. She looked like a woman who had given up on herself.

He expected a snide remark from her but she said, "Do you know anyone I could speak to?"

"I will find out," he told her and reached out to take her hand. It felt icy to his touch. Despite himself, seeing her this way broke his heart. Martin often wondered if he still had any love left for his wife. Tonight he knew he still loved her because he was terrified for her. She was lower than he had ever seen her. He would find a good therapist for her and soon.

Sharon was shocked that her mother had agreed to a therapist and decided that there was some hope. A month later, Sharon watched Mimi pack her bags to leave. She had found an apartment with two other students who were looking for a new roommate. The room was furnished and shabby but clean. It had a bed, desk, and chair. This was more than enough for Mimi.

Sharon was shocked that Mimi's grudge was still going on. Mimi had still not said a word to her mother and was planning to stay this way. Sylvia had approached her several times and asked her to reconsider. She had even apologized which was a rarity for her. Nothing had swayed Mimi even slightly to forgive her mother or resume their relationship.

So, on a sweltering September afternoon, Martin drove Mimi to her new apartment. It was in the McGill University student ghetto, within easy walking distance of school. There was everything she needed in easy proximity.

As Martin walked Mimi up the stairs, he was appalled at the old rickety building.

"Please forgive your mother and come home," he pleaded with her.

"I am sorry dad but I can't."

When he hugged her goodbye, she fought not to burst into tears. Her father looked so old and tired that it broke her heart. She loved him almost as much as she hated her mother.

She could not return to that situation. She was finally free to lead her own life. It would be difficult but she would do it.

Martin pressed an envelope into her palm as he left. She opened it and found it full of hundred dollar bills. It was only after her had left that she fell on her bed and started to cry. She cried like a burst dam. Everything her mother had done to hurt her flowed through her avalanche of tears. It felt as if she cried forever, Then she went to the neighbourhood grocery store to buy some bread and cheese.

She came back to the apartment and chatted with her new roommates over grilled cheese sandwiches that she made for everyone. She felt happy for the first time in months. Everything was going to be fine after all.

On the other side of town, in the posh area of Westmount, Martin stood and stared at his sleeping wife. It was late afternoon and Sylvia was in bed in a deep and weary slumber. She had slept most of the day, gotten up for some water and gone back to bed. Now she was sleeping soundly. She looked very stressed even in her sleep. Her face was furrowed into a frown and her eyes were red and puffy from crying. Her flannel pyjamas hung on her as if she was a skeleton. Her hair was dry and lifeless. He did not know what to do.

He walked to Sharon's room and knocked on the door. She was reading a book and listening to music on her Walkman.

"How's mom?" she asked him.

"Sleeping. Should we go out for pizza?"

It was nearing dinnertime and his stomach was rumbling.

"Sure, I'll be ready in a minute."

As they sat and chewed on delicious slices of cheesy gooey pizza topped with crispy onions, peppers and mushrooms, life seemed like it was fine even if just for a minute. All was blissful until they talked about Sylvia.

"Mom is a mess," Sharon told her father.

"Yes," he agreed, "I have seen her depressed but never this much. I don't know what to do about it."

"Maybe she should see a shrink," Sharon told him. "Do you know anyone that might be good?" Martin knew many medical professionals including a vast array of psychologists and psychiatrists. He remembered that Sylvia had asked him about a therapist a while ago but he had not acted on it.

"I don't think she'll go," he told Sharon."I have tried to steer her in that direction before. She says she will go and backs out at the last minute."

"She can't go on this way, dad," Sharon sighed heavily. She felt like she was the parent and her mother was the child.

"She has lost so much weight and spends all of her time sleeping. I am afraid she is going to die."

Martin was at a loss for words. He honestly did not know what to do to help Sylvia out of this deep and disabling depression. Sharon's words had completely described his feelings. What should they do?

"Maybe we could get Mimi to talk to her again," Sharon said with too much brightness in her voice.

"Remember the last few months of Mimi living here? She is furious with your mother and for good reason. I don't know what we can say or do to help Mimi forgive her."

"Mimi and I are getting together on Friday for lunch. I will talk to her about mom. Maybe I can get through to her."

Martin said, "Try your best, sweetie." He was sure that Sharon was the only one who could get through to Mimi.

The next day was a bright and beautiful Sunday. The September day dawned warm and breezy. There was just a hint of fall in the air. These were the days Sylvia loved best and Martin had a plan. He woke up at 9:00 am and went to the kitchen. There he made some French toast with powdered sugar and strawberries on top and some coffee. He put it on a tray and carried it up to the bedroom. Sylvia was still asleep but not for long. He opened the blinds and sunlight streamed into the room.

"Wakey, wakey," he said but she would not stir.

"I made your favourite breakfast" he continued but she still would not stir. Sharon heard this from her room and wondered if her mother would ever recover.

The next day Martin tried to convince her to see a therapist.

"You are very depressed," he said. "You have lost weight and you are spending all your time moping around. This is not going to help you in any way. I asked you before about speaking to a professional. Talk to a therapist. He will help you feel better."

"I want Mimi back," she told him in a quivering voice.

"You have a much better chance of doing that if you are feeling better," he answered but he did not really believe what he was saying. He had spoken to Mimi numerous times and she wanted nothing to do with her mother now or ever.

"If you think it might help, I will see a therapist." she said in a quiet voice.

"I am so happy you are doing this!" he said. They were sitting at the kitchen table where they had most of their serious conversations. Sylvia had made supper but again eaten almost nothing. She had picked at her food. It was as if she had lost the will to live. Martin hoped that if she received some help, she would also learn how to deal better with both her daughters and with him. He felt a desperate for Sylvia to get help. Everyone in the family needed this as badly as Sylvia did.

CHAPTER 12. SHARON

I don't know how the hell he did it but dad convinced mom to see a shrink. He's not actually a shrink – he's a psychologist. His name is Dr. Wellman which I think is hilarious. I hope he can make my mother well. Personally, I don't think there is a cure for her craziness. Her mother was just as crazy. If it weren't for her own mother scaring her about everything and teaching her to worry about everything, she would have a chance. I think her mother put crazy ideas into mom's head. It must have been difficult being a Holocaust survivor and passing that on to her only child. Maybe Dr. Wellman can teach my mother how to break away from her own mother's craziness This way she can have a decent relationship with both me and Mimi and maybe even my dad.

What kind of mother is she really? She pays all of her attention to Mimi and mostly just ignores me. This used to really bother me but I have now realized that it enables me to do exactly what I please. Besides, I still think that Mimi will never talk to her again. Last week, Mimi and I met for lunch at McGill University. I can't believe I have finally started university. Mimi told me that she still wants nothing to do with mom. It has been six months since mom tried her crazy stunt. Mimi also told me that she and David may get married sooner. They may just have a quiet wedding this spring with a few close people including me and dad. She is not planning to invite mom. That should go over like a lead pipe cracking open a head.

I am majoring in education at university. I want to teach high school English I think. Mimi is majoring in education as well. She wants to teach high school math. She is of course doing great as she does in everything. She gets scholarships every year. This is no great surprise to me. She excels at everything.

As we were gobbling down our smoked meat sandwiches last week, I noticed that my sister had transformed from a girl into a woman. Her sweet face and figure have somehow elongated and she has gone from being pretty to being beautiful. Her sparking blue eyes and stunning smile help a lot. I think she is much happier without mom in her life. And there is David. He is definitely the love of her life. Whenever she mentions him, her whole body lights up. I am envious that she has found someone who will love her for her whole life. I wonder if she realizes just how lucky she is.

David is always so attentive to her. It is as if he knows what she wants before she even tells him. When she is with him, he is completely focused on her. It is as if nothing exists outside their little twosome. He encourages her and he is always on her side. That seems to be the kind of loyalty you would get only from a dog. He is her personal lapdog and he loves her unconditionally.

I would never make a move on him but I wish I could meet someone even half as decent. The boys I meet are all immature. All they want to do is smoke pot and have sex. They are silly little boys while David is a mature man.

I just realized how much like my father David is. They share so many qualities both mental and physical. They are both tall and lean and smart. They are both kind and loving. They like many of the same things. This is probably why mom hates David. I wonder what Freud would have to say about that.

CHAPTER 13

Sharon and Martin were both surprised and delighted that Sylvia was actually seeing Dr. Wellman. Even after she agreed, they didn't believe that she would go through with it. Sharon was sure that her mother would back out of her appointments at the last minute. She had gone for two appointments and scheduled a third. As they all sat across from each other at the breakfast table, Sharon was alarmed by how she looked. Her face was gaunt and her eyes were bloodshot and rimmed by dark circles. She had lost too much weight and was looking like a skeleton with her clothing hanging on her. She was barely picking at her oatmeal. Sharon had made it for her just the way she liked it – with lots of cream, brown sugar and raspberries. She could see that eating was an effort for her.

"How's your oatmeal?" she asked.

"Delicious," she said with no expression in her voice.

"Would you like something else?" she asked.

"No this is great," she insisted.

"Would you like to go out for Greek food tonight?" Martin asked.

He knew this was her favourite.

"I'm not really in the mood to go out."

"I would love some Greek food dad."

Sylvia's friend Marcie had come by and tried to talk some sense into her friend. Sharon had overheard their conversation.

She told Sylvia,

"You have a lot to live for."

"You have a beautiful family that needs you."

"Your daughter will forgive you."

When there was no response she added,

"Get off your ass and act like you're alive."

Sylvia had responded by asking her to leave and was not taking Marcie's calls anymore. Her coping skills were nonexistent and she could not deal with her friend.

Sharon felt terrible about this. Marcie was a great friend to her mother and now they weren't speaking anymore. Her mother's main talent was alienating people and she did it so well.

Martin decided to try some more persuasion.

"The three of us haven't been out for a meal in such a long time. We need some family time."

It seemed like forever until she spoke.

"Well, okay," she said without enthusiasm.

"I'll make reservations at Stavros for 7:00 and I'll invite Ellen and Bob. They can meet us there."

This was Sylvia's favourite Greek restaurant. She loved to go there and order a bunch of succulent dishes family style. She loved the large platters with the skewers, the Greek salad and fried zucchini that was brought to their table. They all shared the huge amount of food with their friends and usually ordered some robust red wine to go with the aromatic food. They had not been there in over six months.

That evening, a wonderful time was had by all. They all dined together on Sylvia's favourite food, laughed and told wonderful stories to each other. Sharon was thrilled to see Sylvia actually eating a meal. She dug into her Greek salad and roasted lamb with lemon potatoes as if she had been on a long famine. They stayed out later than usual but no one minded because it was a Friday night and they could all sleep in on Saturday. Martin had Saturday off work so even he could relax.

Sharon sat watching Sylvia with a smile on her face. She truly believed that things were getting better and hoped that she was right. She hated to see her mother that way. The therapy needed to work.

CHAPTER 14. SHARON

My mom is going to have a fit. Yesterday I went over to see Mimi. She had invited me and David over for dinner. They both looked very excited as if they were about to burst with joy.

As I walked from the car to her apartment, I shivered with cold. The snow was piled high on the sidewalk and there was a major icy chill in the air. This was not unusual weather for Montreal in January which always seemed like the coldest month of the year.

"What smells so good?" I asked.

I shook off my snow boots and walked in the door. David took my winter coat and I removed my boots before saying hi to Mimi in the kitchen.

"I am making chili and homemade cornbread to go with it," she told me. "It helps take the chill off a very cold night."

And cold it was. It was one of those brutally chilly evening when you become numb on the way from the car to the dwelling. I was so happy to be indoors.

"It smells divine," I told her and it did. Mimi loved to cook and everything she made was amazing. David was the main recipient of her food but sometimes she would invite me over as well.

The smell of chili and garlic made my mouth water.

"When will it be ready?" I asked.

"In just a few minutes. The chili is ready but the cornbread is still in the oven."

"Where are your roommates tonight?"

"They all went home for Christmas break. I have the entire house to myself."

“Neato. So what new with you guys?”

“We’ll tell you over dinner,” David answered me.

They were both smiling like the Cheshire cat and I knew something major was about to happen.

Mimi served a salad while we were waiting for the cornbread to finish baking.

As I bit into some crispy lettuce and carrots, I asked them,

“So what’s up with you two?”

David and Mimi looked at me with the smile of two conspirators.

“We have the perfect man for you,” Mimi said.

“It’s about time you stop seeing all those losers and potheads” David added.

“You sound just like mom, David. I am happy with my life. I don’t need to meet anyone new.”

“That’s what I thought you would say. Little sister, it is time for you to be as happy as I am.”

With those words, I decided to hear them out.

“His name is Danny Stein. He is a childhood friend of David’s. He has been going to university in France but he is coming back to Montreal this spring. You have to meet him. He is better looking than David.”

“Hey,” David said, “I am insulted,” but he was smiling as he said it.

“Why would I like him?” I asked them.

“He is just perfect. He is smart and good-looking and he is finishing medical school.”

“Don’t you think we have enough doctors in the family already?” I asked her.

“One more wouldn’t hurt, especially this one. You can bring him to our wedding.”

"Your wedding is in a year and a half from now. We will break up by then."

"No you won't and that's our other news. We have decided to get married a year sooner. There is no good reason to wait. We are doing it this summer instead of the following summer."

"You both wanted a big wedding. How will you pull it off?"

"We changed our minds. We are inviting just a few people. There will be you and dad and David's family and a few close friends."

"What about mom? It would kill her not to come to your wedding. You need to forgive her and invite her."

Mimi had still not spoken to mom and 8 months had passed.

"Not a chance," she said. "I will never forgive her for what she did."

David looked strangely happy when she said that. It dawned on me that he hated my mother. It was no surprise. How could he not?

I could see that arguing would be useless. I felt so sorry for mom. She had acted badly but she needed to be forgiven. Mimi was carrying this grudge way too far for way too long.

As I ate the delicious spicy chili and the melt in your mouth cornbread, I wondered how I would ever tell my mother that she was not invited to her own daughter's wedding.

My mother was going through hell already. Her estrangement from Mimi was more than she could handle. Mom was in no state of mind to hear any more bad news.

At first, I had seen my mom's depression as sort of carte blanche for me to do what I wanted. As time went by, I truly began to feel sorry for her.

For the first time in my life, I hated my sister. She had never wavered in her love or loyalty for me but she was so unforgiving to mom. Yes, it was true that mom had done something very stupid but she had surely learned her lesson. Mimi had everything she wanted. Why couldn't she find it in her heart to forgive our mother?

I was very torn about what I should do. Mimi was not going to budge. Mom was as sad as she would ever be. Mimi was not going to forgive mom in the foreseeable future and maybe never. I wanted to disappear so I would not be caught between them. Maybe I could talk to dad about it. He always seemed to know what to do. Although lately, even he was confused. He had managed to convince mom to see a psychologist which was a good thing. He also convinced her to get out of bed and start doing things again but she seemed so fragile, like a breeze would blow her down.

I will speak to him on the weekend. I need to get him alone but that shouldn't be difficult. I will offer to take him out for a smoked meat sandwich. It is something he really can't resist. Maybe we can figure out a solution for this.

So, two days later, I asked both my mother and father if they wanted to go out for a smoked meat sandwich. I knew if I asked only my father my mother would be suspicious. I also knew that she was still struggling with going out and that she did not like smoked meat sandwiches even though she was a native Montrealer. This was almost unheard of.

"I don't really feel like it," she told me. "Those sandwiches are way too greasy for me."

"You don't know what you're missing," dad told her. "They are the second-best thing in the world next to your cooking."

"I think I'll pass anyway. I have a book I want to finish reading."

"Suit yourself," he told her and we were off.

We dressed warmly from head to toe and were off to Snowdon Deli that had the most delicious smoked meat piled high on crusty rye bread with just enough mustard. The sandwiches were so large that you could hardly fit your mouth around them.

Lately, dad and I had been going out for more and more meals together. Mom wasn't up to cooking or going out for dinner. I didn't mind as I really enjoyed my father's company. Unlike my mother, he was very interested in me and my life. He always asked me questions about university and about my life in general. He told me about his work in emergency and his concern about mom. I sometimes wondered what my mother had done to deserve a man like him. He was also good-looking, as my friends told me.

One friend once blurted out to me, "Sharon, your dad is so hot!" to which I blushed crimson and changed the subject.

Now we were sitting across from each other chowing down on huge smoked meat sandwiches with sour pickles and crispy fries. I was lost in the joy of the moment before I realized that I had something very unpleasant to discuss with him.

"Dad, Mimi is not going to invite mom to her wedding."

He looked like he was going to laugh.

"That can't be true. She must be joking with you."

"She isn't joking. She has decided to get married sooner and have a smaller wedding. She is inviting only immediate family. She told me that mom is not included."

He stopped eating his sandwich in mid bite and put it down on the plate.

"I can't believe that Mimi would be so cruel."

"Believe it," I told him. "She says she will never forgive mom and she wants nothing to do with her."

My father was turning ghostly white. He had lost his appetite which had been huge a minute ago.

"What will we do?" he asked me.

"I don't have a clue," I answered. "Do you think that talking to David might help?"

CHAPTER 15

Martin decided to take Sharon's advice and talk to David. After all, there was nothing left to lose. Martin truly did not know what to do. He had a rule to not interfere in his children's lives. He saw what doing so had done to Sylvia and he did not want both of his daughters to be alienated from their parents. He had managed to keep a very close relationship with both Sharon and Mimi. He did not want to incur Mimi's anger and possible estrangement. On the other hand, he also knew that Sylvia would wither and die if her daughter did not invite her to the wedding. He decided that he had to speak to Mimi but how? Perhaps, he could talk to David first to soften the way. Yes, that was what he would do. He would see if David would ask Mimi to invite Sylvia to the wedding.

He phoned David and left a message for him on his answering machine. He told David he needed to speak to him and could he please not tell Mimi about it. He also told David to phone him at work so Sylvia would not pick up the phone. He felt very deceitful but this was the way it had to be.

Finally, two days later, he was paged at the hospital for a phone call. It was David. When Martin picked up the phone, David sounded hesitant and almost scared.

"Hi David." Martin tried to sound casual.

"Is everything okay?" David asked him with a hint of fear in his voice.

"Yes, everything is fine." he answered without much conviction.

"Could we meet for lunch later this week? I don't have any shifts this Thursday or Friday."

"What is it about?" David asked.

"I would be more comfortable discussing this over lunch. Please say you can come."

"Sure," David agreed but he still didn't sound so sure.

"Please don't tell Mimi about it," Martin added.

They agreed to meet at a café downtown close to McGill University on Thursday at noon. Martin hoped that he could get David to speak to Mimi about Sylvia. Frankly, it was his only hope.

On Thursday, Martin was feeling very nervous. He was not quite sure if meeting David was a good idea. He feared that this lunch might even make the situation worse if that was possible. He put on his warm parka and winter boots and went to the garage to get his car. As he drove downtown, he wondered how his life had wound up so out of control.

When he arrived at the café, he had a surprise waiting for him. David was already there and Mimi was sitting next to him. She did not look pleased. What had David said to her?

He sat down at the table and Mimi immediately said to him, "You should not be making secret plans with David. Everything you say to him you can say to me."

"What is it that you wanted to talk to David about?" she asked Martin who noticed that David seemed scared to open his mouth.

"It's your mother. You need to make up with her and invite her to your wedding. I understand why you are angry with her but she is still your mother. Don't you want your children to know their grandmother? Believe me your mother has paid for her mistake. She is very depressed. She is seeing a psychologist and I think that will help her develop some healthy boundaries. Please give her another chance."

Then a miracle occurred. Mimi said, "Yes. I will give her another chance but only because I love you."

She continued with, “We will have to make sure that mom stops interfering in my life. Otherwise, I will stop speaking to her again.”

David said nothing. He had been mute throughout this ordeal. He didn’t want bad feelings between Mimi and Sylvia but he was angry. How dare Sylvia try to introduce Mimi to someone else? He was a little disappointed that Mimi said she would reconcile with her mother. He knew her mother did not care for him and he resented it greatly. He would just have to learn to live with this family dynamic.

Martin tried not to cry even though his eyes welled up with tears. He felt that this was a new beginning they desperately needed.

“Thank you Mimi, I love you too.” was all he said.

Mimi decided to invite them all to dinner the following Saturday. This would be a test run for her to see if her mother had actually changed.

After this they ordered lunch. Martin and David had burgers and fries and Mimi had a bowl of beef and barley soup. As they ate their food, Martin felt so much relief. Maybe, just maybe, things could still work out and they could be a family again.

When Martin got back home, he phoned Sharon. He told her that Mimi was giving her mother another chance. She would be overjoyed that Mimi would be talking to her again. She wouldn’t be very happy about the fact that the wedding would be small. For a long time, she had been looking forward to large and lavish weddings for her daughters. She had started a special bank account to save for both weddings. Sharon was at school and the house was so quiet. He didn’t have work until Saturday and the entire day was his. He contemplated going to the gym to work out and then he looked outside. It was snowing heavily and looking very frosty. He decided he would indulge in a little nap. He went to his bedroom and lay down on the bed. It felt so good to lie down. He never did this in the afternoon. He snuggled under the toasty down duvet and was soon fast asleep. This was the best sleep he had in a long time. His mind felt clear and relaxed for the first time in a long, long time.

He woke up two hours later with Sylvia standing over him and staring at him.

“Are you alright?” she asked him. “You have been sleeping for a long time.”

“Yes, I am just fine,” he answered, stretching slowly and sitting up in bed. He felt the moment of extreme warmth and comfort after waking up from his nap. He saw the room was now dark. He could smell a wonderful garlic and onions aroma drifting into the room.

“Supper is almost ready,” she told him. “I made a lovely beef stew for a cold winter’s day.” She smiled at him.

“I’ll be down soon,” he told her. He slowly put on some clothing and made his way down to the kitchen. Sylvia was chopping up vegetables for a salad. He was so pleased to see her active again. He hoped his news would help improve her mood even more.

As they sat eating the hot hearty stew and the Panzanella salad, Martin could not help but notice that Sylvia had put on a few pounds. She seemed to have a good appetite and was eating with enjoyment.

“This food is delicious. Where is Sharon?”

“She went skating with her friends. I can’t believe that they went to an outdoor rink. It is so cold and miserable out there.”

“They are young and tough.” he told her and added, “By the way, we have a dinner invitation for the Saturday after this one.”

She hardly looked up from her food until he continued.

“Mimi and David have invited us to her apartment for dinner.”

She looked shocked. “What?” was all she could muster.

“They want to discuss some changes to their wedding plans. They figured that we might as well have dinner at the same time.”

"Are you sure I'm invited?" she asked him.

"Yes, all three of us are. I hope Sharon can make it."

"Why is she inviting me?" Sylvia asked him.

"She wants to see you," he told her.

"What should we bring?" she asked.

"She said a bottle of wine would be fine." Sylvia looked stunned. She did not know what to say.

"Sure, let's go," she said, trying to sound casual and relaxed. Her stomach started churning and she felt like she was going to throw up. As she started to clear the table, she did the deep breathing Dr Wellman had taught her and started to relax. She started to actually feel happy that they were going.

As she was loading the dishes into the dishwasher, Martin heard her humming, something that she hadn't done in a long time. He hoped that this would be the beginning of a better life for all of them.

He was still concerned that this reconciliation might not go well but he was hesitant to say anything to Sylvia. Just maybe she had learned to stop interfering in Mimi's life.

As they were having their coffee, Sharon burst into the kitchen. She was bright red from the cold and had on her warmest woollen sweater. She was just removing her down parka and stomped into the kitchen as if she was on a mission.

"I'm starved. What's for dinner?" she said as she put her winter jacket over the chair.

"We already ate," Sylvia told her, "but there are plenty of leftovers. I will warm up some beef stew for you and get some salad out to get you started."

"Thanks mom. I've been skating all afternoon. I could eat a horse."

Sylvia was amazed at how much Sharon ate but decided not to say anything. She finished both the stew and salad and three pieces of crusty baguette. The three chatted over coffee and fragrant apple crisp with whipped cream as the day turned into evening.

CHAPTER 16. SHARON

We are all invited to Mimi's for supper in a few days. Mom is so excited that she can't contain herself. She has asked dad what she should bring at least a hundred times. She asked me about some outfits she wants to wear. Is this one too formal? Is this one too casual? I think she really believes that this dinner will change everything. I don't feel quite so certain.

For one, Mimi is still pretty pissed at mom. The one thing those two have in common is that they don't forgive easily. They are both so stubborn and they hold grudges like no one else does. I hope Mimi will be able to be friendly and warm. She told me that she is doing this mainly for dad. That is the wrong reason. She should be doing it because she genuinely wants to make up with mom.

Also, dad has not told mom about the changes Mimi and David have made to the wedding plans. I think she will freak out when Mimi tells her. This may totally ruin any chance of peace between them. I think dad should tell her before we go. This way it won't come as a shock. I think he is scared of her reaction which may be worse if she finds out later.

I have been staying put at home as much as possible. The weather has turned pure evil and I feel like my fingers and toes are frozen as soon as I step outside. I still go to university but I mostly stay at home otherwise. This supposedly amazing guy that Mimi and David want to introduce me to is coming to Montreal in a few months. Well, maybe he will be great. They showed me a picture of him as a child when he and David were best buddies. He did look quite adorable in those days with curly blonde hair and mischievous blue eyes that looked like they were up to no good. However, he is not as handsome as David – not even close. That would be impossible.

Staying home in the evening has become so much better since mom started cooking again. I was tired of making grilled cheese sandwiches for me and dad every night. Mom is such an amazing cook. She can make almost anything taste good. Last night she made moussaka with a Greek salad. Was it ever good. I had three servings. If I don't watch it, I will get chunky from her incredible cooking.

All in all, things are better at home for now. I sure hope it continues.

So we all went to dinner at Mimi's and it was better than I thought it would be. Dad had told mom beforehand that Mimi and David were getting married earlier and having a small wedding. She had shrugged off the news and told him that it didn't really matter. This was the first big surprise. The second one was that mom behaved well throughout the dinner.

We arrived at Mimi's frozen and shivering. She took our coats and hugged each of us including mom. Mimi looked radiant. Her eyes were bright and she was glowing slightly from the heat of the kitchen.

"What smells so wonderful?" dad asked her.

"I made roast beef with Yorkshire pudding. I'm sorry but David couldn't come tonight. He has a cold."

Couldn't or wouldn't, I wondered but didn't say anything.

"Supper will be ready soon. Please sit down and make yourselves comfortable." There was a warm glowing fireplace with real flames. The living room was toasty.

"I have some hot apple cider. Would anyone like some?"

All three of us said yes at once. We sat on the old soft worn couches near the fireplace and drank our cider. At first conversation was awkward. We sat in silence for the first few minutes but I broke the quiet.

“So how is school?” I asked her.

“I am doing my student teaching this year and next year I am hoping to have a real class of my own.”

“How are your students?” mom asked.

“They are in junior high so they are a bit wild but lots of fun. I am teaching them some math games and they are really enjoying them.”

“I think the roast is ready. I am going to check on it.”

The living room and kitchen were all one big room so it was easy to watch her do this.

“Where are your roomies?” I asked her.

“Out on hot dates,” she answered. “Dinner is ready. Come eat.”

She had made a memorable meal. The ancient scarred pine table was spread with Caesar salad, roast beef with mixed sautéed vegetables, and Yorkshire puddings. She opened our bottle of red wine and poured some for each of us.

Mimi is a great cook like our mother. I am happy to make anything decent. My specialty is burning food. I always seem to forget about it when I put it on to cook.

We dug into the food like hungry wolves. The conversation throughout dinner was casual and friendly. No one brought up any touchy subjects. We were all on our best behaviour.

I watched us all as if I was a fly on the wall. If someone from a distance was looking at us, we would seem like a normal happy family. Appearances can be very deceiving. As we were eating our dessert, Mimi’s roommate Ellen came into the apartment. Mimi offered her some apple cake and she joined us. Shortly after, her other roommate Lisa came in and also had some apple cake with us.

We couldn’t stay late as dad had an early shift at the hospital the next day. It seemed to take about a half hour for us all to put on our sweaters, parkas, and boots. Dad went to warm up the car as we got ready to leave. Mimi gave both mom and me a kiss and hug before we walked out the door. We left with mom still on good terms with Mimi and all was well for the moment.

On the way home, we chatted about nothing in particular. Everyone was relaxed and happy for the moment. Mom commented on how good the meal was. Dad told her that Mimi got her cooking ability from her. I dozed in the back seat until we were well within our warm garage. I could hardly keep my eyes open. The meal, wine, and car ride had lulled me into a sleepy haze. As soon as we walked into the house, I went up to my room and immediately fell asleep. I had bad dreams of Mimi falling out of an airplane. I heard screaming and crying, although I did not know where the sounds were coming from.

I woke up the next morning dazed and confused but ready to start another day. My legs felt weighed down. I could smell coffee brewing in the kitchen downstairs. I made my way there and mom and dad were sitting and eating scrambled eggs and toast. I went down and joined them. I poured myself a strong cup of coffee and found some eggs still in the pan and scooped them onto my plate. I popped some whole wheat bread into the toaster and went to the fridge for some jam.

Both mom and dad seemed in a fine mood. Dad ruffled my messy hair when I sat down next to him. It seemed like a large weight had been lifted from their shoulders. They sat gabbing about nothing much in general. Dad was fully dressed and ready to go. Mom was still in her bathrobe but fully awake.

Dad said, "Do you want a ride to university? It is still very cold out there." He didn't have to ask twice.

"Yes, sure!" I answered. It was better than freezing my fingers and toes while waiting for the bus.

"I want to leave soon," he told me.

I raced upstairs in a minute and put on my underwear, jeans and woollen sweater. I ran a brush through my wild hair and ran downstairs.

When we were leaving, he drew mom into his arms and gave her a long hug and kiss. It suddenly occurred to me that he really loved her. I had often thought that he married her simply because Mimi was on the way but the past few months had changed my mind. He had shown so much love and concern during her depression. He looked at her with so much tenderness. He had found her a doctor who was helping her.

It also occurred to me that if dad could love mom who was a bloody mess even at the best of times, there was still some hope for me. I had been guilty of loving my sister's man for years and I despaired that I would ever meet someone that I could truly care for. Maybe there was still at least some chance that it would happen. Mimi and David's friend was arriving in two months. Maybe he would make me swoon. I could only hope.

CHAPTER 17

Finally, at the end of February, the snow began to melt and the days began to warm slightly. Instead of warm winter jackets and furry hats and mittens, a person could get by with just a warm jacket and boots. There was slush everywhere and it was easy to get soaked after walking just a block.

Spring was a turning point in the lives of the Miller family. Mimi and David grew even closer and set their wedding date for August 10. Sharon finally met met Danny at coffee with Mimi and David and rather liked him. He was both sweet and charming. He had sparkly eyes and adorable dimples. She had to admit that he was as good as if not better than her soon to be brother in law. He seemed to like her too and they started dating almost instantly. For a reason she could not fathom, Sylvia actually liked Danny or perhaps she had just learned her lesson.

Sylvia put on some weight and started to go out more. She and Mimi even successfully met for lunch and had a good time. Sharon was supposed to come but she had cancelled at the last minute. So the two were together and spoke easily of everything.

As for Martin, he was happy because everyone seemed to be getting along for a change. He decided to work a few less shifts and spend more time with Sylvia. The two went out together more often. They openly told each other what was on their minds.

Since she was feeling better, Sylvia had developed a new insatiable appetite for sex. Martin was thrilled when he would wake up in the morning to being fondled by his wife. All in all, things were definitely much better for almost everyone.

The one exception was David. He was unhappy that Sylvia was

back in their lives and let Mimi know this frequently. He would say things to Mimi to indicate his feelings.

A typical exchange went like this.

“Mimi, your mother is interfering too much in our lives.”

“She is getting better David. Just be patient with her.”

She would shrug it off and he would grow even more angry. He expected an apology from Sylvia but Mimi told him it would never come. As much as he loved Mimi, he was wondering if he should be marrying her. Her family was a disaster and he felt like a victim of this disaster. Mimi had no idea that he was having second thoughts about their marriage. He never told her. If he seemed unhappy, she believed that other issues were causing him to frown and become glum.

Mimi was oblivious to the changes in David. He was moody and taciturn much of the time but she just felt that it was part of his busy schedule. David wondered how she could be so blind to his needs. Sylvia’s behaviour had really put him off and he was pondering breaking off with Mimi.

David was of two minds. He loved Mimi with an intense passion. She was his first and only love. He admired her beauty and her brains. She challenged him on a regular basis and made him a better person. However, he hated her mother. He was sure that Sylvia would eventually destroy their relationship. She had already tried to do so. He couldn't forgive her for trying to find another man for Mimi.

If David was more mature, he might have broached the subject with Mimi. Together they could have come up with a strategy for dealing with Sylvia. However, David was not mature and did not know how to deal with the situation so he kept all of his anger inside. He went to the gym and took his anger out on the punching bags. He imagined each punch to be directed at Sylvia. He thought that this would help but he was just as angry when he came home. It never left and kept building and building until it was like a poison.

CHAPTER 18. SHARON

The unthinkable has happened. Mimi and David broke up. I can't even believe this has happened. She phoned me last night and I could tell she was crying. She told me that David had broken off their engagement. She said that his reason was that he was not ready for marriage. I sat there listening to her crying and unable to say a word.

"What am I going to do?" she asked me in a trembling voice. "I love him so much. I built my future around him. Why did he do this to me?"

"Maybe he is just in a bad mood. Give him a few days to cool off. I am sure he will come to his senses and realize how much he loves you."

"Do you really think he will change his mind?"

"Yes Mimi. He loves you so much. He will come to his senses right away."

Even as I was saying this, I felt confused. The David I knew would never ever break up with my sister. He worshipped her. Briefly I wondered if there was someone else but I did not say a word to Mimi about my suspicions. There was no reason to upset her even more. Then I wondered if my mother had paid him to break off their engagement but I decided not to mention this either. Mom was certainly crazy enough to do this but I believed she had learned her lesson.

"Please don't tell anyone," I told her. "He will change his mind in a few days," but I was not so sure.

"Did you two have a fight recently?" I asked her.

"No," she sobbed, "We were getting along so well. This came right out of nowhere. He just said that he is not ready for marriage. When I asked him to explain, he said that there was no other reason. Sharon, I am falling apart. Please come over!"

So I went to her apartment and held her as she cried. Then we drank an entire bottle of red wine together. I should not have driven home that night but I did. Luckily I did not destroy my father's car or myself. When I got home, I promptly went to the bathroom and threw up. Then I took an aspirin and went to bed. All night I had nightmares of strange figures hurting each other with all kinds of weapons. I woke up hungover and tired.

When I was nibbling at my breakfast, dad said, "You are not looking well Sharon. Are you coming down with something?"

"I have an upset stomach but it is getting better dad. No need to worry." He looked at me as if he knew I had gotten drunk but he didn't say anything. By lunchtime, I was back to my hungry self but what about Mimi? Would she ever be the same again?

This just goes to show that you can never completely trust anyone. David was Mimi's knight in shining armour. I had been in love with him for years. How could such a wonderful man do this to my sister? The answer was that he was not a wonderful man. This was impossible. It briefly struck me that this had to do with my mother. Did she do something else? Did she confront David? Did she threaten David? She had always hated him. Maybe I could find out the answer in a different way.

Well, two weeks have passed and David has still not come to his senses. I am as confused as Mimi is. These two had it made. They supposedly had a strong and loving relationship. It wasn't supposed to end like this without even a real explanation on his part. All he told her was that he wasn't ready for marriage. This is super strange because he was the one who wanted to get married sooner. I will never understand how this happened. I am feeling guilty because my relationship with Danny is going so well. I should break up with him because he is David's friend but I can't seem to do it. I just like him too much. I think I am going to lose my virginity to him. When he kisses me, my entire body trembles and I am breathless. He has a wicked sense of humour and always makes me laugh. I think meeting him is one of the best things that has happened to me.

I don't tell Mimi any of this because she is so upset. It would be like rubbing it in to brag about my relationship when hers has just ended. A side effect of this breakup is that Mimi and mom have been getting closer. Mimi has been in our house crying several times in the past few weeks. It is as if she is looking to mom for comfort.

Mom never says, "I told you so." to her.

I am happy about that. Mom really hates David and she must be feeling so much relief that he is no longer in Mimi's life. Instead of saying anything, mom has been baking brownies and feeding them to Mimi whenever she comes over. Mom makes the world's best brownies. They are filled with oozy chocolate fudge and so delicious. Who said that chocolate was a cure for the blues? Whoever it was had it right. I don't have the blues and I still get to enjoy the brownies. I tend to eat way too much of them. I am already such a fatso that I don't need any brownies.

Well, it all goes like this. Mimi comes over sobbing with her curly red hair wild and blue eyes red rimmed. Mom whips out a plate of brownies and brews a pot of tea and soon they are chatting and laughing like the best of friends. I join them sometimes because otherwise they would eat all the brownies.

Then mom invites Mimi to stay for supper and Mimi says, "I would love to."

Dad arrives and is delighted to see "his three girls" setting the table and helping mom with supper. He is elated when he comes in. His eyes light up when he smiles and he hugs us all. Then we eat an amazing meal and dad drives Mimi back to her apartment.

I am not staying for supper with them tonight although it smells divine. Mom has whipped up some casserole with layers of cheese and chicken and vegetables. I have a date with Danny.

We are gong out for burgers and then to a movie. I could have invited him for supper. Mom always makes enough food to feed two armies but I was afraid it would bother Mimi to see him. So, when he arrived to pick me up, I just waved at them and went out with him as quickly as I could. I didn't think Mimi would make a scene but I didn't want to take a chance.

We went to Harvey's for burgers and fries and then we went to see the movie "Planet of the Apes". I just loved it but the best part was when we went to park on the mountain overlooking the city. We couldn't keep our hands off each other. Danny and I both live with our parents so we had no place to make out but in his dad's car. We kissed and caressed each other like two drowning people searching for air. Then he slipped his hand inside my sweater and undid my bra. He took off both my sweater and bra and started kissing my breasts and nipples. I was so excited that I couldn't breathe. He kept doing this until I couldn't take it anymore. I begged him to stop and he finally did.

We had both decided that our first time would not be in this car. We were planning to go away for a weekend and do this properly in a bed in a nice room.

When I got home, I was surprised to see that Mimi was still there. Mom had invited her to stay for the night and she had accepted. She greeted me in a pair of my old flannel pyjamas which were way too big on her.

"Those pyjamas look better on you than they do on me," I told her.

She blushed and said, "Aw shucks."

Then she went to get ready for bed. We both went to our separate bedrooms to sleep but I was keyed up from making out and it took me a long time to fall asleep.

CHAPTER 19

Sharon walked in on Sylvia having brownies with Mimi yet again. This batch was chocolate chip with cheesecake and she had to admit they had come out splendidly. She couldn't believe what was happening. Mimi was back in her life. David was gone.

"May I join you?" Sharon asked, "or is this a private brownie party?"

"Pull up a chair sis before we eat them all."

"Don't mind if I do."

"Oh my god, these brownies are delicious!"

Sharon was still perplexed about Mimi and David's breakup. She hoped Mimi would get over David and find someone worthy of her. Sharon looked out of her kitchen window at the buds on the trees and the flowers slowly peeking up in the garden. The sun bathed them in light as they spoke. Most of the snow was gone. Sharon's favourite season was spring. It brought with it such hope and promise. Last spring she had believed she might never smile again and now she was hopeful about the future.

What happened next surprised them all. Mimi was discussing her apartment and the fact that her lease would be up soon.

"Mom, my lease on my apartment is ending soon and my roommates are leaving. I was thinking that maybe I could move back home for a while until I find a job. What do you think?"

Sylvia felt this would be the best thing in the world but realized this was not the best thing for her daughter. Mimi was thriving as an independent woman and coming home would be a step backwards for her.

“I don’t think it would be a good idea. You have done so well on your own. You have really grown up these past months. I used to drive you crazy with my demands. I would probably do the same if you came to live here again.”

Both Sharon and Mimi looked surprised, maybe even shocked. Mimi realized that it had been very difficult for her mother to say this and that her mother was right. She could play it hurt but she decided to take the high road.

“You are right mom. It is better if we don’t live under the same roof.”

“You are welcome to visit and to have brownies or whatever you want,” Sylvia told her.

Sharon felt optimistic about her mother’s progress for the first time. Things might still be fine after all.

She had another brownie and decided that it was impossible to have too much love or too many brownies in your life.

CHAPTER 20. SHARON

Mimi and I sat eating brownies and drinking coffee with mom for a few hours. Then mom rushed off to a doctor's appointment. After she was gone, Mimi and I went out to sit on the deck. The sun was strong but it was still a little cool outside so we brought blankets with us. We sat on reclining loungers pretending it was summer when it was actually only early spring. I was a bit cold but I didn't let on because I was young and felt that I had to be tough.

I asked Mimi, "How are you really doing?"

"I still miss David but I am starting to feel better. I don't think I will ever understand what happened but I have to move on with my life. I am looking for a teaching job for the fall. I can't believe I am graduating in May."

"Let's have a hell of a party when you do," I told her.

"Okay."

"I can't believe what happened before. I asked mom if I could move back home and she said no!"

"I think aliens have taken over mom's body. Otherwise, why would she say no?"

"She thinks we will get along better if we don't live together."

"Well, she is right about that. Would you like to smoke a joint?"

"Yes, yes, yes!"

I went to my room and came back outside with a fat joint in my hand. I lit it and we sat on the deck passing it to and from each other and watching the smoke curls in the air blow away in the wind. For some reason, this made us both laugh hysterically.

The sun warmed our faces and we soon forgot it was even cool outside as we fell into a sweet, stoned haze. It was getting late in the afternoon when we went back inside and raided the fridge. We made huge roast beef sandwiches with lots of Dijon mustard on rye bread. It was so delicious. Then we went to my room and listened to music on my bed. Mom found us sleeping on my bed in a euphoric state. If she suspected we were stoned, she didn't let on. Instead, she invited Mimi to stay for dinner which she was thrilled to do.

I can't believe that we actually ate dinner that evening but we did. The roast chicken and vegetables were so delicious it would have been a shame to waste them so we didn't. We ate like two chubby little hogs. It was great that my skinny little sister ate as much as I did.

The next day was a regular university day for me. I wish I was enjoying education more. I think that maybe I went into education because Mimi did. It's not much of a reason. I may have to rethink this latest of the bad decisions I have made.

I was on the bus home from university when I saw David. My heart skipped a beat when I saw him. He was walking along Queen Mary Road looking rather furtive. I rang the bell to get off the bus not knowing what to do. When I got off I could still see him. I thought that it was strange that he was walking on this street at 3:00 in the afternoon. On the spur of the moment, I decided to follow him. I saw him round a corner and I walked a good distance behind him so he wouldn't see me. Was he going to see another woman? Was he a secret spy? He went into a large building. I waited a few minutes and walked up to the entrance. It was a medical centre. It had doctors and dentists in it. Well, that solved the mystery.

The rest of the day I wondered about him. Why had he gone into a medical building? Was he sick? Is that why he broke up with Mimi? I decided to leave that topic alone before I became obsessed. I had spent enough of my life obsessed with him.

CHAPTER 21

Spring was slowly giving way to summer. The days were getting hotter and longer. Flowers started popping up in bright profusion all over the city. The mild spring breezes were being replaced by hot humid summer winds. Sharon was giddy with excitement. She and Danny had been having sex and she loved it. She couldn't wait to see him. Tonight they were going to a play. She could just as easily have forgone the play for sex. Danny's parents were out of town so he had the house to himself. They made great use of it. She came over as often as possible and they went at it eagerly. Last night Danny had tried a new position and she had loved it. Afterwards, they smoked a joint and it made them horny so they had sex again. Then they raided the fridge and sat eating what ever they could find.

Over a bite of a chicken sandwich, Danny, said, "Let's get married. I love you and I want to be with you all the time. We could do this every day."

"We already do it every day. How about if we wait until you finish medical school?"

"Not a bad idea but I am not sure if I can wait until then."

"Let's talk about it again in a year." Sharon figured that if Mimi and David were kaput, she had to be careful. What guarantee was there that things would work out for them? Their relationship was only six months old. It had to withstand the test of time.

Also, she liked Danny and loved having sex but was this enough to base a marriage on? She did not think so.

Sharon realized that moment that she was sore from all the sex. She also realized it was late and she had university tomorrow.

"I need to go home," she told Danny.

He looked at her. She was sitting at the kitchen table wearing only his shirt. She had a smudge of mustard on her cheek. Her skin was glowing and her curly brown hair was a mess. Her eyes were soft and sultry. He had a sudden desire to have sex again. He felt an erection beginning.

He walked over to Sharon and bent down to lick the mustard off her face. Then he bent lower and stuck his face into her naked breasts. He started to suck her delicious nipples and she was soon moaning with desire. In minutes they were back in his bed. He ran his hands over her supple body and then between her legs. She was already wet. His tongue found her labia and dug deeply into it. A minute later, he was on top of her and they were both animals without boundaries. He held her hands down and they both came with a great delight.

Later he drove her home and wondered how he had gotten so lucky. Sharon said that she was so sore she might never recover but she went to bed with a smile on her face and slept very soundly and dreamlessly that night.

Sharon was woken to the sound of screaming the next morning. It was coming from her parents' room. At first she thought they were having a fight but realized her father had gone to work and it was only her mother there. It was a guttural sound that seemed like it was coming from a wounded animal.

She quietly walked into the room. The door was open. Sylvia was lying there screaming and gasping for air.

Sylvia had woken up screaming and unable to breathe. She lay in her bed gasping for air and thinking that she was about to die. She could not breathe in and when she tried she started coughing violently. She tried to pick up the phone to dial 911 but she was unable to do even that. Her heart was pounding in her chest. She wondered if she was having a heart attack. Just as quickly as it had started, the feeling subsided. She sat up in bed taking small breaths and started to shiver. She wrapped the blanket around her tightly as she felt her teeth chattering. It was a warm summer's day but she was chilled to the bone. It dawned on her that a nightmare had caused this. She had dreamed of Mimi getting eaten by a wild lion.

Just then Sharon walked into the room.

"Mom, are you alright?"

"Yes, I just had a bad dream."

"Can I bring you something?"

"A hot cup of coffee would be wonderful."

Sleepy Sharon went downstairs and brewed coffee for them both. She wondered what was going on with her mother.

"Thanks Sharon."

Sylvia took a large gulp of the coffee and felt her cold body start to warm.

"Is there anything else I can do for you mom?"

"No I am fine."

Sharon went to take a shower and start her day. She wondered if she should tell her father about what had happened and decided that this was just part of her mother's recovery. Sharon never realized that her mother's dreams were just like her own.

CHAPTER 22. SHARON

I have always been jealous of my sister Mimi. She has had the better looks, the better grades, the better friends and the better boyfriends. I am reasonably decent looking and she is gorgeous. I look more like my dad. I have his curly brown hair and round face. I am not fat but people say I have a rubenesque type of body. I am quite curvy. Mimi is the opposite. She is slim to the point of almost being too skinny. She has lovely chestnut hair and a finely chiselled face with beautiful cheekbones. She is definitely a classic beauty. Next to her I look like a toad. Let's not forget the fact that mom adores her and just kind of tolerates me. Dad seems to love us both equally. He is the best man I have ever known. I hope my future husband is half as kind as my father. I swear I will never get married because no one will ever measure up to him. He has always been there for all of us He always has something kind to say when I feel really down in the dumps.

My feelings for my boyfriend Danny have changed. I don't care for him as much as I did. He is good-looking and he can't get enough of me in bed.. He is quite loving to me but he is a spoiled brat. His parents are very wealthy and they give him whatever he wants. He went to university in Paris so he could learn to speak better French. This will come in handy for him here in Montreal when he is a doctor. Everyone tells me he is a great catch, especially Danny himself. Somehow I just don't love him and I don't think I ever will. Danny never mentions David. I was hoping he would give me a clue as to why David broke up with my sister who was the love of his life. When I ask him why, he just shrugs. Maybe he doesn't want to betray David's confidence. I miss David. I wish I could see him again. I think I am still in love with him. Sometimes when Danny and I are having sex, I see

David's face instead.

I would never make a move to be with David because it would hurt Mimi too much. Listen to me pretending that I even have a chance with him. He never noticed me even when the three of us had just met. I wonder where he is and what he is doing. Does he have a new woman? I hope he is happy. I still wonder why my mother could not stand him. Did she have a good reason or was he just coming between her and her precious girl?

Well, I can't believe it but David is back. He phoned Mimi a few days ago and said that he wanted to talk to her. She was not at all sure if she even wanted to see him but he was persistent. They met for coffee and talked over their relationship. He told her that he had broken up with her because our mother kept getting in the way of their happiness. He told her that he had made a terrible mistake and that he still loved her. He wanted them to get back together. Mimi was not sure that this was such a good idea. She didn't understand why David had not told her this before. They should have been able to talk about anything she told him. She also said that she did not trust him anymore. So now she is in a state of uncertainty.

She told him that she would have to think about it. We met at school and discussed what she should do.

"I still love him but I don't trust him anymore," she told me.

"I can understand why. You don't have to make up your mind today. Let him wait. He has put you through so much. Do you think he is worth the trouble?"

"He was wonderful. He was always so good to me. I love him. I don't know what to do."

A sob escaped from her.

"Don't do anything until you are sure."

"You always give me the best advice."

"That's what sisters are for," and I blew her a kiss as we rushed off to our busy days.

We hugged and went our own separate ways. Mimi had asked me not to tell mom about this and I understood why. So, for the next while, she would ponder whether her relationship with David was worth another try. I can certainly understand her hesitation. David had broken up with her with no explanation. She needed to decide if she could forgive him. The decision had to be hers alone. Mom might try to pressure her and she did not need pressure from anyone.

In some ways I think I am tougher than Mimi. I know I would never get back with someone after he had broken my trust. I would tell the person where to go but this is David. Maybe just maybe I would make an exception for him.

Mimi decided to give David another chance. She still loved him despite the fact that she did not trust him anymore. She told him that she was not making any commitment to him but that she would give their relationship another try. They would do this slowly and they would start as friends. These were her conditions and she was sticking to them. David agreed, grateful that she would speak to him at all. He said that he realized how stupid he had been to throw over this wonderful woman because of her mother. He would just have to figure out a way to keep Sylvia at a distance. He felt that her influence could only hurt them. When Mimi told him that she and Sylvia were now quite close he was very unhappy but he did not let it show. Instead, he said to Mimi,

“I am so glad you worked things out with your mother.”

“It will be better for our relationship if you two get along,” she told him but he did not believe her.

David somehow hoped that Sylvia would disappear. He sometimes had fantasies about wringing her scrawny neck. When he was over at the Miller family table, he spoke as little as possible. He was sure that Sylvia would twist his every word.

Instead, he sat at the table and eyed Sharon. He loved Mimi but he had a crush on her sister. She had killer curves and she always made him laugh. He sometimes wondered what would have happened if he had met Sharon first.

Sharon noticed that David often stared at her at the dinner table. She wondered why. She thought that it was because she ate too much or weighed too much.

Sharon often enjoyed watching David when he and Mimi were together. He had such an expressive face. He would always look at her mother with a sheer hatred. It almost shone off him. She could have sworn that she caught him looking at her with lust a few times. It was as if he was imagining her with no clothes on. She knew that look well. She had seen it on other men many times. Was it possible that David had a crush on her? She laughed at herself for even believing this was possible.

Mimi had to tell her mother that she and David were back together. Over dinner one evening at home, she broke the news to Sylvia. Everyone had been really enjoying the delicious chicken Parmesan and mashed potatoes that Sylvia had prepared. The whole family was there. Martin, Sylvia, and Sharon all sat around the table enjoying their meal and chatting. Mimi interrupted the meal by saying,

"I have an announcement to make."

They stopped talking and looked at her. Sharon knew what she was going to say.

"David and I are seeing each other again. He asked me to give the relationship another try. We are starting as friends. I hope all of you will give us your blessing."

Sylvia felt a chill go down her spine and was speechless for once in her life.

Their usually easy going father was the first to comment.

"I don't think it's such a good idea. He really hurt you and he could do it again. I used to really like that boy but he has proven himself not to be trusted."

"I will be careful, dad. I won't let him hurt me again. I promise."

"What do you think, Mom?"

"I think you need to do what makes you happy," Sylvia told her.

Sylvia looked like she was going to throw up. She hoped that her words had been convincing. They had sounded hollow even to her. She took a deep breath to calm down. Through the rest of the meal, they discussed other topics but Sylvia felt ill. She was sure this relationship was going to lead to something horrible. It was a premonition right out of her dream. She couldn't shake it no matter how hard she tried. When Sylvia brought out apple crisp with ice cream for dessert, she couldn't eat a bite of it. She said she was too full but she was really struggling to keep from crying. She eventually went to bed and had nightmares all night. At one point, Martin woke her and asked her if she was feeling well. He told her that she had been screaming in her sleep. She told him that it was just a bad dream and he went back to sleep but she lay in bed wide awake and miserable.

CHAPTER 23. SHARON

Well, the two great lovers are back together in full force. Mimi said that they would take it slowly but that's not happening. She and David are together every day and they are back to being lovey dovey with each other. Danny and I went out to dinner with them last week and they were so all over each other that it made me a little sick.

No, I am not jealous of their relationship. If anything, I am worried about it. He ripped out Mimi's heart and I don't want him to do it again. She is letting her feelings for him cloud her logic. I know she loves him but he has shown that he can't be trusted. I am surprised but I agree with mom for once. Last night, she told me that she was worried about that relationship and I said I was too. We promised we wouldn't say anything to Mimi because she would resent us. Mom has learned her lesson. She is interfering less in Mimi's life but more in mine.

"Is your relationship with Danny serious?" she asked me.

"No, not at all, Mom."

"That's too bad. I need a wedding to plan."

I am thinking of breaking up with Danny. He is sexy as hell but I am noticing more and more things about him that I don't particularly like. He can be quite selfish. We always go where he wants to go whether it is out for a meal or to a concert. I asked him to go to a concert featuring The Four Seasons by Vivaldi and he flat out refused. We have done so many things that he wanted to do but he will not go out of his way for me even this once. I think I will ask dad to go with me. He likes classical music and is better company than Danny.

Danny is way too much into smoking pot. I don't mind an occasional toke but this guy seems to smoke every day. Danny's best quality is his sexual desire for me. It never lessens. We have had sex so many times and in so many places. Last week, we went to the library to study for exams. We were sitting next to each other at a large study table. As I was reading my textbook, I felt his hand creep up my skirt. He started caressing my thighs and working his way up to my pubes. I started getting hot there and then. Well, that was enough. We ran to his car, climbed in and we could hardly wait until we got to a secluded street. We did it right in his car and it was hot. I would miss that so maybe I'll stay with him just a bit longer.

CHAPTER 24

Sharon's favourite evenings were Sundays. Sylvia would make a wonderful dinner for the entire family. They would sit around the formal dining room table laughing and chatting. The food would be delicious as always. Sylvia would spend all day on Sundays cooking her family a splendid meal. She would serve it with loving care. At the end of the evening, she would always pack up large containers of leftovers for Mimi to take with her. Last Sunday had started off so well. Sylvia had made lemon dill salmon on the barbecue and it was delicious. Alongside, there were lemon green beans and tabouli and fresh crusty homemade bread. They were digging into their chocolate cake when Mimi said,

"I am so happy to be back with David. I still love him and I hope we can get married someday."

"Are you sure about this Mimi?" her father asked. He was now the one to ask these questions.

"I still love him dad. I always will."

"Remember how much he hurt you," Sharon added. "Can you really trust him?"

"Thank you both for your concern but I am a big girl. I can take care of myself."

"I hope it works out this time. Otherwise, I may have to buy bigger sized clothes."

"Why would you need to do that Sharon?"

"From eating too many brownies."

They both laughed but Sylvia felt no joviality reach into her frozen heart.

No one in the family except Mimi was happy with this news. Martin saw Sylvia's face fall but she didn't say a word.

He said, "I hope it works out for you."

He didn't mean it.

Sharon wanted to take Mimi away and hide her in a castle where no harm would come to her. She agreed with her parents that Mimi reuniting with David was a poor plan. Sharon was relieved that she was no longer in love with David. The main emotion she now felt for him was revulsion.

"Mimi, do you want to go for a walk?"

"Yes, I sure do."

The tension in their home was so thick that you could cut it with a knife. The girls each wrapped themselves up in a warm jacket and off they went. They had been walking together since they were little. It always helped them escape their mother and calm down.

"I'm worried about you, Mimi."

"Why? I am doing so well."

"Are you really sure that you want to take David back?"

"Yes, I love him. I always will."

"I have a bad feeling about this."

"I know you have my best interests in mind but I will be fine."

There was nothing left to say. So on they walked, chatting about everything except what was really on their minds.

CHAPTER 25

Sharon and Mimi were helping Martin plan a large party for Sylvia's 50th birthday. When he brought up the subject of her birthday, she just shrugged and said, "Let's go for a nice dinner with our daughters." Somehow, he felt that this was not enough. They needed some type of celebration in the family so he decided to throw a lavish surprise party for her. He met with Sharon and Mimi to discuss the details. Each had a different opinion. Martin wanted to rent a banquet room in a hotel and have a fancy catered event. Mimi thought a barbecue would be ideal. Sharon thought that they should have the party at Sylvia's favourite Greek restaurant. As Sylvia's birthday was in early September, the weather would still be ideal for an indoor or outdoor event.

As the three were chatting over greasy burgers and fries, Martin had a brainstorm.

"What do you think about having the party at the Château Lucerne?" This was a lovely old hotel just outside Montreal. The hotel had old world charm and wild English country gardens.

"That's a brilliant idea dad," said Sharon. "Mom loves that place. We could have the party in one of the gardens. How will you get her there without her knowing there is a party?"

"I could tell her that we are going for dinner there. She will never suspect a thing. The two of you could come with us. She will think this is for dinner and not have a clue."

"Should we bring our boyfriends? I know mom doesn't care for David. Would bringing him spoil her party?"

"Let's invite both boyfriends to the party but the four of us will go there together."

"Dad, I am not sure that we should invite either of them at all," Sharon told him. "Mom really hates David and I can't invite Danny if David is not invited. Perhaps we could just not tell them about the party."

Mimi looked stricken but she said, "I agree with Sharon. We shouldn't invite either one. They can do without us for one night."

So it was decided. They started dividing up the party tasks. Martin would book the hotel. Sharon would make up a guest list and send out invitations. Mimi would choose the food that would be served at the event. It would all go smoothly and Sylvia would love it, or so they hoped.

Martin went on planning the surprise party for Sylvia. He was concerned that she would notice but Sylvia was back in her other world. Since Mimi had announced her reconciliation with David, Sylvia had been struggling with a deep sadness that was trying to overtake her. It was not just her dislike of him. She had a feeling that the relationship would bring tragedy to Mimi's life. From the moment she had met David, she had felt a vague sensation of danger lurking. As his relationship with Mimi grew stronger, so did her fear and concern. She had felt a lessening when the relationship ended but now the feeling was back and it was darkening her world. She had nightmares about it all the time. It was always the same. Mimi would be lying in a pool of blood. She had discussed this fear with her psychologist many times. He had told her that this was actually a fear of losing her daughter to another person. Although this made sense to her on a logical level, it made no sense to her on an emotional level.

Sharon also had the same premonition. She would dream that Mimi was in danger and Sharon could never save her. She would wake up with her heart pounding and wind up going to the kitchen for something to eat. Usually it was something she shouldn't eat but she didn't care.

One morning, Sharon woke up and went to the kitchen to make

some coffee. She saw Sylvia sitting at the table looking pale and drawn. Her first thought was that her mother was sick.

"Are you okay mom?"

"Yes I am."

"You look like you have seen a ghost."

"It's that dream again."

"What dream?"

"I keep dreaming that something terrible is happening to Mimi. She is lying in a pool of blood or getting eaten by a lion or something else equally horrible."

Sharon gasped.

"I have been having similar dreams. Mimi is always being killed."

Sylvia looked at Sharon with confusion.

"Why are we both having these dreams?"

"We are both scared for Mimi and the damage David could do to her." Sharon answered.

She wondered if that was true. The conversation turned to other topics but left them both feeling very uneasy.

Sharon weighed herself and noticed that she was five pounds heavier. She decided to lose weight by working out at the gym. This just made her more hungry and she ate even more. When she had the dream about Mimi, she ate still more. She decided to wait until her life was less stressful to lose weight. She wondered if that day would ever come.

CHAPTER 26

Sylvia's surprise birthday party turned out to be better than anyone could have imagined. August 28 was a perfect day. The intense summer heat was gone and the day was warm, sunny, and temperate. A slight mild breeze was just enough to make curtains stir slightly. When Martin, Sylvia, Mimi, and Sharon drove to the country, everyone was in a sunny mood. Sylvia was thrilled because she was going out for a birthday dinner with her family. Martin was happy because the plan had gone off without a hitch. Mimi was happy because things were going so well with David. Sharon was happy because she had had wild sex the night before.

Their drive proceeded well and they arrived at the château early. All the guests were waiting and Sylvia was bowled over when they yelled, "Surprise!"

So many of Sylvia and Martin's friends were there and it was a pleasure to see them.

The party took place both indoors and on the lovely manicured grounds. Sylvia was thrilled to see so many long time friends wishing her well.

People mingled and ate delicious canapés in the perfect late summer sun. Then there was a buffet meal with some of Sylvia's favourite foods. There was smoked salmon and all types of seafood. There were multiple salads of all kinds including Sylvia's favourite, a wedge salad with blue cheese. The star item on the buffet was prime rib with Yorkshire pudding. And as if anyone was still hungry, there was chocolate cheesecake and many pastries for dessert.

After dessert, a huge birthday cake was brought out and Sylvia blew out the candles. After that, they danced on the terrace beneath the darkening skies. Sylvia had never felt so loved and cherished.

She and Martin danced a slow dance on the terrace. She fit so well into his arms.

"I love you," he whispered in her ear.

"I love you too," she answered and felt a little surprised that she actually meant it.

CHAPTER 27. SHARON

I can't believe how well things are going in my family. Everyone is speaking to each other and getting along. My mom and dad are acting like they are on their honeymoon. I am used to hearing them argue and now all I hear is the two of them having sex. I say good for them. My mother's craziness has always been a source of trouble in their marriage and she seems a lot less crazy.

Another year of university is about to start and I am not ready. This summer has been so much fun. I have gotten to spend as much time as I want to do nothing. So many of my friends have to work in the summer because their parents insist on it. My dad says I work hard enough at school so I am entitled to spend summer relaxing. I wonder if he would approve of all the pot I smoked and all the sex I had. I am still with Danny. It's not that I like him so much but I just don't want to make the effort of breaking up with him.

Yes, the other lovebirds, Mimi and David, are back in full force. This time dad and mom are both not pleased about it. They think he will break up with Mimi again. I think he has learned his lesson and he will never do anything so stupid again. Well, they are not interfering in the relationship. It is easier for them because Mimi is not living at home. They know Mimi and David are together but they don't know how often they see each other or how serious they are.

They are very serious. David has been staying over with her almost every night. He has again asked her to marry him. This time he wants to elope. I think he is afraid that my parents will change her mind if they get engaged. This is a valid fear as he knows they don't approve of him.

Mimi and I got together last week for coffee. We discussed their relationship.

"David wants to elope," she told me.

"Do you want to elope?"

"I'm not sure."

"Don't let him pressure you."

"I won't."

Meanwhile, I have to go to university and register for my courses. September has been baking so far. I am going to wear my hot pants to registration. Maybe I can find a better boyfriend when I am there.

Well, I can't t believe this happened so fast. When I was registering for my courses, a tall good-looking guy came up to me and said,

"How are you Sharon? It's been a while."

"It's been forever."

I didn't have a clue about who he was or why he was talking to me. This guy was amazing looking. He was tall and slim with the bluest eyes and the thickest auburn hair. I noticed other girls giving him the eye but his eyes were fixed on me.

"Where do we know each other from?" I asked him.

"My name is Alan Goldstein. You sat next to me in French class in 8th grade. We plotted together against Monsieur Rideau. We were going to overthrow the regime he had in class. I always liked you but you never noticed me."

Suddenly the picture came into my head of a short, skinny, pimply boy that sat next to me in French class. He had certainly grown up and blossomed. I never would have taken him for the same person.

"Yes, I remember you," I told him. "We launched some good spitballs together. Are you going to McGill?"

"Yes, I'm in my second year of political science. I am hoping to get into law school. Do you want to go for a coffee?"

So we did. During the coffee in the student union building, I couldn't stop from staring at him as we chatted. We talked for almost three hours and then I realized I had an appointment with the dentist. As I rushed away, I slipped him my phone number. I never once considered my relationship with Danny. I must be a slut.

"I can't wait to see you again," he said as I rushed away. Oh my, oh my, I think I am in love or at least in lust.

I thought of him as I was getting my teeth cleaned. I thought of him after I had gone home. I thought of him when I was eating supper. I thought of him when I was stumbling into bed that night. Every day I would come home and look for a phone message from him and every day I was disappointed. After two weeks of waiting, I decided this dream was not about to become a reality and I moved on with other things.

I still wondered what I had done wrong. I decided that it was his loss instead of mine but the feeling that I had somehow messed up still persisted. I spoke to Mimi and she assured me that Alan was a fool for not contacting me. This, and a plate of mom's fudge brownies really helped heal the pain.

The three of us were sitting at the kitchen table chowing down on the brownies and chatting. It became a weekly ritual in our home. It had started when Mimi and David had broken up but continued and developed a momentum of its own. No matter what else was happening in our lives, on Sunday afternoons we would have our brownies chats. Mom would make a different kind of brownie each week.

The three of us would discuss our week and laugh together. We would eat brownies and drink strong coffee. We decided that this would be an exclusive club with no men allowed. Even dad knew that he was not invited. It had been mom's idea to make this open to just the three of us. I wondered if she did that so that

Mimi would not bring David. No matter what the reason was, our threesome became a great success. We started to talk about personal topics and cheer each other up when we were sad.

I looked forward to our talks through the week. I knew that I would have the Sunday chats and company. Our talks led us through the fall into another harsh Montreal winter. I realized we had been doing this for three months. Mom announced that she and dad were going to Florida for Christmas and would be absent for two weeks but she would leave us brownies so we could continue.

I realized I had been wearing my summer clothes when we started this and now winter was in full swing. On December 15, I walked shivering in the door. I removed my 3 layers of clothes and went to say hello to my mother.

"Hi mom!" I yelled.

"You have a phone message!" she yelled back to me.

I was shocked to see that it was a message from Alan. I wondered whether I should even respond to him. He had waited over three months to get in touch with me. He couldn't have been so interested in seeing me again. On the other hand, maybe there was a very good reason I hadn't heard from him. Maybe there had been a family tragedy or emergency.

I had looked on campus for him so many times hoping to run into him again. McGill University has a large campus but I still looked. I never found him and I eventually gave up hope of seeing him again. My relationship with Danny was still on but my feelings for him were gone. He was just a person to see and have sex with when the mood struck me.

I really struggled about what I should do. Part of me wanted to phone Alan and the other part felt that I should just let it go. I decided to ponder the matter over dinner that night. Mom had made moussaka and a Greek salad for dinner and I dug in. This is why Mimi is so slim and I am round and curvy. I really love my food. Mimi pecks at her food and I devour mine. She was over for dinner that evening and I watched her daintily eating her food while I was having seconds. Danny invariably says he loves to watch me eat. He says it is the sexiest thing he has ever seen. I wonder why.

I did not want to mention Alan at the dinner table so I waited until after dinner and asked Mimi to come to my room.

"I met this dreamy guy named Alan at university in September. I gave him my phone number and it took him three months to phone me. I am wondering if I should phone him back."

"Of course you should. He might have a good reason for waiting so long. If he doesn't, you don't have to get together with him."

"You're right. A phone call is not a commitment. I can just talk to him. I don't have to see him." Mimi was always right except when it came to David. She knew how to put things into perspective.

As we were chatting, Mom called out to me, "Someone is on the phone for you. It is someone named Alan."

My heart did a flip-flop as I went to answer the phone. He had phoned twice in one day. I should at least hear him out.

"Hello," I muttered.

"Hi Sharon, this is Alan Goldstein. We met at registration three months ago. I am sorry it took me so long to phone you. I broke my leg playing hockey and I have been unable to do much of anything. I hope we can still get together."

"Sure why not?"

"There is a classical concert at Place des Arts next Thursday. They will be playing the music of Mozart who is my favourite composer. Would you like to go with me?"

"That sounds good."

"We can go out to eat first. There is a great little Italian restaurant near Place des Arts. Do you like Italian food?"

"It's one of my favourites."

"How about if I pick you up at six? That will give us lots of time for dinner and the concert."

"That sounds fine. My address is 25 Clarke Lane."

"I can't wait to see you. Bye."

I felt like Cinderella going to the ball. I went to the kitchen. Mom and Mimi were talking about how to peel an eggplant.

They stopped and stared when I came in.

"Are you alright? Mom asked. "You are flushed."

"I am fine. I am excited. I just made a date with a great guy." The old version of mom would have quizzed me about him but the new version just said, "That is lovely dear," and went on with her conversation.

Mimi asked me, "What about Danny?" and I just shrugged.

I spent days worrying about what to wear to the symphony. I couldn't decide what to wear. I asked mom and Mimi what to wear. I tried on everything I owned and found it all lacking. I was driving myself crazy. I finally settled on a pair of black velvet pants and a glittery blue sweater. Mimi assured me it looked great on me. Mom insisted that I wear her diamond pendant necklace with it.

By Thursday, I was prepared but I thought of cancelling the date. I had worked myself into such a frenzy that I had chewed off all my nails. I asked myself what was the worst that could happen. The worst would be that we didn't like each other and never got together again. This would not be a terrible heartbreak. I hardly knew the guy.

In university on Thursday, I couldn't wait for my classes to be over. I rushed home and started to get ready even though it was hours until my date. The house was quiet and empty. Mom and dad had left for Florida yesterday. The afternoon dragged by. I busied myself with meaningless tasks until it was time for Alan to arrive.

I heard the doorbell ring and my heart lurched in my throat. I rushed to the door. There he was dressed in a lovely blue shirt that matched his eyes. I really liked the fact that he was early.

"Hello, you look beautiful," was the first thing he said when he saw me.

He asked, "May I help you on with your jacket?"

"Yes please," I said while he put my down parka over my shoulders and on my arms. He was driving his dad's car. Traffic was light and we made it to the Italian restaurant in good time. We chatted like two long time friends on the way. I felt as if I had known him forever.

What should I order?" I asked him.

"Everything is delicious here. I have been coming here with my parents for years and we have tried everything on the menu."

I liked that he got along with his parents.

"Do you still come here with your parents?" I asked him.

"As often as possible."

I ordered spaghetti and meatballs and he ordered the same. He said that he was not trying to copy me. This just happened to be his favourite. I couldn't argue with his good taste.

The food was delicious but the service was slow. We didn't have time for dessert so we rushed off to the symphony. I had never been to a classical concert at Place des Arts before. I was surprised by the music and its ability to make me forget everything else. As the music played, I fell into a hypnotized state where I felt the music directly go into my body. It was like a slow motion dream. Time passed so quickly until we were applauding at the end.

I had enjoyed the evening so much. I couldn't believe that I had been so worried about the date. When he dropped me off at the door, I wondered if I should invite him in but I didn't get a chance.

He said, "Thank you for a great evening," and kissed me quickly and chastely on the cheek. Then he was gone. I wondered if I had imagined the whole evening.

I walked around in a euphoric daze until I realized that a week had passed and he hadn't phoned me again. I had been all ready to fly into the sunset with Alan. I had been ready to break up with Danny for him. I wondered what I had done wrong and decided that this was not my fault. He had done this before after all. Maybe he would come back in three months with another good explanation. At that time, I would say no. As great as he was, it was way too difficult to deal with not hearing from him. I chalked it up to a learning experience and soon forgot all about him. This was helped along by a new family drama which unfolded rather suddenly.

Mimi and David had gone to Las Vegas and gotten married. They came by the house to tell me. They both seemed genuinely happy and content. David said that he had been a fool but he was slowly getting smarter. I was taken aback by the news as I had been telling Mimi to take it slowly but she seemed so glowing and radiant that I did not say a word.

It was Mimi who brought up the topic.

"How are we going to break the news to mom and dad?" she asked me.

"Very carefully," I told her.

"When are they coming back?" David asked me looking a little scared and unsure.

"A week from tomorrow," I responded.

"We'll tell them together," David said.

"Good plan. You just can't let their reaction upset you. Congratulations again. Where will you live?"

"I am moving into David's apartment over the next few days. I don't have much to take so it should be easy. Will you help me move?"

"Of course."

After they left, I was deeply upset. Mom had come so far. She was finally in a good place. This was bound to upset her. The only question was how much. Dad would not be thrilled either. He had started to mistrust David when he broke up with Mimi. Somehow the feeling had stuck but dad tended to be way more diplomatic than mom. He would congratulate them with a big smile whether he meant it or not. What mom would do was anyone's guess.

CHAPTER 28

Sharon looked at her watch. It was almost dinnertime. In an hour, she would be driving to the airport to pick up her parents. They were returning from a two-week winter getaway to Florida.

She was apprehensive about their return. They would find out soon that Mimi and David were married. This was bound to be a disaster.

Sylvia had confided on the phone to Sharon that she had hardly thought of home for the entire two weeks and she was proud of herself for that. However, now, as she was returning, she had a knot in her stomach that just wouldn't go away.

Sharon was waiting for them at the gate and gave them both a big hug. She looked happy and healthy and Sylvia wondered if she was just imagining disaster where there was none. Her mother Fredelle would call it borrowing trouble. She was definitely a pro at that, she thought bitterly.

"How is everything?" she asked Sharon.

"Mimi and I are fine. The house is in one piece. It is bitterly cold out there. I hope the car will start."

It did and they drove home through the chilly night watching the ice fog on the trees and the mounds of snow. Sylvia shivered despite her warm jacket. Her body always had trouble going between two extreme changes of climate. Her mother had said that it was because there was not enough fat on her bones.

Sharon filled them in on everything that was new at home. She didn't tell them that Mimi and David had gotten married. She didn't want to spoil their homecoming and she felt the news should come from the source. This was not going to go over well.

Why should she bear the brunt of their disapproval and possible anger? Mimi had promised that she and David would come over the next day to tell them and that was enough for her.

Besides, she had her own issues to think about. Danny had phoned her from a trip to France and told her that he loved her and wanted their relationship to be more serious. She didn't feel the same way but did not want to hurt his feelings. She had to end their relationship completely, but how?

That evening, Sylvia lay shivering in bed. Sharon brought her a hot cup of tea and Martin brought over a heating pad and tucked it under her. This didn't help so he added an extra blanket on top of her. This still didn't help. She lay there with her teeth chattering unable to warm up no matter how hard she tried. Martin finally got under the covers and put his naked firm hot body against her as he held her in his arms. Finally, the chilliness started to thaw and she fell asleep with him still holding her.

The next morning, Martin was already gone when she woke up. She wanted to stay in bed all day but she had things to do. She needed to buy groceries and make a nice dinner for everyone. Mimi said she was coming over for dinner and bringing David. Sylvia decided that she might as well be gracious to him. She still hoped that they would break up again but she was willing to accept him for now.

At the same time, Sharon was walking to her first class on campus. She shivered at the cold and wrapped her scarf tighter around her neck. She was also wondering how the evening would go. Although this was not her battle, she was very involved in this war. Her mother's hatred of David had caused so many problems in their lives. David had also caused his own battles. She hoped mom would be mature and gracious enough to hear the truth. She arrived in her class, took off her jacket, hat, mittens, and scarf and prepared for a day of learning.

Sharon's premonitions came true. The evening did not go as planned. Later Martin called it a disaster similar to the sinking of the Titanic. He felt he had watched his happy family suddenly sink into misery and despair. Things started off very rocky and went downhill quickly. To begin with, Mimi and David were quite late and Sylvia's beautiful roast dried to a leathery consistency. When they arrived an hour after they were supposed to, she was worried and livid at the same time.

"I am so sorry we are late. There was a terrible accident on the highway and not a car was moving. We had to wait for the police and ambulance to clear the scene." Mimi looked very upset and Sylvia believed her but this did not start things well. Martin hung up their coats and everyone sat down for dinner. The extra hour had wreaked havoc on much of the food. The roast was dry. The potatoes were slightly too crispy and the broccoli was mushy. Sylvia did not even apologize. She sat with a scowl on her face eating and not saying a word. Luckily, everyone was starved and they hardly noticed that the food was not up to par.

Sharon watched everyone eating. They were so quiet. It was as if everyone had lost their ability to speak. She waited anxiously knowing what was coming.

David said, "Great meal Mrs. Miller," and she stared at him with daggers in her eyes.

Everyone could tell that she was in a dreadful mood. They engaged in conversation while she sat numbly at the table. When they were dining on the cheesecake and drinking the coffee, it was time for Mimi and David to make their announcement.

"Mom, Dad, Sharon, we have something to tell you. David and I got married last week. We decided to elope because we didn't want a large wedding. We are both very excited. We hope you will all be happy for us." Mimi was looking right at Sylvia when she said this. Sylvia stood up without saying a word and walked out of the room. They heard her slamming her bedroom door.

"Congratulations," Martin said tepidly. "Don't worry about your mother. She will come around." Even as he said this, he wondered if it was true. "Where will you live?"

"We are living in my apartment, Mr Miller," David told him.

"Soon we are going to look for something larger. My studio apartment is hardly big enough for one person never mind two."

"We should have a party for you," Martin told them.

"Let's wait until mom feels better about this," Mimi suggested. Sylvia did not come out again for the rest of the evening. Martin went to check on her and she was lying in bed looking pale and rigid. This was not the time to talk to her so he left the bedroom.

Everyone pitched in to clean up and then Martin and Sharon walked Mimi and David to the door. No one mentioned Sylvia. They were all waiting to see what would happen. Would the old or new Sylvia emerge? Only time would tell.

That evening when Martin went to join Sylvia in bed, she had not moved. He decided to let her absorb this news in her own way. He got into bed and put his arm around her. Being a doctor had taught him to sleep well and he was out like a light in seconds holding his sleepless and miserable wife.

Sylvia finally dozed off to nightmares of epic proportions. When she woke up in the morning, she felt empty and lost. She phoned her psychologist and made an appointment to see him right away. She prayed that this would help because she felt like she was drowning and she desperately needed help to keep from going under.

Sylvia realized after the phone call that her coping mechanisms were better than before. After her chat with the psychologist, she felt that she was ready to rejoin the world of the living. She felt shaky and upset but she could get on with her life. She was not going to phone the happy couple to wish them well until she was ready to do so. She wasn't sure if she would ever be ready.

Sharon arrived home from school that evening to a smiling mother and a delicious dinner. Martin and Sharon were both relieved to see Sylvia smiling. Throughout the meal, no one mentioned Mimi and David's marriage. The wound was still too raw. Sharon and Martin hoped Sylvia would eventually come to terms with what had happened. He was still smarting from the news himself. Somehow, he had hoped that Mimi would find someone better. He still didn't trust David but he knew that there was nothing he could do about it – especially now. So they went on with their dinner and their lives as before but not really as before.

CHAPTER 29. SHARON

Well, I suppose the easy-going cheerful attitude at our house could not have lasted. Dad's smile seems forced. Mom has lost her appetite and she is losing weight again but at least she is getting out. Mom and Dad now invite Mimi and David over for Sunday dinner and they usually show up. I wish they wouldn't. The conversation is strained and the atmosphere is awkward. Mom looks so miserable when she sees them together.

As for the two of them, they are as tight as ever. They sit holding hands and keep looking into each other's eyes the way people do when they have just met. I envy them. My relationship with Danny is over. He ended it because he thought I wasn't ready to commit to him. He was right. I want a relationship like Mimi and David's with so much love that you can feel it when you are in the same room with them. I want someone who will do anything for me. He looks at her with so much love that it makes me want to cry. I am holding out for the same thing. I may never find it but I am just 20 years old. I figure that I have some time to try. For now, I will just go to university and enjoy life as much as I can. Life is not so easy at home so I spend some extra time at the library. There I can have a quiet read and not have to interact with anyone.

I am thinking of being a hermit for a while. I am feeling tired of being with people and I think my own space would be good. Mimi and I used to be so close but things are changing now that she is married. She and David are looking for a house. They have decided they want to start a family soon and an apartment will be too small. She is already teaching and he is still finishing medical school but I guess they have figured out the money deal. Dad has offered to lend them money for a down payment and

David's parents have as well. They will be fine. I really miss my conversations with Mimi. I miss dropping in on her and smoking pot together. We used to talk several times a week and now I am lucky to hear from her once a week. I have to get used to this. She is in a different role and she has left me behind. I wish it didn't hurt so much.

I am used to being the invisible daughter but now I am also the invisible sister. This gives me way more grief. Mimi and I have a lifelong bond. I thought that nothing could ever break it but I was wrong. I am starting to dislike David as much as mom and dad do. It is not his fault that he and Mimi shut me out but somehow I feel that he wants her all to himself. He must sense the animosity towards him in our house. It is so thick you can cut it with a knife. So he hoards her in hopes that her love will protect him from all the hatred. Who knows? Maybe it will.

CHAPTER 30

Sylvia sat in her psychologist's office having a very difficult conversation with him.

"I feel that I have lost my daughter," she said.

"Why?" he asked.

"She is married to a man I hate. We hardly ever talk anymore. When she is over, it is always with him. Now they are married, and I don't think I will ever feel close to her again."

"Are you close to your other daughter?" he asked her.

"Yes, we are very close." Sylvia believed that even though Sharon might have told a different story.

"What do you think you can do to be closer to Mimi?" he asked her.

"I could stop hating David. I am sure she knows it. I am sure everyone knows it. The problem is that I can't do it."

"Can't or won't?" he asked.

"Does it really matter?" she said.

"Yes it does. You have made a choice to hate David. You can make a choice to stop hating him. Your hatred is making your daughter have to choose sides. She has to side with her husband. You are not giving her a choice."

Sylvia thought about that statement. She thought about it as she was driving home. She thought about it as she was preparing supper. She thought about it when she went to bed that night. By morning, she had made a decision to stop hating David no matter what effort it took.

She would learn to smile at David and really mean it. She would stop glaring at him. She would be interested in his life and his relationship with Mimi. This was going to be a huge effort and she knew it would be difficult at first but she would eventually get it right.

The thought of being nice to David made her feel queasy but the thought of losing Mimi again made her feel even worse so what choice did she have?

As she drove home, she thought of this some more. She had been in drama class in high school. Her teacher had said that she was good at facial expressions. She would have to practice a sincere smile until she really meant it.

That evening, she brought up the topic to Martin over dinner.

"I think we should be nicer to David," she told him.

"Why?" he asked her. He was not so pleased with his son-in-law either. He didn't trust David anymore after his past behaviour had hurt Mimi so much.

"Well, he obviously makes our daughter very happy. Maybe we could use this as a basis for forgiving him. I understand that I am the one who holds the longtime grudge against him but it is not working. Mimi is becoming remote from both of us. We need to be closer to them. What happens when they have children? Don't you want us to be the doting grandparents?"

Martin started at her in silence. He could not believe that his wife was actually preparing to have a truce with David. She had changed so much that he hardly recognized her anymore. He loved the new Sylvia way more than he had loved the other one.

"Yes, I don't suppose it will hurt. How do you propose we make this change?"

"Well, we could start off my smiling at him and including him in our conversations. If we manage that, maybe we can figure out what else to do."

"Okay, let's begin this Sunday when they are over for dinner."

So Sylvia made raspberry crisp for dessert because it was David's favourite and they began their new friendly behaviour.

This was going to work. Sylvia was determined that it had to. Even Martin had agreed that it was necessary to change their behaviour towards David. So, every week when Mimi and David had dinner with them, they went out of their way to be friendly to him. Everyone noticed this. Sharon thought that they were trying too hard and wondered why.

At first, both David and Mimi were suspicious. On their way home, he asked her,

"Is it just me or were your parents behaving strangely tonight?"

"It looked like they had glued smiles on their faces," was her answer.

"Well, the dinner and raspberry crisp were delicious."

"Do you think my parents are up to something?" Mimi was suspicious of both Sylvia and Martin, especially as they had never forgiven David for the past.

"I guess we will have to wait and see."

The conversation then turned to other topics and they arrived home full and sleepy. They went to bed and cuddled. They fell asleep wrapped snugly in each other's arms.

CHAPTER 31. SHARON

Now my mother and father have both gone crazy. They are going out of their way to be nice to David. They are some strange pair crooning over him. It is obvious to anyone that they are acting weird. They give him too much attention. He and Mimi both look uncomfortable. They leave as soon as they can after dinner is over. They always have to be at home early because they have to get up early. While this is actually true, they don't have to leave as early as they do. I think this is all too strange. One day mom and dad hate David and the next day they love him.

Mimi and David are buying a house. They want to start a family. I am happy for them but very jealous. They seem to have everything figured out while I am nowhere. I am still living with my parents and struggling with what I want to do for a living. I know I don't want to teach. We did our student teaching last term and I didn't enjoy it one bit. They both have great careers. She is teaching and he is finally an intern at the hospital. I wonder if Mimi and David will have many children.

I wish I had a boyfriend who cared about me. Since my relationship with Danny ended, there hasn't been anyone. I have gone to some parties but nothing has clicked. I fear that I will be living with my parents for the rest of my life. I am 21 and I don't have a clue about what I want to do with my life. Mom and dad never push me. They never even suggest that it is time to move out but I am restless. I need to do something with my life other than going to university and smoking pot. It is time for me to grow up but I don't know how. Dad says I will figure out what I want. He says there is no hurry to do this as I am still young. Mimi is young too and she has a husband, a career, and soon a family. When will any of these happen for me? I am afraid the answer is never.

I have decided that I need to get out of the rut I am in. How? I could certainly do with getting out of the house and doing something interesting. I am going to phone Mimi. Maybe she can tear herself away from David to have lunch with me. She is still my best friend.

Mimi and I have arranged to go out for smoked meat sandwiches tomorrow. I am looking forward to seeing her.

CHAPTER 32. SHARON

Mimi and I had a wonderful lunch. We ate huge smoked meat sandwiches with greasy fries and talked about everything. I asked her what I should do about the rut I found myself stuck in. She said I should do one thing that is new and different. This seemed like a good idea but I didn't know what to do. She suggested going out and finding a new man. I told her that this was a great plan but I didn't know how.

"There must be events at McGill University. There is always something going on there."

"Well, the newspaper is looking for new people to write stories. I have thought of doing that."

"So what's stopping you?"

"Just plain apathy."

"Well, then get off your butt and go."

So I did. It turned out to be the best decision of my life. When I went to the meeting of the newspaper group, I found a group of kindred spirits. All of us were interested in changing the world for the better. I was assigned to write a story about a guest speaker on campus who was discussing abortion. This was right up my alley. I wrote the story and Andy the editor said it was amazing. He published it without any changes. As the weeks went on, I wrote more and more articles that were published in the McGill newspaper and I began to feel a renewed interest in life. I also realized that I loved writing.

Well, I have finally graduated from university. I am supposed to be grown up but I am not. I don't even have a career. I know the solution to my problem. This summer I am going to find a job and a man. Mimi is the one who is all grown up. She and David want to have a baby. I want to grow up too. The problem is that is is easy for her. I am not the kind of person she is. Nothing falls into place for me the way it does for her. She knew that she wanted to teach when she was 4 years old. She made me play teacher with her every day. She would be the teacher and I would be the student. She would ask me to sit down and then she would teach me something simple. Sometimes it would be how to add up two numbers and other times it would be something like tying a shoelace. I did this willingly as I adored her.

CHAPTER 33

All of her life Sharon had been influenced too much by Mimi. Whatever Mimi told her to do was what she did. When they were children it was even worse. Mimi would tell Sharon to do something crazy and Sharon would oblige. She remembered the time Mimi had told her to eat a lilac from the bushes in their front yard. She had been five and Mimi had been seven. Sharon was hesitant but Mimi told her,

"It tastes delicious and it is good for you."

"Are you sure Mimi?"

"Just eat it Sharon."

"I feel sick."

It was not delicious and it made her throw up but Sharon still blindly followed her sister around. After all, Mimi was the smart and beautiful one. Even at the age of five, Sharon knew that their mother loved Mimi more that she loved Sharon. Sylvia was always praising everything Mimi did and telling her how smart she was. If Mimi drew a childish picture, Sylvia would display it on the fridge. If Sharon drew a similar picture, Sylvia would praise it but Sharon would never see it again. She knew even at that age that her mother had thrown it out. It hurt her deeply that she was not considered as good as her sister. So, a lifelong worship of Mimi and hatred of Sylvia started in Sharon's mind. Sharon also had no confidence. How could she? She was never good enough to measure up.

As she thought of it, she realized that it was time for it to end. She was an adult and had to figure things out. Mimi was busy with her marriage and her life. No one could tell Sharon where to go from here with her life. She had to decide herself – and soon – because floating around was not doing her any good. One thing she knew for sure was that she did not want to teach. She now had a teaching degree but had not looked for any teaching jobs. Her student teaching had been a nightmare and she realized that she had only gone into teaching because Mimi had. She felt like such a dismal failure.

She loved writing for the university newspaper. The editor, a large gangly boy named Andy, loved everything she wrote. He would always praise her and publish her articles verbatim. Sharon wondered if she had some writing talent. Little did she know that Andy had a burning crush on her and would have said anything to get her to notice him. He stayed up nights masturbating to the image of Sharon lying naked beside him. She never noticed him but his crush lasted for years until he met his future wife Marsha who resembled Sharon.

Sharon decided she would keep a journal with her ideas in it. Her school counsellor had told her that a journal would help her know what she wanted.

So for two months she wrote down ideas that came to mind. Sometimes, they made no sense but she still did it. After the two months, she read her journal. Suddenly she realized what it was that she wanted to do. She wanted to write. Journaling had given her more purpose than anything had in a long time. She really loved writing and she would make a living doing that.

She could go to Carlton University in Ottawa to journalism school and start the process. Of course, she would have to apply first. If she got in, she could finally live away from home and learn to do something she really enjoyed. It seemed like a wonderful plan. She would also be less involved in Mimi's life. Maybe she could have a life of her own. The more she thought about it, the more excited she got.

The next day she went to university and picked up the forms to apply to Carleton University for a Bachelor of Journalism. She wondered if she could afford to go to school in Ottawa but she believed that her parents would help her out with that. If they didn't she could always apply for a student loan.

She hadn't been this excited for a long time. She decided she would tell the entire family at this week's Sunday night dinner. She hoped that they would be excited for her. She was sure her parents would be thrilled to finally have her doing something. Mimi and David would be happy for her but in their own universe. This was going to be a new and exciting chapter in her life and she couldn't wait for it to begin.

CHAPTER 34

Meanwhile, on the other side of the city, Mimi was sitting on her sofa at home waiting for the results of her home pregnancy test. It turned out positive. She was pregnant. She didn't know whether to laugh or cry. She really wanted a child and David did as well but lately she was sensing that there was something seriously wrong in their relationship. David was often distant and she was uncomfortable. He claimed nothing was wrong but she knew him too well to believe that.

Her fear was that David was cheating on her. He had lost interest in sex. They hadn't had sex in almost a month. He was now working in a hospital emergency room with many beautiful nurses. Maybe he was seeing one of them. He was often home late and always claimed there had been a new emergency with a patient. Somehow she didn't believe him. Her own father worked in the emergency room and he managed to be home on time.

She wondered if she was just being foolish but knew she wasn't. This was a dilemma. Should she tell him about the baby? Should she leave him? Should she have an abortion? They had been married for just one year and their marriage was already falling apart.

The idea of having an abortion really bothered her but she did not want to raise a child alone. She was in the biggest mess of her life. She wondered if she should talk to her parents but she was also uncomfortable about that. She knew they had never been pleased with her choice and felt that she had let them down. Sharon was her usual confidante but she had been neglecting Sharon lately in an effort to spend more time with David. Would

Sharon even want to talk to her?

Mimi had always prided herself on knowing what to do but she was lost. She decided to talk to David. He was her husband after all. His reaction to the news would be very telling. If he was happy about it, maybe they could still work on their marriage. If he was unhappy, that would mean a different scenario. It would confirm to her that he was cheating and she would confront him about it.

That evening she decided to make a special dinner. David loved lamb. She slow roasted a leg of lamb with rosemary and garlic even though the smell made her sick. She mashed some potatoes with buttermilk and make a large salad. She even forced herself to make an apple pie for dessert.

At six when David was supposed to be at home, she got a phone call. He told her he would be late. There was an emergency at the hospital, he said. At eight, he was still not home. At nine, she threw out the food and went to bed and cried herself to sleep. When he came home and crawled into bed, he smelled of sex with another woman and she knew.

At that moment, her father Martin was wondering what he should do. He and David worked in the same hospital. There were rumours that David and a nurse named Penny were having an affair. He had heard them numerous times. He didn't want to tell Sylvia because he wasn't sure if these rumours were even true. He certainly didn't want to tell Mimi but he was torn. He was sure that David and Penny were having an affair. His wife and daughter had a right to know but he had no business telling them something damaging if it was a lie. He had seen careers and marriages destroyed by lies.

David pulled on his bathrobe and walked into the kitchen. Mimi was sitting on a chair at the kitchen table. As soon as he looked at her he knew that she knew about his infidelity. Her eyes were red rimmed as if she had been crying.

"How could you David?" was all she said.

“I’m sorry, Mimi. I have no excuse for what I did. I’ve been a fool. Please forgive me.”

“How long has it been going on?” she asked him.

“A few months,” he told her and then he realized what a fool he had been.

“How did you know?” he asked her.

“You came home last night with the smell of her all over you. I would have to be crazy not to notice.”

David felt terrible. He wanted what he had with Mimi. That was real. The other was just a stupid fantasy.

“Please give me another chance,” he begged her.

“I always stood up for you. My family didn’t trust you but I told them they were wrong. What a fool I’ve been.”

“It’s not too late. We can still work things out.”

“It is too late. We have been married just a year and you have already cheated on me. That is a record. I want you to leave.”

“Where will I go?”

“I don’t care. I am going to work in a few minutes. I want you gone by the time I return.” She left the room and went to take a shower. Her words had hit David like a brick. He felt the air kicked out of him. What would he do? Where would he go?

Sharon was busy filling out her application for journalism school. She was excited about this opportunity to finally do something with her life. She had just finished having dinner with her parents and she was up to her elbows in forms. There was so much to fill out. Still, she was so happy that she had finally committed to something. Her parents were happy for her as well, although her father had seemed very preoccupied at dinner. For once, it was Sylvia giving her the encouragement.

“You will make a great journalist,” her mother told her. “You have always had a flair for writing. This is a perfect career choice.”

Martin had smiled and agreed with Sylvia but she could tell he was thinking about something else. She had excused herself soon after dinner to work on her application forms. Nothing could stop her now.

The phone in her room rang.

“Hi,” she said in a happy excited way.

“Hi Sharon. It’s Mimi.”

Sharon could hardly recognize Mimi’s voice. Her words were slurred as if she had been crying.

“What’s wrong, Mimi?” she asked her.

“Please come over. I need to speak to you. Don’t tell mom and dad.”

“What is the matter?” Sharon asked again.

“I will tell you when you get here.”

“Is David home yet?” Sharon asked her.

“No, he won’t be home again. We have broken up.”

Sharon was in shock. How could this have happened? These two were meant for each other. She did not want to go out in the cold and dark but it was Mimi. What else could she do?

She asked Martin if she could use his car. She was going to visit a friend.

He said, “Sure, why not?”

She pulled on a jacket and boots and was off in a flash. She sped to Mimi’s house. When she arrived, the door was unlocked. Mimi sat on the sofa looking like a disaster. Her hair was a mess and her eyes were red rimmed. Her clothes looked rumpled as if she had slept in them.

Sharon didn’t say anything. She just walked over to her sister and held her as she cried. After the tears had subsided, Mimi told her the story.

“David was cheating on me. I suspected it for a long time. Last night he came to bed with the smell of sex all over him and I knew." She could not continue because she burst into sobs.

Sharon sat by her and didn't know what to say. She believed her sister but just didn't understand. This was David.

Mimi continued, "I asked him to move out while I was at work. He is gone. I never want to see him again," and started sobbing again.

"Mimi, you are beautiful and smart. You will be fine without him."

"Sharon, there is something else. I'm pregnant."

Sharon felt the world tilt. "Does David know?" she asked.

"No, I was going to tell him last night before everything happened. Please promise me you won't tell anyone."

"Okay, I won't. What are you going to do?"

"As you know, I really want to have a baby but I don't know if I can do it alone."

"You aren't alone. You have me. You have mom and dad. All of us will help you."

Mimi started crying again. Sharon got up and put the kettle on to boil.

"Have you eaten anything?" she asked Mimi.

"No, not recently. My stomach is upset."

"I am going to make you a grilled cheese sandwich and a cup of tea. You need to keep up your strength especially now that you are feeding two."

This brought a smile to Mimi's face. Sharon made them both gooey grilled cheese sandwiches with tomatoes and peppers and they ate. Mimi noticed that the food was very therapeutic. It helped her calm down and relax. Things did not feel as dire when she ate a grilled cheese sandwich. Sharon made two more sandwiches and Mimi ate hers with gusto. Then they sipped their strong hot tea while Sharon fussed over Mimi and kept giving her hugs. It somehow brought them both back to childhood to sit this way together and eat. Their bond was as strong as ever. David had not broken it as Sharon had often feared. If anything, his recent actions had strengthened it.

"Do you want me to spend the night?" Sharon asked her.

"No, I need to learn to live alone. The truth is that I have been doing it for a few months now and I am used to it. I need a good sleep so I can teach tomorrow. I think I will sleep well tonight."

Sharon arranged the comforter on Mimi's bed. She switched on the soft night light.

She led Mimi to the bed and helped her into it, although Mimi was still fully dressed.

"We'll get through this together," she told her suddenly fragile sister.

Mimi was asleep in seconds and Sharon went home. She wondered about whether she should fill out those journalism school applications. She decided to wait until later to decide.

Meanwhile, David had made yet another stupid mistake. When Mimi told him to leave, she was not at all sure that their relationship was over. Sure, she was certainly hurt and upset but she hadn't decided to end her marriage. David did not understand this. He believed that she would never take him back. He realized when he left their house that he had nowhere to go. He was not about to go home to his parents and he had nowhere else. He found himself driving over to his girlfriend's apartment. He spent the night there in misery.

Sharon was having breakfast with her parents. They were in great moods. Sylvia and Martin were planning their next winter getaway. Sylvia had made waffles which were so delicious. Sharon found herself with no appetite in front of waffles with whipped cream.

Her mother was quick to notice.

"Sharon, are you feeling well?" Sylvia asked her. Sylvia knew that

Sharon never said no to food.

"Yes, mom, I am fine. I am just a little tired."

"How is your application for journalism school coming along?" Martin asked her.

"Very well dad. There are so many pages to fill out." She wondered if she should continue with her application. She wondered if she should tell her parents that Mimi was alone and pregnant. She decided to honour Mimi's wishes. Mimi should be at work by now. Hopefully, she had pulled herself together. She hoped that David had come to his senses and asked Mimi for forgiveness. Sharon was fairly sure Mimi would take him back, not because he was so great but because she was pregnant. What a mess this was. For once, she was glad that she was not in a relationship. They were nothing but trouble.

She decided to work on her application. Mimi was at work and Sharon still desperately wanted to go to journalism school. At this point, it would be ridiculous to give up. There were several scenarios that played themselves out in her head.

Mimi and David could reconcile. She thought this one was the most likely. Mimi could have an abortion. Mimi could choose to have the baby on her own which would make Sharon rethink her application.

Sharon reminded herself that she had not even been accepted to university in Ottawa. By the time they accepted her and if they even did, she would know what to do. So she worked diligently on her application with hopes that she could do this. She really needed a victory in her own life right now. She was at loose ends and nothing good had happened for her in a long time. She excused herself and went to her room to work on her application.

She realized that she had left her coffee in the kitchen. As she walked back to it, she heard her parents talking.

In the kitchen, Sylvia and Martin were finishing their coffee. Martin decided that he needed to tell Sylvia what he had heard.

"I think David may be cheating on Mimi," he said. He didn't want to tell her but the evidence was mounting and he had decided complete honesty was the best policy for their marriage.

He saw Sylvia grow pale as if she might be ill. She put down her coffee and stared at him.

"How do you know?" she asked him.

"Right now, it is a rumour in the hospital. I have heard it from a few of the nurses. They say that one of them is having sex with David and bragging about it to the others. I don't know for sure if it is true. What should I do?"

"That bastard! How could do that to our little girl?"

"We don't know for sure that he is."

"I don't think the nurses would tell you this if it wasn't true. They have great respect for you." Sylvia knew several of the nurses that Martin worked with. Sure, they gossiped but they would surely not purposely mislead him.

"I think we should tell Mimi," she told him.

"I don't think that's a good idea. I am going to confront David about it. I will know from his reaction whether it is true. If it is true, we can talk to Mimi about it."

"I never trusted him. I want to wring his scrawny neck. What will Mimi do?"

"Let's not jump to any conclusions until we have the facts." Martin was not a rash man. He didn't want to decide anything until he had evidence. He decided that at work today he would talk to two people. He would ask nurse Mara if she was sure this was true and he would ask David. He needed to get David alone. He would invite David out for coffee and ask him then. There was no use in making a scene at the hospital. If it was true, he didn't want the hospital staff to hear what he was going to say to that little piece of garbage. He was already quite sure that Mara had not lied.

"Please let me know what happens," she told him.

Sharon chose this moment to walk into the kitchen.

"Your father thinks that David is cheating on your sister."

Sharon pretended to be surprised even though she knew the entire story.

"I hope it's not true."

"So do we but he is a little shit. Who knows what he might do?"

Sharon and Martin were shocked at Sylvia's language. She never swore.

She almost laughed at herself for being so kind to him lately. She had welcomed him into the family and look what he had done? Sylvia couldn't keep the thoughts about how David had hurt her little girl out of her head. She had come so far in her relationship with Martin and in her ability to be calm. She was not going to let this stress her out.

She decided some strenuous exercise was in order. She glanced out of the window and noticed that the snow was falling. It was too slippery for a run but she could still go to the gym. She did not want to go out in the snow but her brain was churning and she was spiralling into a dark place. So, she threw on her parka and grabbed her car keys and was out of the door in minutes.

Martin tried to get a moment alone with Mara so he could ask her if David was really having an affair but it was very difficult. The emergency department had been buzzing all morning and none of the staff had a second to themselves. The fresh snowfall had caused several car accidents which kept casualties coming in steadily. That, combined with the stomach aches and headaches and heartaches and cuts and bruises and limb breaks were keeping all the staff rushing from one patient to another.

He completely forgot until lunchtime. He saw Mara sitting in the cafeteria talking with a few other nurses. She looked exhausted. Her curly brown hair had escaped her ponytail and looked liked a mess. Her slim frame looked hunched over like she was carrying extra weight.

He decided not to bother her. She was obviously busy with lunch. She would find her sometime in the afternoon. However, the afternoon was just as hectic as the morning. The snowfall had become quite severe and there were even more car accident victims to attend to. Martin completely forgot about Mara until he was driving home that afternoon. Sylvia will be so mad, he thought to himself. When he arrived at home, Sylvia was not mad. Her morning at the gym had relaxed her and she was pouring all of her anger into pounding chicken breasts with a mallet.

Martin stood and looked at her without knowing what to say. He decided to come right out with it.

"I'm sorry Sylvia but I didn't get a chance to speak to Mara today. The crazy weather had the stupid drivers crashing into each other. I was busy all day."

"Where is Sharon?" he asked her.

"She is in her room working on her journalism school application. I haven't seen her this excited in a long time. I hope it works out for her."

"So do I."

They both knew that Sharon had been restless and depressed for a while. They wanted her to find something that would make her excited and happy. Hopefully, this would be it.

Sharon had not gone on a date in two years. She kept telling her parents that there was no one that she was interested in dating but they wondered if this was part of her depression. Martin had been on the verge of telling Sharon that maybe she should talk to Sylvia's psychologist when she started smiling again. He wanted the smile to stay. He worried about both his girls but Mimi had seemed settled and happy and he felt that she was doing well. He wondered if this was true.

Mimi arrived right on time at 6:00 o'clock. She looked tired and a little ill but no one mentioned it. Martin, Sylvia and Sharon each gave her a hug. Sharon was afraid that Mimi would collapse in her arms and held her tight.

"Dinner will be ready in a half hour," Sylvia told them.

"Would you like some wine while we wait?"

"No thanks mom. I need to talk to all of you. Can we all please go to the family room?"

Everyone followed Mimi. They sat down and waited but Mimi was silent.

Finally, Sylvia couldn't wait any longer.

"Are you feeling okay?" she asked Mimi. As soon as she said this, Mimi started to cry.

Between tears, she said, "David and I have broken up. He has been cheating on me."

So, it was true.

Then the next bomb fell.

"I am pregnant," Mimi told them. "David doesn't know. I never had a chance to tell him and I don't plan to."

Sylvia and Martin were shocked. They expected that David might be cheating but this was a complete surprise. They both wanted to be grandparents but not this way.

"I want to have this baby but I am so scared. How will I do it alone?"

"You won't be alone," Martin said. "All of us will stand by you and help you in any way we can."

Mimi started crying even louder.

"Let's talk about this over dinner. It is ready," Sylvia announced.

They all headed into the kitchen. Mimi ate surprisingly well. Over dinner, Sylvia said that she would help Mimi with the baby anytime she needed a babysitter. Martin pledged his financial support and Sharon said she would spoil the baby rotten. Mimi cried a great deal but also smiled quite a bit. She realized her family would stand by her. She wouldn't be alone. That was a great relief. She would eventually tell David but not now. She would wait until the news would hurt him the most the way he had hurt her.

David came to the house the next morning while Mimi was at work to pick up his clothes. When he walked in, he was surprised that everything looked just fine. He expected that there would be some damage but there was nothing. His clothes were hanging like they always did in the closet beside hers. There were fresh flowers in a vase on the kitchen table. Nothing was out of place.

He packed his clothes and thought about whether he should write Mimi a note. He decided it was the right thing to do. He wrote,

> Hi Mimi:
>
> I am so sorry for what I have done. Please forgive me. I came to take some of my clothes. I will phone you later in the week. I hope we can still work things out.
>
> I will always love you,
>
> David.

He felt so ashamed that he sat down on the sofa and cried. He was the world's biggest fool. ,He had betrayed the best person in the world. He looked at the picture of the two of them on their coffee table. It had been taken at their wedding. They both looked so happy and hopeful. Now he had ruined it all. Well maybe it was not too late. Perhaps Mimi would give him another chance.

David left the house and drove to work. He was nervous about going there. He knew that Martin would be there this morning and he was terrified to face him. His father-in-law had always been kind to him and he felt that he had betrayed him as well. Sylvia must be gloating, he thought. He knew that she hated him. Her recent friendly behaviour had not fooled him at all.

He was also concerned about how to break up with Penny. He knew that he had to do it as soon as possible. He did not love her and was realizing that he did not even like her. She was getting the idea that he was moving in. He would have to move out right away. Whenever he tried to talk to her about it, they wound up in bed. What a weak willed moron he was. Well, he could grow up and change. It was about time that he did.

Mimi got home from work and found the note that David had left her. She wanted to speak to him but she didn't have a clue as to how she could reach him. She wondered where he was staying and decided that she didn't care. She crumpled the note and threw it away. Then she went to cook dinner and have an early night. Although the pregnancy was in its early stages, she was already so tired. She supposed the fatigue was also due to the stress of the ending of her marriage.

"I will take good care of you," she said out loud to the baby in her womb. All through her pregnancy, this would be her mantra. Whenever she felt sad or defeated or hopeless, she would say this to her baby. It sparked the realization that she was now responsible for both of them and somehow always brought her back to a more settled state.

Mimi decided to make a healthy dinner for her and the baby. She didn't have much of an appetite but managed a salad and a small chicken breast. Afterwards she had a mighty craving for ice cream. She took some out of the freezer and couldn't stop eating it.

She slept well that evening. She decided that her problems could wait until morning so she put on a pair of cozy pyjamas and snuggled into her bed. She put her problems aside for the night and immediately fell into a deep and dreamless sleep.

The next morning was Saturday so she didn't have to go to work. She woke up feeling rested and happy until she noticed the empty spot beside her in the bed. Then the realization sunk in once again that her marriage was over.

She phoned Sharon who was already awake.

"Want to get together?" she asked Sharon.

"Sure why not?"

"I am making pancakes for breakfast. Want to join me?"

They had always bonded over pancakes usually made by their father but Mimi could whip up a great batch herself.

"I'll be there in five minutes," Sharon told her. They both knew that this was impossible but it made them giggle.

Sharon found Mimi fully dressed and in a jubilant mood. She looked wonderful. The smell of fresh coffee wafted in from the kitchen.

Sharon poured extra maple syrup on her pancakes and said, "This is so delicious. Don't tell dad but you have outdone him."

"Flattery will get you more pancakes." Mimi giggled at Sharon and plopped two more on Sharon's plate. Mimi's appetite had returned and she was enjoying the food immensely.

They were still best friends. In each other's company, each found a comfort borne of years of being together and knowing each other so well that talk was not necessary. This was a special bond.

"What are you up to this weekend?" Sharon asked Mimi.

"I have some marking to do and otherwise I am just going to relax."

"Did I tell you I finished my journalism school application and sent it in?"

"Wow, congratulations. When will you hear from them?"

"Not until the spring."

The morning passed quickly with the pancakes and chatter. Sharon had some plans with a friend so she left and Mimi got to work on her marking.

As Mimi was settling down to some serious marking, she heard the doorbell ring. When she went to the door and asked who it was, a scared voice said, "It's me David, Mimi. Please let me in."

She opened the door and looked at him. He appeared as wretched as one person could be. He was somewhat dishevelled as if he had slept in his clothes. He had two days of stubble on his chin. He reeked of sadness and desperation. It had been just five days since he had seen him last but she could have sworn that he was a different person. Her impulse to slam the door in his face was overtaken by sympathy for this wretched beast.

"Yes, you can come in if you want to get some more of your belongings. Otherwise, we have nothing to say to each other."

David took off his parka and winter boots and stepped towards her. Was that a tear in his eye or was it just the cold from outside that was making his eye water?

"I'm so sorry, Mimi. I am the world's biggest fool. What we have is real and I have gone and ruined everything. Can you ever forgive me?"

He had quickly come to the conclusion that living with Penny was a disaster. He couldn't stand her anymore. She was a coarse and vulgar woman. She lived in a disaster zone. The only thing she had going for her was her constant desire for sex and even that was getting old. He desperately wanted to return to his sweet and loving wife again but was it too late?

"David, right now the pain is still too fresh. I am not making any promises but maybe later we can talk again. Right now all I want is for you to leave."

He turned and put on his parka and boots and left without another word. He slammed the front door as he was leaving and a gust of cold wind filled the house.

Mimi was shocked at how calm she felt. Somehow the pain of what had happened had settled into a numbness that just wouldn't let her feel anything. She went back to her marking and was pleased that the afternoon went by so smoothly. She never gave David another thought for the rest of the day as she made her supper and crawled into bed with a good book. She woke with the book still on her lap the next morning. She had dozed off reading it and slept so well. Today was going to be better than yesterday, she told herself.

"Good morning," she said to her baby and patted her stomach.

"I love you," she continued. She had started talking to her unborn baby.

"It might be just the two of us but I will take good care of you."

The Sunday went beautifully. She finished her marking early in the day and spent the afternoon making food to take to work for lunch. She needn't have bothered because this was Sunday dinner night at her parents'.

She arrived at their house to the wonderful aroma of garlic and rosemary. Her mouth started watering as soon as she walked in the door. It was chilly outside and Sharon greeted her with a cup of steaming hot chocolate with tiny marshmallows on top. They sat and drank it in front of the fireplace which was throwing so much heat their way. As soon as they were finished, Sylvia called them in for dinner.

"I made roast lemon chicken, lemon potatoes and Greek salad for dinner." She knew Mimi adored Greek food.

"Where's dad?" Mimi asked. Martin's absence was very noticeable at the dinner table.

"He had to do an extra shift at the hospital. They are short-staffed because of Christmas," Sylvia told them. "He should be home in time for dessert."

So the three ate with relish. Mimi could feel the tender chicken melt in her mouth. She loved the tanginess of the potatoes and the bold flavour of the Greek salad. She also noticed how much easier Sunday dinner was without David. Sylvia smiled often and talked comfortably. Things had been very stilted when David had been there.

"Has David tried to contact you?" Sylvia asked her.

"He showed up at the house but I told him that I wasn't ready to speak to him."

"It must have been hard for you," Sharon said and squeezed her hand.

"No, it was strangely easy," Mimi answered.

Just then, Martin walked in with windswept hair and ruddy cheeks. He bent to give Sylvia a peck on the cheek.

"Don't touch me! You are freezing cold!" she yelled but the smile stayed on her face.

"I'll get you some dinner," and she was gone in a flash. So they waited for Martin to eat and Mimi had a second helping of everything.

For dessert, Sylvia had made baklava. It was sweet and syrupy and delicious.

When Mimi was ready to leave, Sylvia insisted on giving her some food to take home.

"After all, you liked the food so much. You might as well enjoy it at home."

Mimi returned home with a week's worth of chicken, potatoes, salad and baklava. She decided that she would alternate this with her own homemade lunches and have a feast. Once again, she slept well with nary a thought of David.

She patted her abdomen and said, "I will take care of you," to her baby and went to bed.

CHAPTER 35

Winter was brutal in Montreal that year. From the middle of December until early in March, there were endless blizzards and sub-zero temperatures. A person could get frostbite in under a minute. Still, Mimi, Sharon, and their parents had a great winter. Mimi became more and more pregnant and more and more large. Her appetite and stomach both bloomed at the same time. Sharon spent a lot of time with Mimi and waited eagerly until the spring to see if she would get into journalism school. Sylvia continued to jog indoors and see her therapist. Her relationship with Martin was going well and she was calming down. Martin was happy because his wife and children were doing well. He and Sylvia had gone to Florida for January and missed some of the worst of winter.

As for David, his winter was quite different. After one more attempt to reconcile with Mimi, he gave up and stayed on at Penny's apartment. She was thrilled that they were together but he was less so. He really did not love her or even like her. He just went through the motions of life with her all the while wondering why his life had gone wrong. He never once took the blame squarely but always made excuses. He did not even know that Mimi was pregnant. He had not seen her in months and had no idea that she was pregnant.

Fate had a way of laughing at David. March 14 was Penny's birthday. She would be 26 and felt it was high time to get married. David said he would take her out to celebrate. He made reservations at Le Choux, a restaurant he and Mimi had frequented in the past. Little did he know that Martin had made reservations for four for the same evening. They were celebrating Sharon's acceptance into journalism school which had arrived in the mail the day before. Everyone was ecstatic.

Sharon and Mimi met Martin and Sylvia at the restaurant at 6:30. There were already some appetizers on the table. Martin and Sylvia had arrived early and ordered some anchovy tarts, fried oysters, and antipasto for everyone to share. They were anticipating Mimi's blooming appetite.

Mimi and Sharon arrived together and joined their parents. Everyone was in fine form. Martin, Sylvia, and Sharon drank champagne to toast a new chapter in Sharon's life. Mimi drank ginger ale and immediately started on the appetizers. The other laughed as they watched her eat. Sylvia especially had no idea that her tiny little daughter could eat this much.

While the Miller family was immensely enjoying their appetizers, David and Penny were trying to find a parking spot by the same restaurant. They finally parked several blocks away and had to walk there in the biting cold and icy wind. While they were trudging through the snow and feeling the icy wind, Penny's mood turned foul. She felt that David should have dropped her off at the door of the restaurant.

They finally walked in the door but before they were even seated, David saw Mimi. She was sitting at a table quite far away chatting with her family and laughing. It was impossible not to notice how pregnant she was. She was glowing with health and happiness. David's world started to spin. He thought he would pass out.

"We need to go," he told Penny and practically dragged her out the door.

"What the hell is going on?" she asked him.

"I am suddenly feeling very sick. I will make this up to you later."

She looked at him and saw his pallor. Her anger melted into compassion.

The next morning while Penny was still sleeping, he quietly got out of bed, pulled on his yesterday's clothes and went to confront Mimi.

Mimi had had a wonderful sleep that night. She was excited for Sharon and had really enjoyed her family's night out. She lay blissfully sleeping unaware that David had seen her last night. She was awoken from this bliss with an insistent pounding at her door.

She glanced at the clock and saw that it was 7:18. Who in the world would come over early on a Sunday morning and pound at her door? She was a little frightened but she assured herself that there was probably an explanation for this.

She slipped into her bathrobe and went to see what was going on. She went to the door and looked through the peephole. It was David looking messy and quite mad. His hair was uncombed and his hat was on backwards. He looked like he might be drunk.

"What do you want David?" she asked him.

"I want to talk to you! Please open the door."

She felt uneasy about this.

"I'm sorry David but I am not comfortable with you coming in." She still believed that David did not know that she was pregnant.

"I know you're pregnant Mimi. We need to talk about it."

He sounded angry and Mimi felt scared.

"I don't want to talk to you about anything David. Please go away."

"Mimi, we have a child on the way. How could you not tell me that?"

"David, you were with someone else. What did you expect?"

David was shivering outside but Mimi still refused to open the door.

"Please leave or I will phone the police," she told him.

"Don't do this," he said with sobs in his voice but she saw him walk away and get into his car and drive off.

She was shaken to the core. How had he found out? No one she knew would have told him. This was a new worry for her. She did not want David in their baby's life. What would she do now? She suddenly felt very tired. She crawled back into bed but found it difficult to sleep again. Finally she drifted back into sleep and slept until 10:02. When she woke up she felt sluggish, tired and confused. What would she do?

Mimi phoned Sharon.

"What's new sis?"

"Are you still hungry?"

"David was here. He knows I am pregnant. He is really angry. What should I do?"

"Are you sure your relationship with David is over?"

"Oh yes, yes, yes!"

"I think you should change the locks on your doors. That way David can never get in."

"What a good idea."

"After this, you should file for divorce. I am coming over."

"Thanks Sharon."

"I love you sis."

"Me too."

So Sharon came over yet again to help her sister. That afternoon they found a locksmith who changed the locks right away. The next day Mimi phoned a lawyer and started the divorce process.

CHAPTER 36. SHARON

I am feeling so much better. I finally got accepted to journalism school. This is something I have wanted for a long time. My life did not have much before. I was between stuff for a long time. I was spending way too much time sitting in my room. Now there are things to do again. I need to get ready to move to Ottawa to go to university. It is still four months away but it will go by quickly.

I became Mimi's birth coach. I have been going to childbirth classes with her. I am learning how to guide her through childbirth and loving it. Mimi is also excited. She is due before I leave so I should be able to be there for her when she has her baby. I am excited about being an aunt. I am feeling a little guilty about the fact that I will be leaving in late August shortly after she has the baby but mom and dad have assured me that they will help her.

I can't believe I used to have a crush on David. He is revolting. He has turned out to be a first-rate creep. He should be the one who is with her but he is too busy fucking that nurse. I never told Mimi I saw them out together. When I was having coffee with friends they were in the coffee shop together. She was looking at him like he was the best thing on earth and he looked bored. She is attractive in a trampy sort of way. She is very tall with wild black hair and too much makeup. She is a little chubby but who am I to talk? I don't think that David is really into her. He looked like he would rather be anywhere else but there.

He told Mimi he wanted to get back together but she decided that she was not interested. If he is serious about getting back together, he should dump the whore and ask Mimi to take him back. Everyone knows they are still together. I don't know where his brains are but they are not in his head. I didn't go over and say anything when I saw them but I know David saw me because I caught his eye. He looked away as if he was embarrassed. He should be embarrassed. What a fool he is to give up Mimi for her.

The strange thing is that David does not like his girlfriend. I could clearly see it in his face. Whenever he looked at Mimi, his eyes would sparkle. When he looks at the whore, his eyes look dead. I sometimes wonder if I should talk to him. If I ask him to give up the whore and try to reconcile with Mimi, he might listen. On the other hard, I don't think Mimi would take him back at this point. She seems happy on her own. She has always wanted a baby. This will keep her too busy to miss David.

Mimi told me that David is being served with divorce papers today. She found out his address and is having the papers brought over there. David's whore will be happy but not him. I bet she wants a commitment. He seems like a good catch. He is handsome and smart and a doctor to boot. Does she ever wonder if he will cheat on her?

I would pay money to see the expression on David's face when he gets the divorce papers. That will be a precious moment.

CHAPTER 37

When David found out that Mimi was suing for divorce, he had a fit as Sharon had predicted. He screamed at Penny and stormed out the door.

Sharon and Mimi sat together in Mimi's backyard drinking lemonade. Sharon could tell that Mimi was feeling at peace with her life. Mimi was tired but quite wonderful otherwise. The spring had finally arrived and she could go out without freezing. She loved the feeling of her baby kicking and moving around inside her and her swelling belly. Sharon loved to touch Mimi's stomach and feel the baby kicking.

"It's going to be a hockey player for sure," she told Mimi.

"As long as she is happy, I don't mind what she does."

"I notice you are using she."

"I am having a daughter. I can feel it."

Sharon laughed as Mimi rushed inside to go to the bathroom.

"I see your daughter is kicking you in the bladder."

The air was still cool and breezy but the sun was showing some warmth. The snow was melting quickly and she could even manage short walks. Mimi was on maternity leave from her teaching job and was hardly ever alone. Sharon was always there feeding her and making her laugh. Sylvia and Martin were also often there bringing her food and encouraging her. Mimi felt so blessed with their kindness. Her friends often dropped by as well. She was overcome by everyone's love and kindness.

She often sat in her backyard on a bench under a tree. She would see the new signs of life in her yard. She watched as the cardinals returned to her bird feeder. She loved the splash of red on their breasts. She watched the perennials she had planted slowly coming up in the garden. She felt the new life everywhere especially in her own body where her baby kicked all the time.

This difficult period of her life was turning out wonderful. Her appetite was great and her cheeks were rosy. She felt so warm and happy and excited about her baby's birth. David was a distant memory and she hardly ever thought of him.

Sharon noticed Mimi in deep thought.

"What's on your mind sis?"

"I need somewhere to leave the baby when I go to work."

"How about mom?"

"She lives too far away."

"How about a day care centre?"

"She will be too small."

"A nanny?"

"I can't afford one."

"Don't worry. You will find someone great to look after your baby when you work."

"I hope you're right."

CHAPTER 38. SHARON

Yesterday, I started cleaning out my room. I have been living there for the whole 21 years of my life and I have so much junk. I found my elementary school report cards and a valentine that my friend Bobby gave me in grade six. I wish I knew who he was. I must have liked him if I kept his valentine for so long. My room is pretty much a disaster. Mom and dad never really forced me to deal with the disorder or clutter. They still haven't asked me to clean it up but I think I really should. I will be moving to Ottawa soon and I will use this room only when I come home. I wonder if I will ever live in it again.

Winter and spring have flown by and it is finally June. Last weekend, Mimi and I went to Ottawa for the day to check it out. It is lovely there. We went to a fifties style diner for lunch and took a walk in the park by the Rideau Canal. The tulips were in bloom everywhere and it was magnificent to see all of their colours. My favourites were the yellow tulips. They say that summer is on its way. Mimi is as big as a house. It is hilarious because normally she is so small and petite. I swear that there is so much weight in front that she may topple over.

Pregnancy really suits her. She glows from head to toe. She seems happier than she has ever been. She must be disappointed about David but she doesn't say anything. It is as if he never existed. She has always wanted to be a mother. This is what is making her smile. It will happen in just two months.

After our walk, she was tired so we sat on a park bench and relaxed. We felt the sunlight on our faces and watched all the mothers with strollers walk by. There were many families with babies and she remarked on the cuteness of every one.

She will be a great mother. She will love her baby fiercely and unconditionally.

I will do the same. The baby will not have a dad but there will so many people who love it. My parents are quite excited. My mom is setting up a room for the baby in their house. Mimi has an adorable nursery ready with pink and blue walls so a girl or boy would be happy there. She was worried about who would take care of the baby but she seems to have found a solution. Her neighbour, Mrs Morrison, will come to Mimi's house to do it. She is a sweet older lady who has raised six children of her own and Mimi really likes and trusts her. She is very competent and the answer to a new mother's dreams.

I think the only fly in the ointment is David. He had asked for visits with the baby. Mimi does not want him to ever see the baby but the lawyer says she has no choice. He is the baby's father and there is no reason to take away his rights as a parent.

I would take them away simply because he is still with that whore Penny. Mimi told me that he tried to reconcile with her a few times but she wouldn't consider it because he was still with another woman. What is wrong with that man? He is a fool.

We drove back to Montreal with the windows open and sang the song "American Pie" over and over again. We sang loudly and foolishly and felt like two children again. It was a wonderful moment.

I am going out in a few minutes. I am going to pick up Mimi and we are off to her prenatal class. This is the last one. I am reasonably sure that I can be a decent birth coach but I am not 100% sure. I have never seen a baby being born before. I hope I don't faint in the delivery room. Mimi is nervous. People have been telling her miserable childbirth stories. Whenever she walks down the street, some stranger accosts her and tells her a terrible birthing story that she doesn't want to hear. Mimi is far too polite to tell them to get lost so she listens. They talk about their 36-hour labours and their intense pain. They always want to touch her stomach. She politely declines. There should be a law against scaring a pregnant woman.

Mimi said to me the other day, "If something happens to me, will you please take care of my child?"

"Yes, of course I will," I told her, "but nothing is going to happen to you."

"I have read that some women die in childbirth," she told me.

"That happens in countries where there is no help available. We aren't in a developing country. We live in Canada. This is Montreal for goodness' sake. You have great doctors and you are young and healthy. Nothing will go wrong."

"You are probably right but it would mean so much to me if you would agree to take the baby if I am not around. David will fight you for the baby but please don't let him have her. I don't want him and the whore raising her. I have drawn up a will naming you as her guardian. This should help guarantee your custody."

She was still calling the baby by a feminine pronoun. I wondered if that meant anything. Did she know she was having a daughter or was she just tired of using the word it?

"Mimi, I promise that if anything happens to you, I will raise your baby."

I was pleased that Mimi thought I was capable of doing this.

"Thanks Sharon. I feel so much better."

At first, I didn't think much about that conversation but as time went by, I started to think about it more. Was I willing to raise her baby? What about my future schooling? I would have to give it up. I was only 21 years old and didn't want children just yet. Then I realized that Mimi was the person I loved the most in the entire world and I would do anything for her. Of course, I would raise her child.

Then I told myself that I was crazy. This was not going to happen. Mimi would sail through childbirth and motherhood and I would be the doting aunt.

The more I tried to convince myself of this, the more I worried. I was starting to feel as if something was going to happen to Mimi. I had no good reason for this feeling but it wouldn't ever completely leave my mind. I started having nightmares about Mimi being in danger again.

After driving myself crazy for a week, I decided that I was probably feeling this way because I was so close to going away and doing what I wanted that I was sure something would happen to spoil it. I realized that I had been depressed and was finally getting better. I didn't remember when I had wanted something as badly as the opportunity to go away to journalism school. My life had been in a slump for such a long time and I was finally feeling motivated. Now that I could finally do what I wanted, something was bound to happen.

My mother believed that there were dark shadows hiding everywhere to steal our joy. I always scoffed at this but obviously some of this craziness had rubbed off on me. Well, I was clearing my room and getting ready to leave and nothing was going to spoil it.

CHAPTER 39

Sharon was so relieved when Mimi's divorce became final in June. It had been an easy divorce with one major issue. Mimi had not wanted David to have anything to do with their baby. Once the lawyer told Mimi that this was not an option, she gave David parental rights to see the baby. Sharon and her parents told her that the baby would need her father even though it was David.

Sharon tried to help as much as possible but Mimi had a difficult summer. She was so large and the weather was so hot and humid. It seemed like she was dragging herself around. It was impossible to sleep because of the humidity and her bulk. She would toss and turn and try to find a comfortable position which did not intrude with her large belly. She would wake up in the morning drenched in sweat and exhausted. Thankfully she did not teach in the summer. Sharon had bought her an electric fan but that just seemed to move the hot air around.

She was moody and glum and very eager to give birth. She was looking forward to being a mother.

Sharon organized a baby shower and their parents brought over a crib and bassinet and set them up.

Sharon was almost as eager as Mimi for her to give birth. Mimi was due in a week and Sharon was due to leave for Ottawa in two weeks. Sharon was very afraid that the baby would be late and she would not be there as the labour coach. She had suggested Sylvia as a replacement.

Mimi had just laughed and said, "Are you kidding? Mom would go off the rails."

Then Sharon had suggested Martin.

Mimi said, “Dad shouldn’t be there. He is a doctor and might try to interfere.”

“Then what should we do if I am away and you go into labour?”

“I will go into labour before you leave. The baby’s head is in the birth canal so I am just about ready to pop. You will be my birth coach and the first person she sees, just as it should be.”

Sharon was running to the phone whenever it rang, sure that she was being summoned to Mimi’s labour. She had taken to sleeping with the phone in her bed. She was ready to leave town. Only one thing was still keeping her in Montreal.

She had a dorm room in Ottawa and she needed to move her belongings there and start university. The room rental started on the 7th of September and she was hoping to leave on the first day of the month. This way she would have time to organize herself before school started a week later.

Meanwhile, David was now finally living in his own apartment. Penny had told him that she was pregnant and he had immediately left. He was furious at her. How could she do this to him?

Later on the day that she had told him that she was pregnant, he had started packing his things. He gave no thought to what he had done to Penny’s life.

That evening, Sharon was at the supermarket buying some groceries for Mimi. Although Mimi insisted that she could do it, Sharon wanted to help her out. The heat was intense and Mimi was as big as a house. The least she could do was buy some food for her older sister.

As she walked down the cereal isle, she saw David. He was walking alone with a cart and looking miserable. He had always been so handsome that it shocked Sharon to see him looking haggard and unshaven. She wondered if she could duck out of the aisle but he saw her. She wondered what he would say.

“Hi Sharon,” he said with forced gaiety in his voice.

"Hi David," she said and tried to walk away but David grabbed her arm.

"How is Mimi?" he asked her.

"Just great. She should be giving birth any day."

"I miss her so much. Do you think she would see me?"

"David, she is not interested in seeing you. She has moved on and you should too."

"Would you please tell her to talk to me?" he asked. Sharon was starting to feel nervous. His grip on her arm had tightened and he looked desperate.

"You are with someone else, David!"

"We broke up and I miss Mimi so much. Please tell her that I love her."

Sharon had had enough.

"Let go of my hand!"

She screamed way too loud. People turned and looked at them.

David let go and walked away without another word, leaving his grocery cart standing in the aisle.

Sharon was shaken. She had never seen him look so lost or wild and she was scared for Mimi. Should she warn Mimi or tell her about the encounter? She decided that honesty was best and she would tell her sister. She noticed that she had a red welt on her arm from his fierce grip.

When Sharon arrived back at Mimi's house with the groceries, Mimi was sitting curled up on an armchair reading a book. She smiled when she saw Sharon but she knew something was wrong as soon as she saw her face.

"What wrong?" she asked Sharon.

"I will tell you as soon as we put away the groceries. Mimi slowly followed Sharon to the kitchen as they started unloading the food into the pantry and the fridge.

"Hey, you didn't buy me any potato chips," Mimi complained.

"You already have two bags. How much potato chips does one pregnant woman need?"

"I can't help it if the baby wants potato chips. She especially likes barbecue chips," Mimi chided.

Mimi ate very healthy food during her pregnancy but potato chips were her downfall. She could not seem to get enough of them. She ate them with her favourite sandwiches and used them for topping salads and everywhere else she could manage. Sharon loved to tease her about it.

"Your baby will be born addicted to potato chips," Sharon said smiling.

They sat down with frosty lemonades in the living room and Mimi could see that Sharon had something on her mind.

"What happened Sharon?"

"I ran into David at the supermarket."

"And…?"

"He was desperate, Mimi. He said he still loves you. He said he wants to see you. He supposedly broke up with Penny. He looked crazy. I was scared of him. I am afraid he will hurt you. He grabbed my arm so hard that it is bruised."

Mimi looked surprised.

"This is David, Sharon. We have known him since high school. He would never do anything violent."

"You never saw him like this. He had a crazed look in his eyes. He grabbed my arm and wouldn't let go."

"It will be fine."

Mimi was sure that David would never physically hurt any of them. Emotionally was quite another story.

"Maybe you should move in with mom and dad and me until you have the baby. That way we can be there easily to take you to the hospital."

"I don't need to do that. I will be fine."

But Sharon wasn't so sure. She tried for a few more minutes to get Mimi to move in with them. She even tried to see if she could move in with Mimi.

"I will be leaving soon. We won't see each other as often. Maybe I could stay here and hang out with you until the baby is born, Mimi. Wouldn't that be fun?"

"No it wouldn't. I go to sleep early every night and hardly do anything. I would cramp your style."

"I have no style for you to cramp," she told Mimi and they both started laughing.

Sharon could tell that Mimi could see right through her and she wasn't falling for this weak excuse to be protected from her ex-husband.

Without wanting to, Sharon suddenly became tearful.

"I am really going to miss you big sister," she told Mimi as she started to sob.

"I will miss you too but you will be just two hours away. We can still see each other often."

"Not as often as we did before."

"Sharon, maybe the baby and I should come live with you."

"I know you are not serious. You are just making fun of me."

Sharon smiled through her tears.

She knew they would both be fine but she realized how close the two of them had been and knew things would not be the same.

Sharon was still nervous about David. She returned home and sat at the kitchen table and listened to a conversation her parents were having.

They were sitting together deep in conversation. They hardly noticed her when she came in. She poured herself some water and sat down at the kitchen table.

“David broke up with his girlfriend,” he told Sylvia. She had been busy peeling some potatoes for dinner and stopped what she was doing.

“Do you think he will try to get back with Mimi?”

“It doesn’t matter what he tries. She doesn’t want him anymore.”

“That worm can be charming and persuasive. What if she takes him back?”

“There is no chance of that. Mimi is smart.”

“I hope you’re right.”

She went back to peeling potatoes and then coated them with olive oil and oregano and put them in the oven. She started working on the lemon chicken but she was still worried. She had to trust that her daughter would make the right decision. She was not going to interfere ever again. It had almost cost her the relationship with her daughter and she could not bear for that to happen, especially with a grandchild on the way.

There would be just her and Martin in the house now. She was already feeling a sense of loss. Martin looked as if he had read her mind.

Martin interrupted her train of thought. “You should see David.”

“What about him?” Sylvia asked.

“He is a disaster. He used to look so good. He has lost weight and he looks so haggard. He is like a shadow of his former self. When I see him at the hospital, I feel sorry for him.”

“Sympathy for the devil is never useful. I say he got what he deserved.”

Sharon who had been quiet until now decided it was time to add her part.

“I saw David at the supermarket. He looked terrible. He tried to convince me to tell Mimi to give him another chance. He grabbed my arm and wouldn’t let go.”

She showed her parents her bruised arm. They gasped.

“I will kill that punk,” Martin snarled.

“He is not worth getting into trouble for, dad.”

Sylvia looked like she was going to be sick.

“I am worried that David will attack Mimi. He is desperate,” Sylvia added.

“I do too, mom.”

“I don’t think that Mimi is in any danger. David still loves her. He is desperate to get her back,” Martin said.

“I hope you're right,” Sylvia added.

With that the conversation ended. Sharon went to her room. Sylvia continued making dinner while Martin sat in the den and wondered if his words were true.

CHAPTER 40. SHARON

I feel like my life is in some crazy suspended dream state. My room is cleaned out and my suitcase is packed. I could leave in a minute but I am still waiting for Mimi to give birth. She is due today but nothing seems to be happening. I phone her so often to ask if she is in labour that she must be getting sick of me. I am getting sick of myself.

I feel like my life is stuck in cement. Mimi has told me to leave but I couldn't live with myself if I left before she gave birth. I think this baby is going to be stubborn just like her mother and aunt. She has already decided that she does not want to come out yet. I can't say that I really blame her. It is warm and safe inside a womb but not as great outside in the world.

I found out from dad that Penny, David's girlfriend quit her nursing job and left town. Dad says he feels sorry for her. Apparently she really loved David and he broke her heart. What a surprise. That man is a menace. We should run him out of town. Didn't they used to tar and feather people? I would love to see David tarred and feathered.

It is a fabulous August. The weather is just right. Montreal can be stifling at this time of year with its intense heat and humidity. This August is mild and sunny with just a hint of a breeze.

I have taken up jogging. Mom says jogging calms her down. I have started going jogging with her a few times a week. She puts me to shame with how quickly she can go as I pant along. She says I will get stronger and better as time goes by. I wouldn't mind. She is right. Jogging is helping me calm down as we all stand by on baby alert.

Mimi's due date has come and gone. She is now three days late.

She tells me not to worry; the baby will come when it's ready. I can't stand the idea of leaving until her baby is born. She tells me that she can do fine without me. She has mom and dad and friends who will be there for her but it is not the same. Mimi and I have been bonded since we were little children. We have been through so much together. I can't stand the thought of not being with her when she gives birth.

The days are passing and nothing is happening. She is now a week late. My classes start in a week. I am a nervous wreck. I need to leave but this whole thing with Mimi is still keeping me here. I feel like I will never get out of town to start university.

Mimi is calm and beautiful. She has a glow and a calmness about her that annoys me. Nothing seems to bother her. I suggested some methods I had heard about to get her to go into labour but she laughed at me.

"Calm down Sharon," she laughed, "Things will be just fine."

The two of us have been going out for ice cream every afternoon. Mimi says the baby wants it but I know it is her. We have tried every flavour in the shop. We sit at a picnic table outside and slowly eat our cones. I am surprised that she can still get up onto the bench That girl is enormous. It is especially obvious because she is normally so slim. If I ever get pregnant, you wouldn't even be able to tell. I am chunky at the best of times. I am hoping that after I get to university in Ottawa, I can scrub off a few pounds.

After our ice cream, we go for a stroll in the nearby park. Our stroll is short as it is still so hot and humid and Mimi cannot walk far these days.

We return to her cool house and she lies down for a nap. After that, I return home and fret. Mom tells me that I am worrying far too much.

"You would think that you are the one having the baby," she said to me the other day.

"Everything will work out just fine," she told me.

I will have to wait and see.

CHAPTER 41

Sharon was dozing in her sparse bedroom. She had promised Mimi that she was leaving tomorrow no matter what happened. It was mid-afternoon on August 26 and stiflingly warm. She had the window cracked open but it did little to ease the unrelenting heat and humidity. She lay in a T-shirt and shorts in her bed. She was exhausted. Last night she had not slept well.

Thoughts about her sister's overdue pregnancy had kept her awake. When she had finally fallen asleep, she woke to a ringing phone. However, it had stopped before she answered it. All of her family was waiting eagerly for Mimi to have her baby but Sharon was beyond eager. She was stressed. She wanted to be there for the event but she had promised Mimi she would leave for Ottawa tomorrow. It was probably just as well. She was driving Mimi crazy with her love and concern. Soon, Mimi would run her out of town on a rail.

So she was taking a little time to have an afternoon nap. Tomorrow would be a long day. Her forehead dripped with perspiration and the rest of her was no better. Still she fell into a heat induced dreamy sleep. She dreamed that Mimi had twins and that they came out of Mimi as adults. She woke up laughing at her foolish dream.

She went to take a shower and prepare for dinner. Sylvia was making a family dinner for Sharon's last evening in Montreal. She was preparing some of Sharon's favourites like Greek salad, lemon oregano chicken and strawberry cheesecake. Sharon sang in the shower as she thought of the dinner ahead. Soon Mimi would arrive and the whole family would be together.

"Hi everyone!" she heard Mimi yell as she opened the front

door. Mimi went straight to Sharon's room and walked in. Sylvia was grateful that her daughters were so close although she sometimes felt left out. She tried to concentrate on putting together the last few details of the meal.

Martin came into the kitchen and said, "I can't wait. Can I have some now?"

She kissed him on the cheek and said, "Not a chance. Wait your turn like everyone else."

Sylvia was feeling a little tearful about her youngest, her baby leaving home. Martin had been trying to cheer her up and his kitchen silliness was designed to do that. She smacked him lightly on the rear as he left the kitchen.

The table was set in a most glorious way. There was a centrepiece of lovely flowers and the fancy silver cutlery gleamed. The napkins on the table were a forest green and matched the fine green leaves on the bone china. The table was laden with more food than they could ever eat.

"Dinner is ready!" Sylvia called out and everyone descended on the dining room.

"Mom this is amazing," Sharon said as she came to the table.

Sylvia felt the tears welling up in her eyes as everyone was seated. Both of her girls looked wonderful. Mimi had the blush of pregnancy and seemed to glow from head to toe. Sharon looked so adult and so beautiful. She couldn't believe that these two smart self-assured women had recently been her babies.

Martin said, "Let's make a toast to Sharon's new life."

He filled the wine glasses with sparkling grape juice and everyone made a toast to Sharon. Next came the appetizers. The appetizers were spanakopita, Greek meatballs, and dolmades. Sylvia had made everything from scratch and the food was delectable. Everyone couldn't stop eating them.

"Pace yourselves," she told them with a twinkle in her eye. "This is just the beginning of the meal."

“Everything is delicious, Mom,” Mimi told her between mouthfuls of the Greek meatballs.

“It’s just your pregnancy talking,” Sylvia answered and they all laughed.

“Sylvia, you have truly outdone yourself,” Martin told her.

He helped her clear the table and they both brought out the main course. There was Greek lemon oregano chicken, lemon potatoes, Greek salad and fried zucchini. Sylvia served each dish on a platter and everyone passed each item around and served themselves.

The scent of the food was intoxicating. The conversation was relaxed and happy as everyone ate.

“I am so stuffed that I will never eat again,” Sharon said.

“I am serving chocolate raspberry cheesecake,” Sylvia replied.

“Well, maybe I could have a small piece.”

Just then, Mimi doubled over with pain.

“I think the baby is coming,” she said quietly.

“Are you having contractions?” Martin asked her.

“Yes.”

Sharon was so excited. She would be there for the birth.

“Let’s time the contractions,” Martin said.

So, they sat for a brief time noting the intervals between the pain. When it became obvious that the time between the pain was just six minutes, they decided it was time to go to the hospital.

“Let’s all go,” Sylvia said.

So they took Martin’s car and drove to the hospital. Mimi was looking pale. Her contractions were still making her double over.

“Hey, it wasn’t supposed to hurt this much,” she said as she lay in the back seat with her head on Sharon’s lap.

"Who told you that?" Sylvia asked. She didn't like the pain on Mimi's face or the fact that she was struggling. She hated to see her daughters suffering.

They parked in emergency and walked Mimi into the hospital.

"Hello Doctor Miller," said the admitting nurse.

"My daughter is in labour," Martin told her.

A wheelchair was brought out and Mimi was whisked away with Sharon beside her holding her hand.

Sylvia and Martin sat nervously in the waiting room. Martin had been told not to interfere and he would not even go close to the delivery room unless he was asked. Mimi lay in the delivery room sweating profusely.

Sharon mopped her face and waited as the young Doctor Miriam Gold examined her. Doctor Gold was a tiny elfin woman. She always seemed to Mimi to be too young to be a doctor but her father had said she was the best.

Mimi felt like she was going to explode. The contractions were coming fast and furious and she couldn't contain her moaning.

"Mimi, I am afraid that you are only 2 centimetres dilated. We have to wait until you are 10 centimetres dilated until the baby is ready."

Just as she said this, Mimi's water broke and there was a gush all over the sheets.

"I'll get the nurse to give you fresh sheets," she told Mimi and smiled.

"How long will it take for me to become fully dilated?" Mimi asked through gritted teeth.

"Not long, we hope," Doctor Gold answered and she was out of the room.

Mimi started to cry. Sharon was shocked. Mimi was always so brave. Nothing ever bothered her.

"Would you like to play checkers?" Sharon asked.

She was hoping that this would distract Mimi.

“No, I can’t do anything,” she stammered, crying even more.

Suddenly, she gripped Mimi’s hand even tighter as another contraction made her wince.

Mimi could not be consoled. Sharon tried funny stories and jokes but nothing worked. She brought Mimi ice chips to suck on.

After two hours, another doctor came in to check what was happening.

“Sorry, you are still only two centimetres dilated,” she told Mimi.

Mimi started to cry again and the doctor said the baby would come when it was ready. She offered Mimi pain medication but Mimi flat out refused.

Sharon went to the waiting room to give her parents an update. It was midnight and Sylvia and Martin were looking sleepy.

“Nothing has changed. This is going to take a while,” she told them. “ You might as well go home. I will let you know when something happens.”

Sylvia and Martin reluctantly went home for some sleep and Sharon returned to Mimi’s room and tried again to amuse her sister and help her through her labour.

Sharon remembered that Mimi loved books so she decided to read to her. She had just started a novel called “Fifth Business” by Robertson Davies. She started reading the first chapter to Mimi and Mimi visibly relaxed. She still gasped with every contraction but was able to pay attention to the novel. Sharon was exhausted and her eyes threatened to close but she still kept on reading.

Finally another doctor came to check Mimi.

“You are fully dilated,” he told her. “We can take you into the delivery room now.”

This time Mimi cried with joy. She was so relieved that this was finally going to be over.

“Thank you,” she said to the doctor, although she didn’t know why.

When they reached the delivery room, it was already 7:00 in the morning. Mimi had been in labour for what felt like forever and she was eager for it to end.

“Push,” the doctor said and Mimi pushed.

“I can see the baby’s head,” the doctor told her. A moment later the baby slid into the doctor’s arms.

“You have a beautiful daughter,” the doctor told her.

Mimi held her new daughter to her breast and immediately felt an overwhelming love for her. There were tears in Sharon’s eyes as she watched Mimi holding her daughter.

Mimi handed the baby to Sharon who held her and thought that this was life’s biggest miracle. Then the doctors took her away.

While Mimi was being cleaned up, Sharon went to phone her parents.

She forgot that it was 7:30 in the morning. She had been up all night and had lost all sense of time.

A groggy sounding Martin answered, “Hello.”

“You have a beautiful new granddaughter, dad. She weighs 8 pounds and 3 ounces. Mother and baby are doing well.”

She could hear Sylvia in the background asking her father if everything was alright.

“Yes, Sylvia, we have a granddaughter.”

She could hear her mother say, “I am so happy.”

“I need to go back to Mimi now. I’ll phone you soon.”

Sharon returned to Mimi’s room. Mimi was lying in bed with the largest smile on her face.

“The nurse says we can eat now. I am starved. There are some sandwiches in the fridge down the hall. Get me ten.”

Sharon found sandwiches and juice boxes for them both and returned to the room. She brought them over to Mimi.

Sharon noticed that Mimi looked exhausted. It was no surprise considering she had been in labour all night.

"What kind of sandwiches do we have?" Mimi asked her.

"This one looks like chicken salad and this one is cheese."

"I'll take the chicken salad," Mimi told her.

"How are you feeling?" Sharon asked her.

"Tired and sore," Mimi said with a smile in her voice.

They started eating the sandwiches hungrily. The doctor brought the beautiful baby girl and put her in a bassinet by Mimi's bed.

Mimi's face suddenly turned pale.

"Oh my god, what is it?" Sharon asked her.

"Get a doctor! Something is wrong!" Mimi screamed.

Sharon ran out into the hall and found a nurse. They rushed back to the room and Mimi was lying pale and unconscious on her pillow. She looked dead.

Sharon could feel a panic rising up in her.

The nurse quickly examined Mimi.

She took off the sheets covering her and there was blood everywhere.

"She is hemorrhaging," she told Sharon in a cool voice. We have to get her into surgery immediately.

Before Sharon knew what was happening, the nurse and doctor had wheeled Mimi away and Sharon was left in the room with the bassinet with Mimi's baby, sitting and crying.

Just then, Sylvia and Martin came into the room holding a large bouquet of flowers.

"What happened?" Sylvia asked when she saw Sharon's stricken face.

"Mimi started to hemorrhage. They took her down for surgery," she told them between sobs.

Sylvia looked like she would faint and Martin had to grab her to steady her.

The baby started to cry. Sharon picked her up and cuddled her and her parents met their new granddaughter for the first time. Sylvia and Martin both had tears in their eyes.

All three sat in the room with the baby for what seemed like forever. Finally, a doctor came in and told them.

"Mimi will be fine. We were able to stop the bleeding. She lost a lot of blood so it will be a long recovery for her. She will need someone to take care of her and the baby for several months."

Sharon decided at that moment that she was not going away to school. Her sister and niece really needed her and she would not let them down.

It is amazing how a life can change in an instant. Suddenly, nothing mattered to Sharon except for Mimi and the baby. There was nowhere she needed to be and nothing she needed to do. Her role in her sister's life was the only one that mattered.

The first task was to name the baby. Sharon knew the names that Mimi had favoured so she chose one. She knew that Mimi was especially partial to the name Jennifer so Jennifer it would be.

"Hi Jennifer," she told her beautiful baby niece as she held her and cuddled her. Mimi was still unconscious but she was slowly coming around.

For the next few days, Sharon spent most of her time at the hospital. When she was there, she was either cuddling Jennifer or holding Mimi's hand. Mimi did regain consciousness but she could hardly move.

Sylvia and Martin tried to convince Sharon to go to Ottawa.

"We can take care of Mimi and the baby," Sylvia told her.

"Please don't miss this opportunity," Martin added.

"You have been waiting so long for this."

"I can't leave with Mimi so sick and the baby needing me," she told them. There was an expression of complete determination on her face. They could see that it was futile to argue.

So Sharon's life changed completely but not in the way she had imagined. Jennifer was ready to leave the hospital but Mimi was far from ready. So Sharon took her home to Mimi's house. Her room and crib were waiting for her.

Sharon loved Jennifer as if she was her own. She kissed her and hugged her and cuddled her constantly. Mimi had really wanted to nurse her child but of course that would not be possible. So Sharon made formula and gave it to Jennifer.

Jennifer was the most beautiful baby in the world as far as Sharon was concerned. She was pink with beautiful blue eyes and a tuft of blond hair. Sharon had to admit that Jennifer looked like David.

She decided she had to let him know that he had a daughter. She dialed his number.

"Hello David, this is Sharon."

He sounded like he had just woken him.

"Yes, what is it?" he asked with a slurry voice.

"Mimi gave birth. You have a beautiful baby daughter."

"Can I come to see them?"

"Well, Mimi is still in the hospital. She had some complications but she is doing better. Jennifer is at home with me. You can come to see her."

"I will let you know," he said and hung up abruptly.

What is wrong with him, Sharon wondered.

She didn't know that David had started to cry and was too embarrassed for her to hear. He was so happy that he had a daughter and he was overcome by tears he couldn't explain.

Sharon fed Jennifer again and then changed her diaper. In a moment, her mother was coming over to look after Jennifer while Sharon went to the hospital to visit Mimi. The baby was wonderful. She gurgled and chirped and hardly ever cried. Sharon cuddled Jennifer and put her down in the crib.

She heard the doorbell and went to let in her mother, who was returning from seeing Mimi.

"How is the baby?" Sylvia asked.

"She is perfect mom. How is Mimi?"

"She is so weak. It scares me. She can hardly speak."

"I know Mom. She will get better soon."

Even as she said this, she wondered if it was true. Mimi had rallied very little. She seemed no better. She managed a weak smile but it was evident that even that was an effort.

Sharon wanted to bring Jennifer to see Mimi but the doctors would not allow it. So instead she went to visit Mimi and told her all about the baby. If that didn't make her perk up, she didn't know what would.

After she visited Mimi in the hospital, Sharon returned to Mimi's house. While her mother was feeding Jennifer, Sharon phoned the dorm and cancelled her dorm room. Then she phoned the university and withdrew from her courses. If she thought about it, she would have been very depressed but she decided there was no time right now for regrets.

CHAPTER 42. SHARON

Jennifer is almost a month old. She is a beautiful sweet baby. She takes her formula happily and sighs contentedly when I cuddle her. The two of us have gotten into a routine. Between changing diapers, feeding and cuddling, I find my days are quite full. Somehow I feel like Jennie, which I now call her, is mine.

The university told me that I could start in the winter term in January when I told them what had happened. I don't think that will be possible. Mimi is still not doing well. When she was recovering from her bleeding, she developed an infection. She had raging fever and was almost delirious. She kept asking me to look after Jennifer if she died. I kept saying that I would but she would be fine. I wish I believed it.

She is finally over that infection but the doctor says she is too weak to go home. She hardly has an appetite. Mom has been bringing her treats and she seems unable to eat them. The doctor threatened her that he would put her on an IV if she didn't eat more.

Yesterday, I went to visit her. I try to go every day. She was sitting up in her bed staring into space.

"How are you feeling?" I asked her.

"The same," she said without even looking at me.

"You need to get well soon. Jennie needs you to come home."

"She has you."

"It's not the same."

"Here are some pictures of Jennifer, Mimi. She looks just like you."

"She is beautiful," Mimi answered in a whisper.

Since Mimi had been ill, she had become so quiet. It was as if she was slowly disappearing.

"I brought you some chocolate truffles" I told her.

"I'm not really hungry. I just had lunch," she said listlessly.

"I guess there will be more for me," I said and popped one into my mouth. The old Mimi would have demanded some but this one was not interested.

"I brought you a book to read. It is a great mystery novel."

"Just put it in my bedside table. I will get to it later." Her bedside table was crammed with books and snacks that had not been touched. I did not know what else to do. It felt like she had given up.

"Your daughter needs you. I need you," I said to her.

She was only half listening to my conversation and fell asleep while I talked. I was terrified that she would die. She should have been well by now. I had spoken to my father about this and he said that the healing process was taking longer than expected. She would heal on her own time, he told me. I was not so sure.

David never contacted me after I told him he was a father. I should not have been surprised but I was. Wasn't he interested in seeing his child? I used to think I was in love with him. I couldn't understand why I had ever even liked him or my sister had ever married him. He was revolting. He did not care about his own daughter. What kind of man was he?

I thought Jennie was better off without him.

Someday she will ask about her father and Mimi will have to tell her something. I am not sure what she will say. Mimi will know what the right thing is; she always does.

CHAPTER 43

Such a short time ago Sylvia had seen both her daughters as smart young women that were doing what was right. Now she wondered what would become of them. The only thing that helped her was running. She would come home and collapse.

Today it was not working for her. No matter how much she ran, nothing felt better. She ran home and felt just as terrible as she had when she left. She stepped into a hot shower and let the warmth permeate her sore body. After the shower, she got dressed and went to the kitchen. She was going to bake Mimi's favourite chocolate chip cookies to bring to the hospital. She had been tempting Mimi with treats for a few weeks to no avail. Mimi seemed to have lost her appetite and she had always been slim. She was looking positively skeletal at this point.

It had been so easy when they were little. A bandage and a kiss seemed to cure most pains. Not anymore. Both her children were struggling and she could only hope that they found their way. So the cookies were her way of controlling something. Maybe Mimi would actually eat some of these cookies.

Sylvia took the cookies out of the oven and decided to bring them right to the hospital before they even cooled. She placed them on a platter and covered them with tin foil. They smelled wonderful. She drove right to the hospital and went into Mimi's room.

Mimi was sitting up in bed and reading. She looked pale but there was finally some animation in her face.

"Hi sweetheart, I brought you some chocolate chip cookies," she told Mimi expecting that she would say that she was not hungry.

Instead, Mimi said, "They smell wonderful mom. I would love to have some."

Sylvia was sure that she was going to start crying. Her baby was coming back.

"Sharon brought me some lovely pictures of Jennifer yesterday, mom. Would you like to see them?"

"Yes, of course."

"Please take them out of the bedside table."

Sylvia took out a pile of colour photos of her granddaughter.

"Isn't she beautiful?" Mimi asked.

"Yes, she is. She looks just like you."

Mimi nibbled on chocolate chip cookies as they thumbed through the photographs.

"I especially like this one. She looks so cute in that pink striped sleeper."

Sylvia realized at that moment why Mimi was feeling better. Her own daughter was making her smile and restoring her will to live.

"Mom, the doctor says I can go home next week."

"That is the best news I have heard in a long time."

Sylvia said a silent prayer of thanks.

"Sharon wants to stay until I get my energy back."

"That's a good idea," Sylvia said but she wasn't sure if it was true. Sharon really needed to get on with her own life.

Still, she was so grateful that Mimi seemed to be feeling better. She noticed that Mimi had eaten four cookies. This was so much better. She stayed for about an hour and then went home to make dinner for herself and Martin. She felt so much more calm and happy than she had in a long time.

Sharon phoned them later that day with the best news.

"Mimi is coming home tomorrow!" she blurted out in a loud voice. She could hardly contain her excitement.

"That's great, Sharon," Sylvia said.

"The doctor has told her to still take it easy for a while. She is still weak from the infection. But I think being home with me and Jennie will be the best medicine."

"You are right about that. Maybe you can go away to Ottawa for the winter term."

"Maybe," Sharon sighed.

Sylvia was not convinced. Well, at least Mimi was doing better. Maybe she could persuade Sharon to leave soon. She would just have to take it one day at a time.

"Who was on the phone?" Martin asked her.

He was stretched out in a large black leather reclining chair reading the newspaper.

"That was Sharon. She phoned to let us know that Mimi is coming home tomorrow." She expected him to be delighted but instead a frown showed on his face.

"What's wrong Martin? I thought you would be so happy to hear this."

"I am happy that Mimi is doing better. I just don't think she is ready to be released from the hospital. She is still so weak and she has lost a lot of weight. It is hard work caring for a newborn and I think it will exhaust her before she is well."

Sylvia couldn't believe that she was hearing this. Still, Martin was a doctor. He would know what was best.

"What should we do Martin?" she asked him.

"Nothing. I am probably just worrying too much. Sharon will make sure that Mimi is doing well and help Mimi with the baby."

"I brought her chocolate chip cookies today. She ate half a dozen."

"Well, keep feeding her and she will feel better."

Sylvia went into the kitchen and started mixing flour for bread. Then she left it on the counter to proof and made more cookies. This batch was chocolate fudge. She looked at the clock and realized with a shock that it was 10:00 pm. Time to go to bed. She went to see how Martin was doing. He was sleeping in the recliner with the newspaper on his lap. She folded the newspaper and gave him a gentle kiss on the cheek.

"Is it morning?" he asked her.

"No we are going to bed now," she told him and he got up slowly. She put her arm around his waist gently and they ambled to their bedroom.

CHAPTER 44. SHARON

In the past year, I have felt so much like I was living in a dream. There was an unreality to my life that was so strange. It was like I was in a place somewhere between two lives. I felt like that just before I was supposed to go away. Now I am feeling that way again. I have been cast into Mimi's role as a parent to Jennie.

I have spent a beautiful month bonding with her while feeding her and caring for her. I have grown quite attached to her. I feel like she is my own baby. This is bound to end soon. Later today, my parents are bringing Mimi home from the hospital.

I have washed her bedding and filled the fridge with her favourite foods. I think it will be no time at all until she is up and I am the invisible daughter again. I am used to this role. I have spent 21 years in it. I am always there but not really noticed by anyone. Mimi will be grateful but she will take up her own duties again. Where will I be at that point?

I will be nowhere in a life which has little meaning. I have phoned the university and told them that I will be starting the journalism course in the winter. I need something that is my own. I can't live in my sister's shadow anymore. I will have to find a place to live. I gave up my dorm room when Mimi got sick. When she is a bit stronger, I will go to rent a place. I have to do this for myself. I love my sister but I am not her keeper.

Mimi is finally home. She seems to be eating well and she loves holding Jennie but she is still so weak. She seems unable to do anything. When she walks from the kitchen to the bedroom, it seems like a big effort. She has been home for a week and I was hoping that she would be so much better by now. She still isn't able to care for Jennie or do much of anything else. My responsibilities have doubled because I am now looking after Mimi as well.

Dad has offered to hire a nurse to live with Mimi and the baby until Mimi is well. Mom suggested that Mimi and Jennie move in with them. I know this would not work for Mimi. Mom would drive her crazy after a while. So I stay here torn with a desire to leave and wracked with guilt that I cannot desert my sister and niece. I don't know what to do. Last week, I turned 22 and no one noticed. A 22nd birthday is a time for real celebration. It is a transition into adulthood.

Everyone is so worried about Mimi. I can't believe my own family forgot my birthday. I can understand Mimi forgetting because she is sick. But mom and dad? How did they forget?

My friend Annie wants to take me out for my birthday. She says we can get high and eat ourselves into a frenzy. It is the best offer I have had in a long time. I will ask mom to come in and look after Mimi, and go out for an evening. I think that a slave – even this one –deserves an evening off.

So, mom has just arrived with dad to help Mimi look after Jennie. Mom is carrying a large box in her hands.

I am just about to kiss them and go to meet Annie when mom says, "Hey just hold on!"

"What is it mom?" I am afraid if we start talking I will never get out. Mimi is perched on the sofa with a blanket over her and I desperately want to leave.

Mom opens the box and takes out the largest chocolate cake ever.

It could feed 20 people. It says, "Happy 22nd birthday Sharon," on it.

"I am sorry that we are a day late," my father tells me.

"It is double chocolate fudge, your favourite," my mother tells me.

"Can I get the first ten pieces?" Mimi asks.

"I am sorry but I have to go and meet a friend," I tell them.

"Not yet," says my mother.

She picks up a shopping bag full of wrapped boxes.

"You need to have a piece of cake and open your gifts."

I know that I am being rude but I feel that I really need to leave Mimi's house. I am desperate to get out.

"Thanks, but I have to go," I tell them.

I grab my coat and leave before anyone has a chance to say another word.

I get into Mimi's car and speed away from the house. I am feeling like the walls are closing in on me. I know this was a lovely gesture but I am tired of always being there for all of them. I need to finally break out on my own.

CHAPTER 45. SHARON

Annie was sitting and waiting for me at the bar when I arrived. She looked wonderful. Her blonde hair fell softly around her face. She was slim and well put together. I, on the other hand, was a shapeless blob.

"Rough day?" she said when she saw me.

"My parents came in with cakes and gifts. I had to leave because you and I already had plans."

"Let's drink to your birthday," Annie said.

She was looking especially stylish tonight. She had on a white silk shirt and tight black jeans. She was so slim she could get away with it. I would look like a hippo in that outfit. Her blonde hair was in a ponytail. I noticed men giving her the eye. How could they not?

In contrast, I was wearing a loose fitting ratty green sweater and old tattered jeans. We looked like Beauty and the Beast.

"Two screwdrivers for me and the birthday girl," Annie said to the bartender.

He brought them right to us and she paid. She said tonight was on her.

We drank them and then everything looked a little bit brighter.

"I have dinner reservations at La Bastille," she told me with a smile.

"Oh my, you have to make those so far in advance. How did you get us in?"

"I have my ways," she told me with a wink.

When we entered the restaurant, I felt like I had been whisked away into the past. The centuries old former prison building had thick walls, a dimly lit interior and medieval furniture. As I sat on my high back chair, I was so excited to be there.

"Did you have to have sex with someone to get us in here?" I asked her.

"You'll never know," Annie said with a giggle in her voice.

I ordered escargot and scampi and Annie ordered a Niçoise salad and steak frites. She also ordered a bottle of red wine for us to share.

I was a little worried. "How can you afford this?" I asked her.

"I just got a job," Annie said bubbling over with excitement.

"I am going to be a buyer for Eaton's. The pay is not bad and the benefits are wonderful."

"Wow, I am so excited for you."

I was happy for her but wondered even more about myself. My friends were finishing university and starting careers and I was not even close. At this rate, I would never have a career. I started to feel guilty about feeling this way when Mimi really needed me and stuffed the feelings down. This was my evening and I was going to enjoy it.

The wine and food helped to make me forget everything that was troubling me. By the end of the meal, I was in a soft drunken haze.

"Let's go for a nightcap," Annie said. "There is a bar around the corner that has a jazz guitarist and great drinks."

So we went out again to the bar and listened to music. I was already quite buzzed but I had one more drink.

"Let's go back to my place and get stoned," Annie suggested.

"I think I am already quite high. Thanks so much Annie. You are a great friend."

I hugged her goodbye.

"I am going to go home and to bed."

I foolishly drove back to Mimi's house. I guess I made it in one piece because I woke up at 3:00 am to Jennie crying. I was lying fully dressed on my bed. My head felt like it was stuffed with cotton and my body ached.

I got up slowly, noticing my head was throbbing. No wonder. I had been drinking way too much. I slowly sat up and went to give Jennie her bottle.

The next day was difficult. I felt as if my entire body was aching and sore. Mimi was listless.

She told me, "Mom and dad were hurt that you left last night."

"I had plans Mimi. Even a slave deserves some time off."

"Do you feel like a slave?"

"Yes, sometimes I do. I am here all the time. No one including you remembered my birthday until it was over. I deserve to celebrate."

"I am sorry you feel this way. I did not decide that this would happen." After Mimi said this, she looked like she would cry.

I could not give in to the guilt that was consuming me. I had to say something.

"I think you and Jennie should move in with mom and dad. I really want to go to Ottawa."

"Sure," she said but looked very unhappy.

I decided at that minute that it was time to do my own living. Mimi would recover at mom and dad's as well as she would with me. I was going away to university finally.

"I will stay until the end of the month," I told her. "Then I am off to Ottawa."

She just nodded. She looked exhausted even though she had slept for many hours. My heart broke for her but I had done enough.

I went to get Jennie and brought her to Mimi's waiting arms. I had to admit that she was a perfect baby. She cooed and cuddled and ate and slept well. I would miss her.

As I prepared lunch for myself and Mimi, I thought of David. He had never made an attempt to contact any of us after I phoned him and told him that he was a father. He had fought Mimi for parental rights and was not exercising them. Well, it was his loss. Jennie had enough people to love her.

As Mimi and I ate our tuna sandwiches, she seemed even more subdued than usual. She hardly said a word about anything. I wondered if she was dreading living with mom and dad. I decided not to ask her. I was already feeling guilty and it would be far too easy to stay with her and Jennie indefinitely.

I loved them both so much but I needed to love myself. It was time for me to start living my own life.

When we were having our coffee after lunch, Mimi said to me, "You have made the right decision to go to school in Ottawa. Jennie and I will be fine. Maybe I won't have to leave this house. I am getting stronger all the time."

"You are certainly improving," I told her.

I wasn't at all sure whether I was telling the truth. She was certainly eating better and moving around more but she was still weak. Maybe the thought of living with our parents would make her rally more quickly.

So, once again, I started getting ready to leave. The month went by quickly and soon it was almost time to leave. Mimi was doing well so my guilt started to dissipate. She had taken over Jennie's care almost completely and her cheeks had a healthy glow for the first time in many months. She had gained some weight and was looking more like her old self.

"Please promise me that you will ask for help if you need it," I told her.

"As if mom will give me any choice," she laughed.

Yes, this was the old Mimi resurfacing. I was so relieved.

At the end of November I moved out of Mimi's house. I was not starting university until January but I was eager to leave. I had leased a small one-bedroom apartment near campus by phone and sent in the damage deposit and first month's rent and I was eager to be on my own. I had been living with other people for such a long time that I longed for my own space.

I rented a U-Haul truck to move some of my items to my apartment. Mom had given me an extra bed and a small table with a few chairs. She had also insisted that I take some dishes, cutlery, pots, and pans. I had purchased a second hand car. Dad had helped me choose an old Valiant. It was homely but reliable. As far as I was concerned, I now had everything I needed.

The day I left was cool, crisp, and sunny. There was already snow on the ground. The trees were lined with magnificent hoar frost and looked magical. Dad had helped me load the u haul and I had a promise from my apartment superintendent to help me unload it.

I drove with a smile on my face. I turned on the radio and listened to loud music as I drove. I was feeling more free and alive than I had in so long. On the way, I stopped for a quick lunch and then continued. The roads were clear and clean and I made it in good time.

I rang the superintendent's bell and he greeted me. Mr. Oakes was quite young and adorable. I guessed him to be about 30. He had a bright smile, olive skin, beautiful chocolate coloured eyes and curly black hair. He walked with a slight swagger. I was instantly attracted to him.

"Hello Sharon. I have been waiting for you," he said.

He even had a sexy voice. It had a hint of a drawl in it.

"Hello Mr. Oakes. I really appreciate you helping me unload the truck."

"No problem. Please call me Mike."

So Mike helped me move my stuff into the apartment. I looked to see if he had a wedding ring on but he didn't.

When we were done, he refused my offer of money for the job.

"Thank you, I really appreciate your help."

"My pleasure, I hope we can see each other again soon."

"I think it can be arranged," I said and walked up the two floors to my apartment.

My apartment was small and plain but I loved it. It had real hardwood floors that gleamed. There were a pink fridge, stove, and sink that made the apartment look like it belonged to a woman. I spent a few minutes hanging up some clothes and went out to buy some dinner. I returned with a pizza and sat alone and ate it relishing every bite.

Mike had assembled my bed and I put some sheets on it. It had been a long day and I was tired. The quiet all around me was like music to my ears. After living with my parents and then Mimi and Jennie, I was so grateful to have a space of my own and no one to answer to.

I had to return the U-Haul in Ottawa tomorrow and get some groceries. I also had to get my telephone set up so I could be in touch with my parents and my sister. Somehow this all seemed like a faraway dream.

I unpacked some towels and soap and took a long hot shower. The bathroom was small and everything was crowded together but the shower was strong and hot. Then I slipped into bed and fell asleep before my head hit the pillow. I dreamed that Mike and I were together in an arena watching a wrestling match. It wasn't a romantic dream but it wasn't scary or upsetting either.

I woke up to the bright sunlight streaming into my bedroom. For a moment, I wondered where I was. Then I remembered that I was in my own very first apartment and it felt wonderful. I had a busy day ahead but I didn't mind. Everything I was doing now was for myself.

After getting dressed, I went to a phone booth and phoned Mimi.

She answered quickly with a bright and chirpy, “Hello.”

“Hi, it’s Sharon. How are you feeling?,”

“Sharon who?,”

“Very funny. Are you okay?,”

I wondered why I had phoned her but old habits die hard.

“I am feeling great. I have lots of energy. I just fed Jennie and made myself a large breakfast. You’ll never guess what happened. I just had a call from David. He wants to come see Jennie. Do you think I should let him?”

“I guess you have to. He is her father after all.”

“I suppose so,” she sighed.

“Listen, Mimi, I have to get myself organized today so I am going to take off. Please tell mom and dad that I am fine.”

“Thanks for phoning. I love you. Bye.”

I felt a little lump in my throat at her words and then went off to conquer my day.

I spent the day in thrift stores buying little odds and ends for my apartment. Mom had supplied me with almost everything that I needed but I bought a colourful tablecloth, some extra towels, a salad bowl, some dishtowels and a few picture frames.

As I sat in my apartment, I enjoyed every second of my new-found freedom. I noticed that my windows did not have blinds or curtains on them. I wondered if I should go to the trouble of buying some. I was up on the third floor and my windows looked into a quiet courtyard. I liked the sun streaming into my window.

I wondered if I would be lonely being on my own for the first time. After all, I had always been with others. My reverie was interrupted by a sharp knock on the door.

“Who is it?” I asked knowing that there was only one person who might be at my door.

"It's me Mike," came the answer.

I opened the door and there stood Mike with a big grin on his face. He was holding several sets of Venetian blinds in his hand.

"I was wondering if you might need these. They come with the apartments but some tenants don't want them. I could put them up for you right now."

"I can't believe you are here with blinds. I was just wondering if I should buy some."

He smiled at me again and at that moment I fell in love with him. I never believed in love at first sight but I never felt this way before either. I felt like I would love him for the rest of my life.

As our relationship progressed, Mike and I developed a bond and he always seemed to show up when I needed him the most. This first time it seemed magical but later on it was almost a daily occurrence that I grew to expect.

Mike stood on a chair and put the blinds up in the living room, kitchen and bedroom windows.

He wore jeans and a T-shirt. I could see his muscles rippling under his shirt. I watched him and lusted after him. I wondered if I had been without a man for too long.

When he was finished, I suddenly felt bold and said to him, "I don't know Ottawa very well. Perhaps you could show me around."

He smiled again and said, "How about this weekend?"

"That would be great."

A few days later, we were skating together on the Rideau Canal. Later that day, he took me out for dinner at a local Italian restaurant that served wonderful pasta dishes. The next day, we went out for breakfast together. After we had eaten our omelettes, we went back to my apartment. He kissed me on the lips and I threw my arms around him. I led him into my bedroom and pushed him on the bed. After that, we tore off each other's clothes like animals and had the most intense sex of my life. I was out of breath when it was over.

We lay in the tangles of covers and clothes and cuddled. I had never felt so alive or happy in my life.

A short time later, I dozed off. I woke up to Mike fondling my breast and we were at it again. Later, we sat and chatted.

Mike came from a large Italian family. He was working at this job and finishing his law degree at the same time. He was hoping to open a firm with his brother Gianni.

"How did you wind my with your last name?" I asked him. "It is not very Italian."

"My father died when I was very young. My mother's new husband Robert Oakes adopted all of us."

There were five children. I thought that Robert must have been a great guy to adopt his new wife's children.

As if he had read my mind, Mike said, "My dad Robert was a wonderful man. He died five years ago. We still miss him so much."

"My family is having a big birthday dinner together on Sunday. Would you like to come with me? I think they would love to meet you."

"Sure why not?" I answered.

I wondered if it was too soon but it felt right so I figured why not? Mike's family lived in a large two-storey home on a tree lined street in Hull. His mother Lucia charmed me as soon as we met. She was a tall statuesque woman with curly black hair and a winning smile. I wondered how this woman who looked 30 years old could be mother to five adult children.

"Welcome to our home, Sharon," she said.

She threw her arms around me. Mike's brothers and sisters were all there. His brother Gianni looked just like him. His sisters Maria, Lina, and Linda bustled around me and teased me.

"What do you see in this oaf?" Linda asked.

"Tell us about yourself," Maria said.

This party was a celebration for Gianni's birthday. He was turning 25. He was the second-oldest child after Mike who was 26. All of Mike's siblings were there with their spouses.

"We are glad that Mike finally found a girlfriend," Lina told me.

Her husband Roy who looked so familiar stood with his arm around her.

Mike's mother Lucia passed around appetizers in the living room. There were all types of antipastos and arancini. Everyone seemed so comfortable and happy with each other. The wall was covered with family pictures of Mike and his siblings at every age.

The furniture was well-worn and comfortable. We soon went to the dining room for dinner. The meal seemed to never end. There were salads and soups and three different main courses and five desserts followed by a birthday cake for Gianni.

After dinner, everyone sat in the living room once again and Gianni opened his gifts. Later we left and I felt wonderful.

"I could see that my family loved you," Mike told me. I smiled at him as we rode back to my apartment in his car.

I compared my family to his. We had some happy moments but so much of our time together was fraught with arguments and grief. I remembered all the meals we had with my mother screaming at my father. These people genuinely loved and respected each other.

When we got back to my apartment, I was feeling ready for some sex. He put his arms around me and said, "I love you Sharon. I know we have not been together very long but I have never been so sure of anything in my life."

I looked into his sparkling coal-black eyes and said, "I love you too, Mike."

Then he lifted me and carried me to the bed. In the bed, he tenderly removed my sweater and bra and started stroking my breasts. This led to us both naked kissing each other in a frantic and frenzied way. When he was on top of me, I thought I would explode.

Later that night, we lay with my head on his chest and I felt so happy and safe with him. I realized that I did love him. I wondered how I could have gone from miserable in Montreal to ecstatic in Ottawa so quickly. I decided to relish every second of this newfound joy.

My relationship with Mike was going surprisingly well. I adored him and his large and crazy family. Every Sunday, I went with Mike to his family for dinner. There was always an occasion to celebrate. There were so many of them that it was invariably someone's birthday or anniversary. I was always welcomed with open arms by everyone.

I especially enjoyed my relationship with Mike's mother. She was always so sweet to me.

"You are like my daughter," she told me every time I saw her.

She plied me with food. At the end of every dinner, she would insist that I take some food home with me.

I would return with pastas, salads, and desserts that Mike and I would eat throughout the week.

"I am going to be your chubby little girlfriend," I told him.

"I will love you no matter what you weigh," he teased and pinched my thigh.

"Hey, who said you could do that?"

"Who said I couldn't," he replied and gave me a sloppy pasta kiss.

We both started to laugh as he licked the pasta sauce off my face.

We were inseparable. Mike was over every day and slept over most nights. The only times we were not together were the times he was studying or working in the building.

My schooling would begin soon and then everything would be different – or would it? I hoped we could study together. I couldn't get enough of him. I wanted him to be with me 24 hours of the day.

Our first fight was an unexpected surprise. I had told my family I would come home at Christmas to spend time with them. I was especially looking forward to seeing Mimi and Jennie. Mimi was telling me how well everything was going for her and the baby. I wanted to see it for myself.

I told Mike that I would be leaving for Montreal to see my family on December 20 and return a week later. To my surprise, he was angry.

"You can't leave then," he told me.

"Why not?"

"My family always has a big celebration together," he told me. "They would miss you."

"They have known me for such a short time. They have each other."

"It won't be the same without you. Can I convince you to stay?"

"My family needs me too. My sister was very sick. I need to make sure she is well. I miss her and my niece. I also miss my parents."

"Maybe I can still convince you to stay," he said.

I had been sitting on the sofa looking at a magazine. He walked over to me and pushed me down on the sofa. Before I knew what was happening, he was pulling down my jeans and pushing himself inside me. I was hardly ready and this was painful.

He held my hands down and pummelled me roughly as if he was trying to hurt me. He thrust so hard I thought I would cry.

He finally came and plopped down on top of me. I was still wearing my sweater and I was aching.

"Did I convince you?" he asked me.

"No, you practically raped me you asshole. I don't want to ever see you again. Leave my apartment now before I call the police."

He looked genuinely shocked. “I’m sorry, Sharon. I would never hurt you. I thought the sex would make you want to stay here with me.”

“You need to leave right now,” I told him with tears in my eyes.

“I’m sorry. I love you,” he pleaded with me.

He left and I bolted the door. It was still five days before I was due to leave but I decided to go the next morning.

I was devastated. I had a tearful night and I hardly slept. The next morning, I got up very early and packed my bag. I threw on my winter parka and was out the door just as the sun was coming up. I was feeling that the only safety I could find was back home. After I returned, I would find another apartment. So much for being in love. I felt like a fool. I sneaked out of my apartment as if I was being watched.

The morning was a brutally chilly December day. Snow and ice covered my car. I rushed to scrape off the windshield terrified that Mike would come out. By the time I scraped off the ice and snow, I was chilled. I prayed that the car would start. It started in an instant. As soon as it was warm enough, I put the heat up to full blast. I stopped at a coffee shop and had a coffee and a muffin. Afterwards I found a phone booth and phoned my parents. After all, I was coming five days early. Maybe this would not work for them. If it didn’t, I could always stay with Mimi and Jennie.

“Hello,” my father answered in a groggy voice.

I suddenly realized it was 8:30 on a Sunday morning. Of course, they would still be asleep.

“Hi dad, it’s Sharon. How are you?”

“Great Sharon. It is great to hear from you. We are so excited about your visit.”

If I had woken him up, he made no mention of it.

“I’m sorry I woke you dad.”

“I was just getting up anyway.”

I loved my father. He was always so happy to hear from me.

"Dad, I would like to come home today if you don't mind. I am feeling lonely and I want to be at home. Would that be alright?"

"This is your home too Sharon. You never have to ask."

"I will be there by lunchtime."

"We can't wait. Drive carefully. I love you."

"I love you too dad. See you soon."

So, when I arrived home at noon, mom, dad, Mimi and Jennie were all at the kitchen table. It was laden with enough food for ten people. I was so happy to see them.

They crowded around me and hugged me. Then my dad pulled out a chair for me.

"Let's eat," he said.

I sat down with my family and it seemed as if the last month had never taken place.

Mimi asked, "How is your new sweetie Mike?"

"We broke up."

No one asked me why. For that I was so grateful. We sat and chatted about everything. Dad loved his new shift at the hospital. Mom was planning a trip to Florida for them. Mimi was thrilled with her improving health and Jennie's giggle.

Everything was just about perfect. After we stuffed ourselves, Dad helped mom clean up and Mimi put Jennie down for a nap. I had to admit Mimi looked wonderful. She was glowing with energy and health. She had gained some more weight and it suited her.

"I have something to tell you," she said, "but please don't tell mom and dad."

"What is it, Mimi?" I asked her.

"David has been coming to see Jennie. He has really changed. He wants to get back together and I am thinking about it."

My heart sank. I was feeling a bit queasy. I wanted to yell at her and to shake her but all I said was.

“Be careful. Don’t let him hurt you.”

“I won’t Sharon, I promise.”

We had had a lovely afternoon but it was tainted in my mind. How could she ever consider going back to David? Didn’t she remember the things he had done to her? I was also feeling sick about what had happened with Mike but I put him far out of my mind.

That evening, after Mimi and Jennie had gone home, I sat in the family room with mom and dad. They were looking comfortable together as if the two of them really fit. This had not been the case ever before. I always felt as if mom was waiting for him to make a mistake so she could yell at him. Now they sat together. He was reading the paper and she was knitting a purple blanket for Jennie and she was leaning against his back. They both looked so content.

I also noticed that dad was getting grey streaks in his hair. He still looked so handsome but the grey made him look even better. Why couldn’t Mimi or I meet someone as wonderful as our father?

For some reason, I was exhausted. I read for a while and then excused myself and went to my old room. The bed felt like home and I was asleep in seconds. The next morning, I woke up late. I could smell the most delicious aromas from my room. When I went to the kitchen, no one was there but there was some fresh brewed coffee in the coffee maker and a pile of cinnamon buns in a bowl on the counter.

There was a note from mom:

> Welcome home, Sharon. Dad is at work and I have gone to see my therapist. Help yourself to anything you want.
>
> Love,
>
> Mom

I wondered why my mother had gone to see her therapist. It was a cold miserable snowy day and she could have stayed at home where it was warm and safe. She must really feel that she needs his help.

I was interrupted from my thoughts by the phone ringing.

"Hello," I answered.

"Hi Sharon, it is Mike. Please don't hang up."

He sounded very shaky like he was almost in tears.

"How did you get my phone number?" I asked him.

"I remembered your father's name and looked it up in the phone book."

"What can I do for you Mike?"

"I phoned to apologize about what happened. If I had known I would upset you, I never would have done it. Please give me another chance."

"I'm not sure Mike. Maybe."

"Please, Sharon, I really love you. I would never intentionally hurt you."

His pleading was making my heart lurch. I was softening but not quite ready to forgive him.

"Maybe after I come back to Ottawa, we can talk."

He sighed with relief.

"That would be so wonderful Sharon. Can I phone you again?"

"I would prefer if you didn't. I have a lot of plans."

This wasn't true but I just didn't want to talk to him again for a while. If I kept talking to him, I would weaken and take him back. I was not at all sure if I wanted to.

We said goodbye and I went to eat another cinnamon bun. Then I decided to go to mom and dad's bathroom where a scale stood by the tub. Mom liked to weigh herself every day. I didn't know why. There was not an ounce of fat on that woman. Between her jogging and work-outs at the gym, she never gained weight. I was a different story. I had only to look at food to put on the pounds. I guess my excessive eating had something to do with it.

So I breathed in and weighed myself. To my surprise, I had not gained any weight. In fact, I was two pounds lighter than last time. I decided not to worry about my weight anymore. After all, I would be eating well at home. No need to think about it. A more pressing issue was what I should do about my relationship with Mike. He had always been gentle and kind to me except for the one isolated incident.

Thinking about the relationship was confusing me so I vowed to put it out of my mind until I went back to Ottawa. An answer would present itself to me.

I wanted to get together with some friends. I phoned Annie and a few others that I wanted to see. Annie invited me over for dinner the next day. She said we had a lot to catch up on. My friends didn't know about my relationship with Mike so there were no questions about it, which was a relief to me.

As I was leaving a message on the phone for my friend Lisa, my mother came in. She was wearing her beige winter parka and carrying two bags of groceries. Her face was flushed from the cold and she looked happy. She placed the groceries on the kitchen table and went to hang up her jacket and gloves. Then she returned to the kitchen. She started to unload the groceries into the fridge and pantry. I noticed she had bought some smoked salmon, bagels and cream cheese.

"Would you like fresh bagels with lox and cream cheese for lunch?" she asked me.

"Would I ever! Thanks mom."

She sliced fresh hot sesame bagels and put cream cheese, lox and a tomato slice on each. Then she brought them to the table for us to enjoy.

As we sat together eating she asked me, "So what happened with Mike? I thought you really liked him."

I wondered if I should tell her.

"He was very sexually aggressive to me. He really scared me," I blurted out before I could censor myself.

She smiled.

After a few minutes, she said, "I think sometimes men get carried away. Did he hurt you?"

"No, but he really scared me."

"Sharon, how does he treat you otherwise?"

"He is wonderful to me."

"I think you should give him another chance. He made a mistake but he really seems to care for you."

I was shocked. My mother was telling me to forgive and forget. Who was this woman?

"Maybe, mom. I haven't decided yet."

"Do you want some coffee?" she asked me.

"Yes, mom."

And just like that, the subject was closed. I was so surprised that my mother had told me this. She held grudges against people for years at a time. Maybe she was mellowing. Maybe I should as well.

CHAPTER 46

This period of having Sharon home and Mimi and Jennie visiting every day was a time of great joy for the Miller family. Although December was cruel and bitter, there was so much joy and love between everyone. Mimi was finally healthy. Jennie was a beautiful happy baby who was fussed over by every member of the household. At four months of age she was thriving. Sharon was thrilled that she was finally going to be starting her studies in Ottawa in January. Sylvia was so happy to have everyone around. She was learning to let go of her past fears and neuroses and finally enjoying her family. Martin was thrilled because his family was happy. This brought him the most satisfaction. His relationship with Sylvia had improved tremendously in the past few years. If it weren't for Sylvia's meddling mother, things could be even better.

He and Sylvia were going for a three-week trip to Florida in January. He loved to do this yearly trip. They would bask in the sun and swim in the warm water. They would have frequent sex in their hotel room. This was his favourite part. Sylvia had a renewed libido as she started to feel better. She was even a little wild sometimes. He loved this side of her. He couldn't wait to see her in her bathing suit walking on the beach. She looked so vital and happy. He loved her now more than he had in the past. Their marriage had been shaky at times but it was finally on solid ground.

During this time period, Sylvia hosted a Chanukah party for the family. They invited Martin's parents and Sharon and Sylvia spent days preparing for it. She fried dozens of latkes and bought gifts for everyone. She set a buffet table in their dining room with smoked turkey, latkes, coleslaw, rugelach and various drinks. Everyone was in a wonderful mood and enjoyed themselves. Sylvia was happy that day. She couldn't get over the beauty and sweetness of her granddaughter Jennie and held her and sang to her. This was a great honour.

The afternoon was almost perfect. Mimi had not yet told her parents that she and David were seeing each other. This was the afternoon that she broke the news to them. Her timing was not always the best.

As she was sitting and chatting with them, in the warm family room with the blazing fireplace, she told them,

"Mom and dad, I have something to tell you."

"What is it Mimi?" Martin asked.

"David and I are seeing each other. We want to give this relationship another chance."

Her parents looked like they had been struck by lightning.

"Aren't you going to say something?" she asked them.

Martin spoke first. He was the more subtle one.

"Why would you do that Mimi? He has done nothing but hurt you time and again."

Sylvia piped in, "He was sleeping with that nurse when you were pregnant."

Sharon added, "He dumped you twice Mimi. What makes you think that he won't do it again?"

"I know Mom. It's just that he is Jennie's father. I don't want her to grow up without a dad."

"I hope you know what you are doing," Martin added.

"Please be careful," Sylvia told her.

"I am going into this with my eyes wide open. David is not going to hurt me again."

Sharon was watching this discussion with interest. She had been sitting on a chair in the dining room eating latkes slathered with applesauce. She heard the conversation and felt proud that Mimi had stood her ground but she shared her parents' concerns. She felt that David was not to be trusted. She wondered what had happened to David's girlfriend. She had seemed to disappear completely. Her father told he that one day Penny was at the hospital working and the next she was gone without a word. That was strange considering that Penny had been so in love with David. Why would she disappear into thin air?

Sharon decided she needed to find out the answer to this question. Could David have done something to Penny? Could he have killed her and buried the body? As a doctor, he must know what to do about bodies. She chided herself for even thinking this. David had been a terrible husband but he was not a killer. However, Penny's whereabouts could be very important. Sharon had to protect Mimi and this information might help her accomplish this.

She would ask around and she knew exactly who to ask. Mary, the head nurse in the emergency ward, knew all the gossip and scuttlebutt. She also knew the entire Miller family. She had been a friend of Martin's for years.

Sharon knew her father was not a gossip but perhaps he could ask Mary. After everyone was gone from the party and Sylvia was cleaning up, Sharon asked her father, "Dad do you know what happened to David's girlfriend?"

"She went back home to where ever she was from, some little town in Nova Scotia I think. Why do you ask?"

"Don't you think it was strange that she just up and left?"

"Not really. People leave all the time. Working in the emergency ward is not for everyone. Some people find it too stressful."

"But she was so in love with David. How could she have just left? Perhaps you could ask Mary about it?"

"I did ask her and that was what she told me."

At this point, Sharon decided that this topic was not worth

pursuing. Her father was probably right. There was no great reason behind Penny leaving the hospital and Montreal.

Sharon should have pursued this matter further. If she had, she would have found out that David had impregnated yet another woman whom he had then deserted.

Sharon sat in her bedroom at her parents house and packed her suitcase. She stared out the window at the huge maple tree that was covered with a silver coating of hoar frost and sighed. It had been a wonderful visit but it was time to go to Ottawa to start school. She smiled at the memory of the New Year's party her parents had made. It seemed like everyone that they had ever known was there. There were friends of Mimi and Sharon and their parents, neighbours, and relatives. It seemed as if there were 100 people crammed into the house. The warmth of the guests and the blazing fire in the hearth were a contrast to the wild snowy night. Sylvia had made platters of finger food including crispy chicken wings, vegetables with dip, and puff pastries filled with all kinds of vegetables. Sharon had sampled everything.

At midnight, Sylvia and Martin had toasted everyone and there were hugs and kisses all around. At this moment, Sharon had felt an acute longing for Mike. She so badly wanted to kiss him and wish him a happy New Year. Instead, she kissed and hugged Mimi and Jennie who could hardly be counted as second best. Jennie and Mimi matched each other in glittery purple shirts that Mimi had made. In that instant, Sharon decided to give Mike another chance.

As she readied herself to leave, she decided to phone him.

He picked up the phone on the first ring.

"Hi Mike, it's Sharon. Happy New Year!"

"Sharon, happy New Year to you. How are you doing?"

"I am fine. I'm coming back to Ottawa this morning."

"Please drive carefully. The roads are very icy."

She felt touched by his concern. She inwardly smiled.

"Sharon, would you like to have dinner with me this evening when you get back?" he asked her.

"Sure, why not?"

"I have really missed you. I will cook for us. I will make us a delicious meal."

"Sounds good Mike."

"Please come to my apartment for 6. We can catch up and have some wine before dinner. I can't wait to see you."

"I will see you at six. Bye Mike."

She was touched by how excited he sounded. She knew that Mike really cared for her and decided that he definitely deserved a second chance.

The drive back was slow and treacherous. The snow was falling heavily and the visibility was poor. It took her almost four hours for the usual two-hour drive.

When she got back to her apartment, there was a vase of beautiful roses on her kitchen table. There was a bag of fresh and aromatic cinnamon buns on the table. When she opened the fridge door, there was a fresh casserole inside. She took it out. It had noodles and cheese and tomato sauce and garlic and smelled like heaven. She warmed some up and ate it for lunch. She wondered how Mike had managed to pull this all together in such a short time and she was grateful that he had.

She filled the bathtub with hot water and lowered herself in. As the steamy heat warmed and relaxed her, she felt so grateful to have Mike in her life. After the bath, she decided to lie down. She snuggled into her bed and fell into a deep slumber. The drive had worn her out. She woke up in the late afternoon. Her room was filled with the shadows of the descending dark. She slowly got out of bed and dressed for her dinner at Mike's apartment. She decided that her black lace bra and matching panties would work well this evening. She could do with some sex on her terms.

She had missed sex with Mike and was hoping to resume it as quickly as possible.

She knocked at his apartment door. He answered right away and drew her into a deep hug as soon as she walked in the door.

"I am so happy to see you!" he told her with the largest smile on his face.

Sharon noticed he had a bit of flour on his nose. His wild curls were all over his forehead. He had a slight sheen of sweat on him. She wanted to take him into the bedroom immediately but restrained herself.

"I am glad to see you too," she said in a more subdued way. "What smells so good?"

"I am making lasagna and Caesar salad. Would you like some wine?"

"Yes."

He poured each one of them a glass of red Italian wine and they sat down on the sofa.

"Dinner will be ready in just a few minutes."

"Did you have a good Christmas Mike?"

"It was not bad. There were a lot of family gatherings and too much food. How about you? How was your Chanukah?"

"A lot like your Christmas. Lots of family and food. My parents made a New Year's party. They invited everyone we ever knew. It was great!"

"How are your parents?"

"They are fine. They are going to Florida for a three-week vacation tomorrow. They are escaping the cold. I am so envious of them."

"How are your sister and your niece?"

"They are both doing well. The only problem is that my sister is seeing her ex-husband again."

“Your parents must be angry.”

“Yes, they are. I am not too happy about it either. David is bad news.”

“No one can tell Mimi what to do. Maybe she wants Jennie to have a father.”

“Maybe.”

Sharon was so touched that Mike cared to ask her about her family.

She heard the timer on his stove ding.

“Dinner is ready,” he said.

They sat down at the table. Mike brought a huge baking dish with lasagna out of the oven, then took a wonderful garlicky Caesar salad out of the fridge and served them both.

“Thank you for the lovely flowers and food you left in my apartment,” she said.

“I thought you might be hungry after your drive. How was the drive?”

“Actually quite dreadful. There were practically whiteout conditions on the highway. It was wonderful to get back to your flowers and food and to my toasty apartment. This lasagna is delicious. Did you make it?”

“No, my mother made it. I did make the salad and the dessert.”

They ate and chatted like nothing had ever happened. Mike had made some chocolate mousse for dessert. He served it with coffee.

“Yummy dessert Mike.”

“I am glad you like it.”

After dessert, Sharon was expecting Mike to get affectionate but he didn’t. He held her hand but made no effort to even kiss her. This would be a waste of her sexy underwear. When she turned toward him, he kissed her on the cheek. She realized he was being careful and it touched her heart.

Mike kissed her gently and chastely on the cheek and she went to her own apartment to sleep. She was both disappointed and touched by his behaviour. She thought of going back to his apartment and seducing him but she was tired so she went to bed instead.

CHAPTER 47. SHARON

Today I am finally living my dream. I started university! I had registered for my courses before and I went to buy books and had my first three classes. Walking across campus was an exhilarating experience. The cold and wind was brutal but I still had fun exploring the campus. I almost slipped a few times on very icy paths. I found a café on campus that serves great strong coffee just the way my mother makes it. I found all my classes without any trouble.

I went to the Foundations of Journalism, Journalism Ethics and Reporting classes. The number of students in each class floored me. I was not used to rooms with hundreds of students. The professors were such a long distance away. So far, I have enjoyed everything. My professors are quite interesting and I am so looking forward to learning more.

I had a long day and was quite tired and a little chilled when I got back to my apartment. I had walked to and from campus. Although it was a short walk, the intense cold got right into my skin and bones. My fingers and toes were numb.

I ran a hot bath and climbed in. After sitting in the tub for a long time, I finally felt warm. Mike had invited me for dinner tonight but I had declined. I knew I would be tired after my first day of classes. I also thought it would be more healthy if we took things a little more slowly this time. I was also afraid that if I saw him I would jump on him.

I put on my warm pink flannel pyjamas with the teddy bear print and took out the casserole that Mike had left me when I first arrived back. I spooned some out for myself and heated it in the microwave. I sat on the sofa and watched my small TV as I ate my dinner. I watched "All in the Family" and I couldn't stop laughing at Archie Bunker and his antics.

After TV and dinner I was ready for bed. I slipped under the covers and brought a good book into bed. I wanted to read for fun. Very soon I would be reading for university and I suspected a mystery novel like this one would have no time in my life. So I read for quite a while. I didn't remember falling asleep but I woke up at 7:40 am the next morning with the lights still on in my bedroom and the book sitting on my chest. I was ready for another day of university and life.

It is taking some time getting used to going back to school. The campus is vast. I keep slipping and sliding everywhere I walk. I already have a pile of homework and readings to do. Still, I am happy that I decided to do this.

Mike has been wonderful. He has been making dinner for us several times a week. We have resumed our sex and it is even better than it was before. We often sit together at my kitchen table or his and study and do our assignments.

Mike even bought me a little portable typewriter. We both take turns typing up our assignments on it. It sits on a shelf beside the kitchen table always ready to be used.

I spoke to Mimi yesterday. I have been keeping in touch with her as often as I can. I am concerned about her budding relationship with David. I had to admit that she sounded so happy when we spoke. She told me,

"David has been coming over often to see Jennie."

"Has he been coming over to see you too?" I asked her.

"Well, we are part and parcel of the same thing."

"Are you taking him back?"

"I am not sure. I think maybe we have been through too much. He wants to come back but I am not ready."

"Take your time. Don't let him pressure you."

"I won't. How is your sexy guy?"

"Just as hot and sexy as ever."

"I am drooling at the pictures you sent. Where were they taken?"

"Couldn't you tell by the photos? We were skating on the Rideau Canal."

"Is he good to you?"

"He is wonderful."

"Don't let him hurt you."

"I was about to say the same thing to you."

"Bye Mimi."

"Bye pipsqueak."

I laughed as I hung up the phone receiver. I went back to my reading for tomorrow's class. The shadowy dusk was settling over the city. The bare trees outside my window were bathed in a silvery glow. Soon, it would be dark and I would be in bed. I had an actual physical longing to have Mike beside me in bed, for his warmth and comfort. With a shock, I realized that I still loved him.

He would be arriving soon with some greasy burgers and fries. We would cuddle on the sofa and read some homework. Then we would go to bed early because it was dark and cold but also so we would have enough time to savour each other's bodies. Ah, life was good!

My daydream was interrupted by a knock on my door. I opened it to my handsome curly haired lover and his bag of delicious smelling food. He looked wonderful in his navy blue ski jacket with his curls escaping the red toque on his head. He was covered with a light dusting of snow and his face was bright red from the cold.

"Hi Sharon, I hope I didn't keep you waiting too long."

"You are right on time," I said and took his jacket and hat and hung them up.

The bag of food was heavy and covered with grease spots.

"Thanks for the food. What are you going to eat?" I told him taking the bag and putting it on the kitchen table.

"Very funny," he said in his husky voice.

He pulled me to him for a long hug and kiss.

"Hey you are freezing cold!" I yelled as he embraced me.

"Let's eat. I am starved," was his answer.

So we took the burgers and fries and salt and ketchup and vinegar out of the bag and started gorging on them immediately.

"Let's get a house with a fireplace," he said as I watched the burger juices drip down his chin.

"Sure. How about a butler too?"

"Why not?"

We made fast work of dinner and settled down together over hot chocolate to do our readings together. We went to bed early and had a wonderful time engaged in mind-blowing sex. I swear that the sex with this man was getting better every time. I had an insatiable lust for him that he was happy to reciprocate.

Afterwards, I put on my pink flannel pyjamas with the teddy bears and we fell asleep with Mike's arm around my shoulder.

CHAPTER 48

As well as everything was going for Sharon in Ottawa, things were not quite as happy for Mimi in Montreal. Mimi was struggling. She had returned to work full time. She really had no choice. There were two to support now. She was finding it difficult to work all day and look after Jennie when she came home. Jennie was at day care all day and when Mimi picked her up, she seemed to need so much attention. She acted as if she had not seen her mom in a year. She was whiny and Mimi still had an evening's work ahead of her. She had to make dinner for herself and feed the baby and there was always something to do with teaching that she brought home. By the time Mimi went to bed at 11:00, she was so exhausted that she couldn't see straight. The next day was much the same.

The only break she had was on weekends. David would come over on Saturdays and take Jennie for the day. As soon as he left, Mimi would go back to bed and sleep for several hours. When he returned with Jennie, he would bring something for dinner for the three of them. It was usually some Chinese takeout but Mimi was grateful for anything.

David would often broach the subject of the two of them getting back together. He would always start the same way.

"What do you think of the idea of having me here all the time?"

She would answer, "I am not ready."

He would reply, "If I lived here, I could help you with Jennie and with the cooking and household chores."

"Don't be so romantic," she would joke.

"You know I love you. I always have," he would answer.

"You have a strange way of showing it, David."

At that point, Mimi would change the subject. She would be tempted to ask him why he broke up with her twice but decided this was a subject best left alone.

She was grateful for the Saturday help. Sometimes she wondered if she could even manage without it. This was the one day that she had a break from everything she had to do.

That cold brutal winter meant so many different things to the members of the Miller family. Sylvia and Martin went away for a trip to Florida to temporarily escape the vicious cold. They basked in their tropical paradise, walked together, played tennis and ate wonderful food. Their relationship was better than it had ever been. Sylvia's therapy had managed to help her calm down and see things in perspective. She had a renewed love and respect for Martin. She could not believe that she had thought she married the wrong man. He was kind, loving and strong. Somehow she had mistaken his kindness for weakness. She knew that her mother was responsible for putting strange ideas in her head and she was learning to tune out Fredelle's crazy ranting.

Sylvia was unhappy about the fact that Mimi was giving David a second chance but she decided to leave it alone. On their first week in Florida, she noticed that Martin was overly tired. He slept well and stayed active but he had trouble getting out of bed in the morning and had to have an afternoon nap. When she asked him about it, he smiled and said,

"Don't worry sweetheart. I am just getting old."

"When is the last time you had a checkup?"

"Maybe last year."

"I think it was two years ago. Promise me you will make an appointment when we get back to Montreal."

They were in bed at the time of this conversation. Martin looked at his wife's slim, fit, naked body and knew that there was one good way to temporarily silence her. He put his arm around her and kissed her passionately. He began kissing her neck and breasts and the conversation ended for the moment.

Martin was also feeling quite positive. He was concerned about Mimi reconciling with David but he resigned himself to the fact that there was nothing he could do about it. He was thrilled that Sharon had finally started university in Ottawa. She was smart. She would do well now that she was focused on what she really wanted. He adored Sylvia. He felt that he was finally getting to know her. She had kept so much of herself hidden for so long. Now she confided in him about everything and he was so happy that this was happening. He was more attracted to her than he had ever been. He loved looking at her taut lean body and even the little lines that were forming around her eyes and the grey streaks in her hair did nothing to diminish this.

He had noticed that his energy level was not what it should be. He had had to decline some tennis games with Sylvia because he was tired and needed a rest. Even though he slept soundly, he sometimes woke up tired. He decided that he was getting old but promised Sylvia that he would have a check-up when they returned to Montreal.

Sharon was feeling better than she had in years. Every day was a delight. She enjoyed every one of her courses, even the boring ones. She was picking up little trinkets and furniture that were making the apartment feel more and more like home. Just the week before, she had been in a thrift store and found a lovely blond teak dining room table and four chairs. Mike had bought her four woven purple place mats to go with the table. She thought that the combination was quite outlandish and beautiful at the same time. She called it "thrift store chic."

The best part of her life by far was her relationship with Mike. He was a kind giving boyfriend and a passionate lover. Every day brought them slightly closer. She loved and liked Mike. Their relationship was just what she wanted and needed. She could see them being together for a long time. However, Mike was getting too serious. He spoke of moving in together and getting engaged. Sharon felt that she was way too young to even consider marriage but she understood how Mike felt. He was older and looking to put down roots. He was almost finished his law degree and he wanted to find a job, buy a house and start a family. Sharon knew she was not ready for this but she did not want to lose Mike. So when he brought up the subject she told him she was just not ready yet. She wondered how long he would wait for her to be ready.

Mimi phoned Sharon one Wednesday evening.

Sharon was alarmed. She knew that Mimi was exhausted in the evening.

"Is everything alright Mimi?" she asked.

"Yes, I am so tired but fine. I want to talk to you about David."

"Did he do something awful again?"

"No, he has been wonderful. He comes over on weekends and helps me with Jennie. He has been so sweet and wonderful. I think I should give him another chance."

She heard Sharon gasp.

"Are you sure that this is a good idea?"

"No I am not sure of anything but I still love him."

Sharon fought the urge to tell Mimi that David was a creep. She fought the urge to tell her that she had heard from their father that David was dating some of the nurses and having rough sex with them. She fought the urge to tell Mimi that she could do so much better. She realized that her sister was in a difficult position as a single parent and needed help.

"I love you and I know you will make the right decision," was all she said. Later she wondered if she should have said more.

That very Saturday, David came over with red roses and dinner for them to share. He had brought rotisserie chicken, potato salad, coleslaw, and a lemon meringue pie. Mimi was overjoyed by the fact that he had remembered to bring food she really liked. She cautioned herself to be careful. Soon they were eating and laughing and talking as thought they had never been apart. Mimi almost forgot what he had done to her.

That evening after they had gotten Jennie to sleep, David asked Mimi,

“Would you like a back massage?”

“Oh yes,” she told him without thinking about it.

He rubbed her back through the warm red cotton sweater she was wearing. She sighed with pleasure as his hands loosened all her muscles and bones stressed from the week before. His hands had always been quite magical.

Before she realized what was happening, his warm healing hands had found their way under the sweater. He started rubbing her bare back and in the process he undid her bra. He was soon massaging her breasts and she was trembling with desire.

A moment later, he gently removed her sweater and started kissing her face and shoulders and breasts. She was overcome with desire but suddenly her common sense snapped back.

“David, I am really enjoying this but I am not ready. We are just starting to become close. I don’t want to be intimate yet.”

He looked like a disappointed little boy.

“I understand,” he said. “I will wait for as long as it takes.”

He pulled her sweater over her head again and kissed her forehead. Before they could discuss this further, there was a cry from the bedroom. Jennie had woken up.

“I will go see what she needs,” David said.

She was relieved. She needed to cool off. She hadn’t had sex in a very long time and her hormones were in overdrive. It would have been so easy to have sex with David but she was glad she hadn’t done it. She put on the kettle and made two cups of tea. David was back quickly.

"She needed changing and then she went right back to sleep," he said.

"Would you like a cup of tea?" she asked.

"Yes, please."

So they sat and sipped their tea. Afterwards, she told him she was sleepy and David left to go home. She had enjoyed their evening together but she decided that she had to be on better guard than she had been that evening. She still did not trust him and she would be damned if she was going to let him hurt her again.

She had the desire to phone Sharon in Ottawa again but it was late and Sharon was probably sleeping or having sex with her own honey. She decided to go to sleep instead because she needed all she could get and Jennie would be up soon. She usually fell asleep in seconds but had trouble dozing off. The attempted sex had aroused her and she was wide awake and ready for more. Still, she was not yet ready to re-consummate their relationship. Eventually, she did fall asleep but was up again to Jennie's crying at 3:00 am.

She took Jennie to her bed and nursed her. She smelled the soft delicious blonde tufts on Jennie's head and watched as she nursed eagerly. The past few months had been difficult but Mimi was grateful every day for this beautiful miracle. She looked at Jennie and felt the deepest love she could imagine. She knew that she would fling herself in front of a car if Jennie was in danger. She would do anything to keep her child safe.

Suddenly the tears started falling from her eyes. She felt so blessed that she was overcome with emotion. Jennie didn't even notice the salty teardrops that were falling on her head. As she continued to nurse, Mimi wondered if David loved Jennie. She was his daughter and he seemed to have genuine affection for her but was this a ploy to get back with her? She laughed at herself for her own vanity. David was a handsome successful doctor. He could have his pick of women. She wondered again what had happened to Penny. Somehow, she felt that knowing this information would help her.

She was still so attracted to David. He had mellowed and become even more handsome. He claimed that he had always loved her and he had temporarily been a fool. Now he wanted them to be a family and to have more children. She just didn't feel very sure about his intentions. She knew that David could charm almost anyone but was he sincere? Even if he was sincere, would be still feel that way in a few years or would it just take another sexy woman to lure him away? She remembered well how lonely she had been during her pregnancy and her subsequent illness. If it wasn't for Sharon, she felt she would not have survived.

She was happy that Sharon had gone away to school but she missed her so much. Everyone had always believed that Mimi was the tough and bright one but she knew that this was a myth. Sharon had been the glue that had held her together so many times in her life. Sharon was always making sacrifices so that Mimi could be happy and well. She had the capacity for so much caring that Mimi was sometimes worried that Sharon would give too much.

Sharon had dated a succession of losers that Mimi felt did not even deserve to be in her presence. Now this Mike in Ottawa was her newest man. Mimi and the family had never met him but she could tell Sharon really cared about him. She hoped that Sharon was being treated well. Sharon, like Mimi, could be very naive in a relationship. Someone with a charming manner and no substance could hurt them both easily.

She changed Jennie and put her back in the crib. As she was returning to bed, the phone rang. She knew it couldn't be good. It was 3:30 am.

Panic was rising in her throat. She picked up the phone.

"Hello?"

"Hi Mimi, this is mom. Your father had a heart attack. We are at the Royal Victoria Hospital. He seems stable now but I just wanted to let you know."

"Jennie and I will be right there." She hung up the phone.

She got dressed and threw on her warm winter jacket. She bundled Jennie into her pink snowsuit and they were out the door in minutes.

Sharon was sleeping soundly with Mike's body entwined with hers when the phone rang. She reached out to her bedside table and picked it up.

"Hello," she said in a voice heavy with sleep.

"Hi Sharon. It's mom. Your father had a heart attack. The doctors seem to think he will be just fine. You don't need to come. I just thought you should know."

"Of course I will come. I will leave right away. Bye mom."

Sharon sat up in bed. She was now fully awake.

"What is it?" Mike asked her.

"My dad had a heart attack. I have to go to Montreal."

"I'll drive you," he said.

"You don't have to," she replied half-heartedly.

"Yes, I do. You are upset. You are in no condition to drive."

"Thank you, Mike," she said with tears in her eyes.

He kissed her forehead and hugged her. Then he brewed strong coffee for them as they got dressed. He poured it into a thermos for the road. Shortly they were out the door driving the two hours to Montreal to the hospital on the pitch dark scary highway. Sharon felt chilled the whole way there. She babbled incessantly to Mike and shivered even though she was drinking hot coffee and the car heater was blowing very hot air at her. She shivered and perspired at the same time.

"I can't believe my father had a heart attack. He took such good care of himself. How could this have happened? What if he dies?"

"Everything is going to be fine," Mike told her even though he didn't have a clue.

He was struggling to drive safely during yet another heavy snowfall. The windshield wipers could hardly keep up with the thick dense snow. The highway was nothing but a black band of snow and ice. He hoped that they would not wind up in a ditch somewhere.

When they finally arrived at the hospital three hours later, they walked down the hall to see Sylvia, Mimi, and Jennie. Sylvia looked pale and drawn. Her face was grey and her eyes were swollen and red rimmed. She had aged years that night. Mimi lay sleeping on the sofa with Jennie lying on her chest, both in heavy jackets. They looked almost comical.

"Hi Mom, how is dad?"

"We still don't know. They haven't told us anything.,"

The frantic tone of her voice woke up Jennie who started to howl. Mimi woke up confused and started looking around as if she didn't know where she was.

"Mom and Mimi, this is Mike," Sharon told them.

"Hello," Mike said.

He couldn't think of anything else to say. Sharon took Jennie and cuddled her and the baby immediately stopped crying. Mike thought about what a wonderful mother she would make.

"Can I get you anything?" Mike asked them.

"No, thanks," Sylvia and Mimi said in unison.

Just then a doctor came walking down the hall towards them. Sharon wished she could read his expression.

"I have good news," he said. "It was a mild heart attack. He will be fine."

Sylvia started to cry, to the amazement of Mimi and Sharon.

"When can we see him?" she asked the doctor.

"You alone can say a quick hello but that is all. He is sedated and very tired. The rest of you can come back tomorrow."

Mike and Sharon looked at each other. They couldn't rush back to Ottawa but where would they stay?

It was as if Sylvia had read their minds.

"You two, come back to the house. You can both stay in Sharon's room. Sharon, you have the key. Why don't you both go back there and I will meet you there after I see dad? Mimi, you and Jennie should go home. You are all looking tired."

Sharon was relieved and exhausted. She gave Mimi and Jennie a hug and said, "See you later."

Mimi took Jennie home and Sharon took Mike back to her childhood home. He was struck by the size and opulence. This was a mansion.

"I can't believe that mom said we should stay in my room. She really has changed. I am so glad my father is going to be okay."

She started babbling constantly. When they got to her room, Mike slowly and gently undressed her and tucked her into her bed. She was asleep in a minute. He undressed and crawled in beside her and they both slept like this for several hours on Sharon's single bed in her childhood room, close in space and time as two people could be.

Mike woke up confused the next morning. Where was he? What were these movie posters and chenille spreads doing there? Then he remembered. Sharon was still fast asleep lying on her side and snoring lightly. He realized that they had forgotten a change of clothes. So he quietly put on last night's clothes and left the bedroom. He went down a long hallway towards the smell of fresh coffee. Sylvia was there at the stove scrambling some eggs in a pan. She was wearing a bathrobe that was so loose on her. She looked almost ghostly to him but she was smiling as she worked in the kitchen.

"Hello," he said so he wouldn't startle her.

"Hello Mike. Please help yourself to some coffee."

Mike poured a cup of coffee and added some cream and sugar.

"Would you like some coffee Mrs Miller?" he asked her.

"No, thank you. Please call me Sylvia."

"Are you an early riser Mike?" she asked him. "It's just 8:05."

"Yes. I have always been."

"Sharon likes to sleep in but I suppose you must know that. Would you like scrambled eggs and toast?"

"Sure. How about if I make them for you?" Sylvia looked like she was going to collapse any second.

"Yes please," she said and sat down heavily in a chair.

"How is Dr Miller?"

"He seemed fine last night. He said he was feeling good but he never tells me the truth. The doctors say he can come home in a few days. He has been so tired. I should have known."

"Nobody could have known, Sylvia."

She started to notice why Sharon would like this young man. He was so calm and reassuring that she was starting to like him already. His dimples were also quite adorable, she decided.

So Mike scrambled some eggs and made some toast and he and Sylvia sat having breakfast and chatting like two old friends.

When Sharon made her way to the kitchen an hour later, Sylvia had gone to the hospital and Mike was in the kitchen on the phone.

It was Sunday and they were due at his mom's house for dinner.

"No, her father is okay. He is going to be fine." she heard him tell his mother.

"We may or may not be back today. Don't expect us at dinner tonight. I will see you next week. I love you ma."

Sharon poured herself a cup of coffee.

"This tastes horrible."

"It's been standing too long. I will make a fresh pot."

"How's my dad?"

"He is doing great. We are going to see him later this morning. Would you like some scrambled eggs?"

"Yes."

So Mike made a second breakfast that they ate together and Sharon put their clothes from yesterday in the washing machine after finding a bathrobe for each of them.

"Have you ever had sex in a single bed in a girly room filled with posters?" she asked him.

"No I don't think so." He was surprised that she wanted sex. He supposed it was the tension in her seeking release.

She grabbed his hand and pulled him into the bedroom and slammed the door shut.

"We have 45 minutes until the wash is done. Let me help you with your bathrobe."

She untied his bathrobe and hers. She pushed him on the bed. Before he knew what was happening, she had her mouth on his penis and was licking and sucking and caressing his testicles. He felt like he would explode. He was kissing her stomach and breasts and everywhere and in minutes he was inside her pushing hard and having the wildest sex they had had up until now.

Later they lay holding each other and Sharon heard the bell signalling the laundry was finished. She went to put it into the dryer and they took a shower together and washed each other's backs. By then the clothes in the dryer were ready and they dressed and went to see her father in the hospital.

When they arrived in his room, it was filled with flowers. Sharon had never seen so many colourful arrangements of roses, daisies, carnations, baby's breath and so many more. Martin was sitting up in bed joking with Sylvia. He looked like the healthy one with his ruddy cheeks and the glint in his eyes. It was Sylvia who looked ill. She was pale and drawn and looked like a ghost.

"Hi dad, this is Mike," Sharon said.

The two men shook hands and Mike said, "It's good to meet you Dr Miller."

"It's good to meet you too, Mike. Call me Martin."

"How are you feeling Martin?"

"Actually quite fine. Last night I thought I was having indigestion but it wouldn't go away. Sylvia insisted we go to the hospital."

Sharon reached out and hugged him. "I'm glad you did."

"This is not the best way to meet, Mike, but I am still happy to meet you."

"I am too."

"What's with all the flowers, dad?"

"Well, as you know, I work in this hospital. Everyone knows me so they all sent flowers."

"What did the doctor say about your heart attack?"

"It was very mild. He thinks it will never happen again if I take care of myself."

"I am so relieved dad. I can't bear to lose you."

"That won't happen. I will walk you and your daughter down the aisle when you both get married."

Sharon noticed how quiet Sylvia was. It was as if she was in a trance.

"Are you alright mom?"

"Yes, I am fine. It was your father that had the heart attack. There is nothing wrong with me."

Sharon thought this was a strange answer but then her mom was strange.

Mike stood and watched Sharon interact with her father. She was so loving and solicitous to him. He wondered what his life would have been like if he hadn't lost his own father such a long time ago.

"How long will you be in the hospital, dad?" Sharon asked.

"They are sending me home tomorrow. I am supposed to take it easy for a week. You two don't need to be here. You should go back to Ottawa. Your mom will take great care of me."

"Are you sure dad?"

"Yes I am. It is wonderful that you came but I am feeling fine and you have to get back to your studies."

Just then a sleepy looking Mimi trudged into the room. She looked exhausted. Her face was pale and her eyes were red rimmed and half closed.

"Where is Jennie?" Sharon asked.

"She is with David for the day. How are you feeling dad?"

"Just fine. Everyone is fussing too much."

"You had a heart attack Martin," Sylvia piped in. "We are all concerned about you."

Sharon decided that this was their cue to leave.

"We are heading back to Ottawa. I love you dad."

"I love you too baby," he told her.

They hugged and everyone said their goodbyes. Then Sharon and Mike were on the road again. Today's mood was so much lighter.

The snow had stopped and much of the highway was ploughed. They had an easy drive back and were still in time for Mike's mother's weekly Sunday dinner with the family.

Sharon was a little wound up from the stressful weekend. She was atypically quiet during dinner and did not eat very much. Most of the guests were too busy to notice but Mike and his mother did notice. Both decided not to say anything to her because she looked very fragile and vulnerable.

Mike's mother kissed them goodbye and they drove home. On the drive, Mike was really starting to feel concerned. Sharon was in her own little world and he couldn't seem to reach her.

When they arrived back at her apartment, Mike asked her,

"Would you like a cup of tea?"

She burst out in huge, heavy sobs and she looked like she was going to explode.

She was unable to speak. He sat with his arms around her while she cried and cried. He realized at this moment that she had been holding in all her tension and now it was finally coming out like a bursting pipe.

After she stopped crying, Mike took her hand and led her to the bedroom. He undressed her and tucked her into bed. Then he crawled in beside her and held her again until she was asleep. After he was sure she was sleeping, he got out of bed and went to the kitchen. He put some leftovers into the fridge and did some homework. He was behind in school and he needed to catch up. He hated the feeling of falling behind. His schedule was already too packed. With the building maintenance, university and Sharon, he had to keep on top of things or hell would break loose.

Sharon had a wonderful sleep that night. She did not even remember going to bed. She woke to an empty bed. She went to the living room and saw Mike still fast asleep on the sofa with a law book in his lap.

He had been so wonderful to her on the weekend. It was now his turn. She brewed some coffee and started making French toast.

He woke up sleepy and confused but soon they were sitting together at the kitchen table having their first of many coffees of the day.

Shortly after, the phone rang. Sharon looked at it afraid to answer it but she did.

"Hello?" she said tentatively.

"Hi, it's Mimi."

"Is everything okay with dad?"

"He is doing great. He wants to go home. He says the food at the hospital is lousy."

"He's right."

"Don't you need to get to work Mimi?"

"It's a professional day so I don't have to go in. Jennie is sleeping so I thought I'd give you a call."

"What is it that you want to talk about?"

"Your boyfriend."

"What about him?"

"I want him."

"Well you can't have him."

Mike was looking at her in a puzzled way while he drank his coffee.

"He is so adorable. Those dimples. That curly hair. The way he dotes on you. How did you get so lucky?"

"I don't have a clue."

"Keep him pipsqueak."

"I plan to."

"Gotta go. Jennie is crying. Bye."

Sharon went to the table and hugged Mike and poured him another cup of coffee.

"Is everything okay with your dad?"

"Yes it is. That was Mimi saying a quick hello."

So they drank their coffee and ate their French toast and prepared for their busy days ahead with the comfort that they would have each other at the end of the day. Sharon smiled to herself as she realized that she already felt married to Mike. She wondered if she should marry him. She was just 22 years old and felt a little young to make such a commitment. She was sure she would never find another person that she loved as much or who treated her as well.

Right now she was still in a state of shock about the weekend. She decided it was not a good idea to think about this until she calmed down and returned to normal. Her father had told her never to make a major decision when she was very emotional. This advice had served her well on numerous occasions. She thought that she should heed it now.

CHAPTER 49. SHARON

I am worried about my father. When I was growing up, he was always my hero. As much as mom was crazy, he was always the sane and loving parent. This was especially true when Mom went to see her own mother. After mom went to see grandma, she would always be in a foul mood for days.

Her mother always drove her crazy. She would criticize everything she did and make her feel unworthy. It is horrible to say but I felt relieved when Grandma Fredelle died. It still took years for mom to get better but she eventually did.

Sometimes, when mom came home from seeing her mother, Dad and Mimi and I would escape from the house for a while.

In the summer, he would ask, "Who is up for ice cream?"

"I am!" I would yell.

"Me too, me too," Mimi would echo.

"You don't need any ice cream. I am making dinner," would be my mother's response.

We would ignore her and pile into the car and off we would go.

We would stop at a little ice cream parlour that had the best and most creamy ice cream in Montreal or so I believed. Mimi and I would order banana splits. Dad would order a hot fudge sundae. We would sit there talking and laughing as if we didn't have a care in the world.

Afterwards we would drive to the local park and dad would push us on the swings as we yelled for more.

Eventually we had to go home to mom's miserable mood. It was never fun leaving the warm sunshine for the icy chill that greeted us when we came inside.

Now my father has had a heart attack and I am terrified. He looks great and the doctors claim he is fine but what if they are wrong? What if he has another heart attack and dies? My world would be broken without him.

Mom would go truly crazy and wind up in a hospital. Even though she is much better than she used to be, there is always some craziness lurking behind her eyes.

Every time the phone rings, I am convinced that my father has died. Mike says I am driving myself crazy and he is right. I need to stop making a catastrophe out of everything. There are enough real problems to worry about.

One of my real problems is that Mike keeps talking about marriage. The other night when we were in bed dozing off to sleep, he said,

"Wouldn't it be great if we could do this every night?"

"We do sleep together every night," I told him.

"You know I don't mean that. I mean that we should be together all the time, get married, start a family, plan our lives."

"I have enough trouble planning my day."

"Let's go to sleep Mike. It is late and we have busy days tomorrow."

He sighed and went to sleep but I knew it was just a matter of time before he brought the topic up again. I wondered how I would handle it when he did.

CHAPTER 50

Sharon and her family were finally in a better rhythm. Each one was finding a way to live well. Sharon was finally at school, her parents were thriving and Mimi was enjoying Jennie. David was still pressuring her to get back together but she wasn't about to give in so easily.

Sharon still wondered about Penny. Why had she disappeared and what had happened to her? Would she resurface in their lives?

Sharon had suspicions that there was more to the story of Penny leaving than met the eye. She was positive that Penny's disappearance had something to do with something David had done and that this information would prove important. She had asked her father to ask the nurses. No one really seemed to know what had happened to Penny.

She decided to investigate on her own. She went to the hospital to visit her father and take him out for lunch. While she was waiting for him, she said hello to many of the nurses. She was thrilled to see them. She had known many of them since childhood. They hugged her when they saw her. Each one remarked about what a beautiful young woman she had become.

In each conversation with a nurse, Sharon managed to slip in a question about Penny. In each case, she was met with a shrug or "I really don't know."

She gave up when she saw her father walking towards her with a big grin on his face.

"Where to dad?"

"How about a burger?"

"I have orders from mom that you are not allowed to have a burger."

"Okay, let's go to Lester's and I will have a salad."

"Much better dad. I love you."

"I love you too Sharon."

And off they went with Sharon none the wiser about what had happened to Penny.

CHAPTER 51

David whistled as he walked down the hallway in the hospital. He had been feeling angry and frustrated for a long time. He was angry with himself for the way he had treated Mimi and their daughter. He should have stood by her and never cheated on her. When he thought about it, he realized that he had gotten married too young. He and Mimi had been together since high school and she had been the only woman he had slept with.

Somehow this had woken an urge in him to cheat. Truth be told, he felt it was Penny's fault. She had flirted with him shamelessly and he had given in to her. He was well rid of that little slut, he thought. Since his breakup with Penny, he had had quite a number of flings. None of them had meant anything to him. Now he knew that he should have stayed with Mimi.

The first time that he saw his infant daughter, he fell in love in a new and special way. He felt such a burst of love for her that it threatened to swallow him whole. He wanted to spend every moment with Jennie. He also loved Mimi. She was every bit as beautiful and vibrant as she had been in high school. Her beauty had deepened from a sweet childish glow to the full brightness of a beautiful young woman.

He had spent several months trying to convince Mimi to give him another chance. He didn't blame her for not trusting him. He had spent as much time as possible with Jennie and tried to see if he could combine the visits to be with both of them. Mimi was taking her time trusting him but he felt he had finally made some headway the night before.

When he was over to visit them both, Mimi invited him to stay for dinner. They had a great time laughing and chatting. Later he was tired and Mimi said he could stay over. She made him a bed on the sofa and he stayed there for the night. In the morning, he made French toast for Mimi and Jennie and himself. They laughed as they watched Jennie getting more food on herself than in her mouth. The conversation was easy and friendly. After they ate, he went home.

Mimi had made no move to take him back but she was slowly coming around. She was very hostile to him at first. She didn't even want him to see Jennie. Now she was slowly getting more and more friendly. This time he slept on the sofa but he was sure that next time he would sleep in Mimi's bed with her and he would knock her out with his lovemaking. He had learned a thing or two and he was quite sure she hadn't been with anyone else since their divorce. Yes, Mimi was in for a big treat. He hoped this would cement their relationship.

He whistled as he walked in the door of the emergency department. He went to get a cup of coffee in the staff dining room and then to his locker to put on his scrubs. As he was walking to the ward, he saw Mary McPherson. Her broad and stocky body was hard to miss as was her limping gait. He had never liked her. He felt that there was something sneaky about her close-set black eyes and constant smirk. She had always been cool to him but she had turned downright hostile since Penny had left. She never even said hello to him. Today, she seemed positively elated to see him.

"Hello, Doctor," she said to him with a broad smile on her face. She stepped in front of him blocking his way.

"Hello Mary." He wondered what she could possibly want from him.

"I got some exciting news. Penny and her daughter, I should say your daughter, are moving back to Montreal. They will be staying with me. I can't wait to see them."

"That's nice Mary," he said but his face fell. She noticed his expression change from elated to scared and it made her happy.

"I imagine they will be wanting to see you" she said and continued her stroll down the hall whistling as she walked. David was angry. What the hell was Penny doing coming back to Montreal? Well, she had a daughter but was it his child? For all he knew, she might just pretend it was his so she could ensnare him.

David knew that Penny's return would mean trouble. He knew it would affect his life. He decided right then and there that this did not need to be his problem. Each could live their own lives without interference from the other. He would just ignore her and go on with his plans. This couldn't be that difficult. He had done it once and could do it again. He had no idea of the wrath of a woman scorned and what it could do to his life.

Mimi was breathing a sigh of relief. Her school term was almost finished for the year. It was already May and June would be her last month of teaching until September. She would have two whole months of leisure and spending time with her lovely cherubic daughter. The spring weather was beautiful. The trees and flowers were already blooming. The bitter chill had been replaced by warmth and calm.

She was feeling better than she had in a long time. Winter had been a struggle but spring and summer were definitely turning out better. She had to admit that David was part of the change for the better. He visited every week and often took Jennie over to his own apartment. Jennie adored him. She would coo in his arms and smile up at him with her big blue eyes sparkling.

David was very persistent in asking Mimi to reconcile. She had been adamantly set against it at first but she knew she was weakening. She needed someone to help her out and Jennie needed a father. She still did not trust David but wondered if she should give things another chance.

Mimi's real sadness was that Sharon was not coming back to Montreal for the summer. She was doing so well in Ottawa. She had finished the year with straight A's and was thriving. Her relationship with Mike was getting serious. Mimi missed her younger sister painfully and still felt the hole Sharon had left. They spoke often but it wasn't the same. Sharon was coming for the Canada Day long weekend in June. Maybe they could talk. She needed Sharon to tell her not to get back with David. She felt the void left by Sharon was just large enough for David to slip into.

The phone rang just then.

"Hi big sis. How's it going?"

"You must be psychic. I was just thinking about you. I need you to persuade me."

"Sure, I can persuade you of whatever you want."

"I need you to tell me not to take David back."

"And here I thought it would be challenging. The guy is a creep. He dumped you twice. He dumped you when you were pregnant. He was cheating on you. He will cheat again. You have even more to lose this time. You have so much going for you. So many men would adore you and Jennie. You are young, smart and beautiful. Find a man who deserves you."

"Thanks Sharon."

"No problem. How is my favourite niece?"

"Growing more every day. She misses you. So do I."

"Come visit me this weekend!" Sharon blurted out.

"Where would we stay?"

"With me of course. You can have my apartment. I will stay at Mike's but this invitation comes with a warning. He and his family will feed you until you can't move."

"That is the best idea you have had but Jennie and I have plans with David."

"Dump him. Come to see me instead. The food and company will be better."

"Where will Jennie sleep?"

"Leave that to me. I will figure something out."

"Yes, we would love to come."

Both sisters were excited when they got off the phone. Sharon would get to see Mimi and Jennie. Mimi would get to see Sharon and her apartment. It was a perfect arrangement for everyone except David.

When Mimi phoned him to cancel, he was upset.

"What do you mean that you are going to Ottawa? We had plans."

"Sharon needs my help. We will just have to reschedule. Bye David." She hung up before he could respond.

So, Mimi and Jennie were going on an adventure. Mimi was so excited. It would be easy for her to get her own things ready. All she had to do was throw some clothes and toiletries into a bag. Jennie was an entirely different matter. There were clothes and blankets and diapers and formula to pack. By the time she was finished packing Jennie's stuff, changing her and feeding her, she was starting to change her mind. She was tired. All she wanted to do was to take a nap.

Instead, she bundled up her smiling baby and put her in her car seat. She packed two suitcases in the trunk – one for her and one for Jennie – and she was off.

It was a magnificent spring day. The sun was shining brightly casting a magical glow on the new leaves and grass. The snow was finally gone and everything was in bloom. It was Mimi's favourite time of year. Spring always seemed to hold the promise of new beginnings.

Jennie snoozed in her car seat while Mimi drove. Mimi listened to the news on the car radio. She was surprised that Canada had a new Prime Minister. Joe Clark had beaten Pierre Trudeau. She was shocked. She had thought that Trudeau was doing well.

Mimi had missed Sharon so much in the past several months and she was elated by the idea of spending the weekend with her. She had not been so delighted at David's reaction. He had acted like a petulant child. She wondered if she should end her personal relationship with him. He could still see Jennie but maybe not her. She was of two minds about this. He was so helpful to her when he was trying to win her back. She knew this would end if she told him she would not take him back.

She decided not to think of him this weekend. This would be an easy task. She changed the channel on her car radio and the song "Imagine" by John Lennon was on. She had always loved that song. She started to sing along and focused on the music and the road. That was enough for her at this moment.

When she arrived in Ottawa, she carried Jennie up the stairs to Sharon's walk-up apartment. Before she could knock on the door, Sharon opened it up with a huge grin on her face.

"Hi Mimi," Sharon said and took the sleeping baby from Mimi's arms. She had a white crib all set up in her living room and she placed the baby in it without a pause. Jennie just continued to sleep and Sharon ran to Mimi and gave her a long hug.

"Welcome to my humble abode," she told her sister.

"It's beautiful," Mimi told her and she meant every word. Sharon had always had a flair for making any space look like home. She had plants all over the room. There was a comfy large beige couch with a bright pink blanket draped over the top. The small round pine kitchen table from their mother was adorned with bright purple place mats and a pink blooming African violet. The wall was full of pictures of her, Jennie, their parents, Mike and Sharon. This place really looked like home.

"Where did you get the crib?" Mimi asked.

"Are you kidding? Mike has a large family and extended family and they have millions of children. I could get you anything with the snap of a finger. Mike assembled it for you last night."

"You thought of everything. Thank you."

"You're welcome sis. Are you hungry?"

"Yes I am."

"This is compliments of Mike's mom." She took out a huge pot of lasagna. The smell of garlic and tomato started to permeate the air making Mimi's mouth water.

She stuck it into the oven to heat up.

"What is this nonsense I hear about you thinking of getting back with David?"

"Well, I have been so lonely and he takes good care of Jennie."

"Those aren't good enough reasons to take him back. There is no reason good enough to take him back."

"You're right, pipsqueak, but I miss you so much and he steps in and helps fill the void."

"I miss you too but David is not your answer."

"You are right as usual. Let's not talk about him. Let's enjoy our time together instead."

"It's a deal."

Mimi noticed that Sharon looked wonderful. She was wrapped in a glow that seemed to exude happiness. Sharon noticed that Mimi looked a bit pale and had lost a few pounds. Well, she would take care of that.

"Where's Mike?"

"He is doing some repair work for a tenant. He will join us later."

She took the lasagna out of the oven and spooned a huge helping onto Mimi's plate.

Mimi tasted it. The blend of noodles and cheese and sauce was so delicious that it melted in her mouth.

"Oh my god, this is amazing. How do you keep from gaining weight?"

"I think the sex helps," Sharon told her and they both burst out laughing.

Just then, Mike walked in and joined them. He kissed Sharon tenderly on the forehead and helped himself to lasagna.

Mimi thought they looked like a married couple. They seemed so comfortable with each other as if their relationship was effortless. Mimi sighed at the beauty of it.

"How are you Mimi?" he asked her.

"I am just fine. This lasagna is delicious and I am thrilled to be here."

"That's great. I'm sorry but I can't stay long. I have some work to do."

He finished eating, excused himself and left.

"I think he is giving us some alone time," Sharon said.

Jennie woke up a few minutes later. She smiled broadly when Sharon picked her up and started cooing happily. Sharon changed Jennie's diaper and Mimi fed her. Afterwards they put her back in the crib and she fell asleep.

Sharon showed Mimi to the bedroom.

"This is your space."

The bed was made up for her and it looked so comfortable. Mimi realized that she was exhausted.

"Do you mind if I have a nap, Pipsqueak?" she asked.

"Sure. I will look after Jennie when she wakes up."

"What a great offer."

Sharon tucked Mimi into bed as if she was a child and went to the living room. She was in the middle of a novel and she couldn't wait to get to it again so she started reading. She dozed off on the sofa.

Mike hurried through his chores so he could go back to Sharon and her guests. When he arrived back at the apartment, he noticed that every one of them was sound asleep. He smiled at the scene and went to the building's workroom where he was busy with his own project. He was building a cradle out of oak. He had decided that this would be a good project. It would be a work of art and impress Sharon. Then he would tell her that the cradle was for their children and propose. He hoped it would work. He really wanted to marry her and he was dying to have a family. He knew that he would never find anyone else that he loved as much. She was everything to him. She was smart, funny and beautiful. His family adored her too. He felt as if they were already married.

He hoped this would help her decide to marry him. He knew she was only 22 and had not had much experience with men. He was 28 and ready for a commitment. He hoped that she was as well. So he started carving the design on the handles and whistled a tune to himself while he worked.

When he returned to Sharon's apartment, all three were gone. There was a note that read:

> Hi Sexy:
>
> We went for a walk in the park.
>
> Love, love, love,
>
> Sharon

He even loved the way she signed her notes. There was nothing Sharon could do wrong as far as Mike was concerned. As well as being kind and loyal to her own family, she was wonderful to his. She greeted his mother with a hug and kiss every time they were together. She chatted endlessly with his sisters and played with their children. Last week, he found her massaging his mother's shoulders after dinner.

"Her shoulders were tight and I was helping," she told him. His mom had been smiling like a Cheshire cat while this was going on. Well, Sharon did have the magic touch. She could make him tingle simply by holding his hand.

Mike had not dated many women. He had had quite a few offers but had accepted few. The truth was that he did not find most women to his liking. There was always some flaw that made someone unacceptable. As soon as he had looked at Sharon for the first time, he had been smitten. Those velvet brown eyes, that magnificent smile and those unruly curls attracted him immediately. He wondered at the time about what her fatal flaw might be. But as time went by, he liked her more and more. She made him laugh, she stimulated his intellect and she stimulated his body. There was only one of her and he wasn't ever letting her go.

He went over to his mother's house to say hello.

"Hi Ma, how are you?"

"I'm fine baby. How is Sharon's visit with her sister going?"

"So far so good, ma."

"Are they all coming for Sunday dinner?"

"I will ask and let you know."

"Mikey, could you look at the dishwasher? It isn't working properly."

"Sure, anything for you."

He left with more food for everyone to eat. He went back to Sharon's apartment with a casserole of eggplant Parmesan, a Panzanella salad and a bowl of fruit salad.

When he arrived, All three were back. Sharon was sitting on the floor handing blocks to Jennie and Jennie was throwing them in the air. Mimi sat on the sofa drinking a cup of tea and looking exhausted.

"Hi everyone," he said. "I come bearing more food."

"Thanks, babe," Sharon said. He sat down with her and Jennie and became part of the game.

"Mom wants to know if all of us can come to Sunday dinner," he told her.

"What do you think Mimi?"

"Do you think that Jennie and I should be heading back? After all it's Sunday night."

"You don't teach in the summer and I am not working. Jennie's employer will let her stay. Stay a few more days. What's the hurry?"

"Do you want to return to Montreal so you can see David?" Sharon was never one to mince words.

"Not a chance. We will stay for a few extra days."

"Yay."

So it was settled. Mike was happy that Sharon would get Mimi and Jennie for a few extra days. Sharon was happy that he had mentioned dinner to them so they would stay a few extra days. So she decided to reward him.

That night he lay in bed reading waiting for Sharon to join him. She came to bed wearing a black see through bodysuit that showed everything. He let out a deep sigh when he saw her.

"You like?" she asked him.

She slowly pulled her bodysuit off and it fell on the floor. She crawled into bed and lowered herself onto Mike. Before he knew it, he was wildly kissing every part of her and then inside her panting and groaning. Afterwards they both slept very, very soundly.

In the next apartment, Mimi was sleeping like a log on Sharon's bed. Jennie had had a good day and was out like a light.

The person who wasn't sleeping so well that night was David. He was worried about Penny's return. He felt so close to being with Mimi again but he knew that Mimi would never take him back if she knew that he had a daughter with Penny. What should he do? He tossed and turned but an answer would not come to him.

He finally decided to tell Mimi the truth. She would find out anyway. The emergency room was a den of gossip and someone would tell her father. It wouldn't be long until the news got back to her. She would be devastated if she heard it from someone else. It might as well be him.

He just hoped that this would not destroy his chances of Mimi taking him back. He did not know that Mimi was talking to Sharon about this throughout the weekend. He did not know that Sharon had already convinced Mimi that she should never even consider him, and Mimi was sure that Sharon was right. He did not know that things were over between him and Mimi forever and this news would not even surprise her. She would mainly feel sorry for Penny and her baby and urge David to spend time with his other daughter.

The visit to Ottawa went by quickly for everyone. On Wednesday, Mimi was humming as she and Jennie drove back to Montreal. She was in a better mood than she had been for months. It seemed as if troubles could just slide off her shoulders. The day was bright and brilliant. She could smell the new flowers and the buds on the trees had turned to leaves and flowered.

She carried a sleeping Jennie into her house and put her gently in her crib. When she returned to the living room, she noticed that the light on her answering machine was flashing. She was surprised. Everyone knew she was away so who would phone her? She hoped her father was okay. She still worried that he could have another heart attack.

She pressed play. There were five messages. Each one was from David. He kept asking her how she was and whether she was home from Ottawa. He kept telling her that he wanted to see her and to speak to her. She erased the messages and felt angry. Who was he to leave her five messages? She had decided on her Ottawa visit that she would tell David that there was no chance that they would reconcile. Now she was more and more sure of her decision. She decided to ignore his messages and have a relaxing evening. She didn't owe him anything. He would just have to wait for their conversation.

Mimi sat down and read a book while Jennie was sleeping. When Jennie woke up, she fed her and played with her. She did not think about David once that evening.

The next morning, she had barely woken up and was feeding Jennie when the phone rang.

"Hello," she said in her sleepy slurred voice.

"Hi Mimi. It's David, how are you?"

"A little tired. We had a busy time in Ottawa." She was annoyed to hear from him. He had left so many messages and now he was bothering her when she was hardly awake. What was wrong with this man?

"I need to speak to you. Can I come over?"

"This is not a good time David. We are both half asleep."

"How about if I come for lunch and bring you a smoked meat sandwich?" He knew that this was one of her weaknesses.

She was about to say no but she realized that there was not much food in her fridge.

"Okay," she said feeling a bit put out.

She was suddenly craving a giant smoked meat sandwich.

"I'll be there at noon," he told her and hung up before she could change her mind.

Mimi showered and put on some jeans and a T-shirt. She put a cute little pink dress on Jennie.

She started to tidy up the living room and the bell rang. The morning had passed quickly.

She opened the door and there stood David with his arms laden with all kinds of bags. The greasy one smelled so wonderful that it made her mouth water.

"Hi David, come on in."

"I hope you don't mind. I brought some sandwiches, fries, coleslaw, coke, and lemon meringue pie."

She wanted to hug him but refrained.

Jennie was in her playpen. David put the food on the table and went to pick up and hug Jennie. Mimi had to admit the two of them had a bond. Jennie lit up whenever David was near.

He picked her up and cuddled her. She smiled up at him with her big blue eyes.

“How’s my best girl?” he asked her.

She cooed at him.

He put her back in her playpen and went to sit at the table where Mimi was putting the food on plates.

Mimi’s eyes grew wide when she put the smoked meat sandwiches out on plates. They were enormous.

“Where did you get these?”

“From Schwartz's of course.”

She was impressed by the fact that he had gone all the way there for sandwiches.

“This is delicious David. Thank you,” Mimi said as she tucked into all the food.

“I’m glad you like it.” He was hesitating eating his own food.

“I have something to tell you, Mimi.”

Mimi noticed that David was looking quite stressed.

“What is it?” she said starting to feel alarmed. She put her sandwich down.

“When we were married, I was seeing Penny. I regret this so much.”

“This is old news, David.”

“Well, Penny got pregnant when we were together. She moved home to Nova Scotia. She had a baby daughter. They are moving back to Montreal.”

Mimi looked like she had been hit by a truck.

“Did you know that she was pregnant when she left?”

“She told me but I didn’t believe her. I didn’t even know that she had had the baby until recently.”

“How did you find out?”

“Mary at the hospital told me.”

"So let me get this straight, You left me when I was pregnant and got someone else pregnant. You left me alone when I was pregnant and then you left her alone when she was pregnant. Am I getting this right?"

"Well, I didn't know for sure that she was pregnant."

Mimi felt queasy. Her food was threatening to come up.

"I hope this doesn't affect our chances of getting back together again," he told her.

Was he delusional?

"David, there was never a chance of us getting back together again. Now I think even less of you than I did before. You are a horrible person. Please leave now."

"But Mimi, I love you."

"Go to hell!" she screamed. "If you don't leave now, I will phone the police."

He didn't say another word. He simply picked up his car keys and walked out the door. As soon as he left, Mimi went to the bathroom and threw up all her food. Then she returned to the kitchen and threw everything else into the garbage.

She couldn't believe the nerve of this man. She wondered if he had impregnated anyone else. She actually felt sorry for Penny, whom she and Sharon had dubbed the whore. Perhaps she was a whore but she didn't deserve this. Perhaps she was just another innocent victim of David's.

She put Jennie down for her afternoon nap and lay down in bed.

By evening, she was better. She fed Jennie her dinner and managed to eat some toast. She wondered why the things that David did could still bother her so much. She realized that she did still care about him and part of her was still holding out hope for the relationship.

David had been the only man that Mimi had ever loved and the only man she had ever had sex with. She remembered him from high school. They used to walk down the hall together holding hands oblivious to everyone else. Even in those days, she already loved him. They decided that they were going to spend the rest of their lives together. They were going to live in a house with a wonderful garden that Mimi would tend. They would have many children and live happily ever after.

She cried for a long time. She felt exhausted but somewhat better after she was finished. She went to check on Jennie and then went to her bedroom. She couldn't quite sleep so she read for a while until sleep overtook her.

The next morning, as soon as she woke up, she phoned Sharon.

"Hi pipsqueak," she said.

"Hi Mimi, how's it going?"

"Not bad. Thanks for the great time in Ottawa."

"My pleasure, sis. I detect a weird tone in your voice. What is going on?" Sharon knew Mimi so well that she could pick up on small nuances that no one else could detect.

"It's David. He came over yesterday afternoon and brought me lunch. He also brought me the news that he has a baby daughter with Penny. He has never even seen her but she and Penny are moving back to Montreal."

"What a bastard. I wonder how many other children he has waiting in the wings. What are you going to do?"

"I never want to see his lying face again but he is Jennie's father. He can have a relationship with her. I am not doing him a favour. I want it for her. As for the two of us, there is no chance of us ever getting back together."

"Good. If you ever weaken, I will tell you this story again."

"I miss you pipsqueak."

"I miss you too. We need to get together more often. It is a short drive between Ottawa and Montreal. You can come up anytime."

"I don't want to interfere in your relationship with Mike."

"You are not interfering. He loves you and Jennie. His family loves you and Jennie. I think his mother wants to adopt you."

"That sounds good right about now. I am going to see mom and dad today. They are taking me and Jennie for brunch."

"Is mom still acting a bit crazy?"

"It's no act but yes."

"Give them my love. Tell them I will phone tonight."

"Bye Mimi."

"Bye pipsqueak, I love you."

"Love you too."

Sharon hung up the phone and went back to bed where Mike was waiting for her with no clothes and open arms.

"Is everything okay?" he asked her.

"Let's talk later," she told him and gave him a passionate kiss. A moment later, her bathrobe was slipped off her shoulders and they forgot about everything except each other and the moment.

After the sex, Sharon told him about Penny and her baby. She found herself feeling sorry for Penny. It must have been difficult for her being pregnant and alone. Now she understood why Penny had suddenly left.

Mimi dressed for brunch with her parents. She put on a bright red shirt and some lovely gold hoop earrings that Sharon had given her. She had hoped that the brightness would make her feel better but nothing was working.

She heard her doorbell ring. It would be her parents, although it was a bit early for them. She ran to the door and opened it. It was a delivery man with a large colourful bouquet of flowers of all sorts. He handed it to her and left.

She read the card. It said: Mimi, I am so sorry that I ever hurt you. Please give me another chance. I will always love you. David

She was just about to throw them in the trash when the doorbell rang again. This time it was her parents.

"Hi Mimi," her mother said.

"You are looking beautiful," her father, always the gentleman, added.

They came in and Sylvia immediately noticed the flowers.

"Who are they from?" she asked Mimi.

Mimi went to get Jennie so she could put her in her car seat for the drive to the restaurant.

She answered her mother as she was buckling Jennie in.

"They are from David, mom."

"Are you thinking about getting back together with him?" Sylvia asked.

"No, especially since I found out that he has a child with Penny. Did you know dad?"

Both her parents gasped.

"No I didn't have a clue. I heard that Penny was coming back to Montreal but nothing about a child."

"Yes, there is another daughter. He left Penny when she was pregnant just like he left me."

"What a piece of dirt he is. I'm glad you found out." Martin said.

"I am too," Sylvia added. " This will end your notions of a possible reconciliation."

"Let's go now," Mimi said lifting Jennie into her car seat. "I need to get out of the house."

She was surprised by the anger in her own voice.

They arrived at the restaurant twenty minutes later.

They had a wonderful brunch. The buffet table was laden with more foods than one person could ever eat – and eat they did. Sylvia was even restrained enough to not mention Martin's overindulgence in the dessert table. He had taken a piece of chocolate cheesecake, lemon meringue pie and trifle. She watched him eat it and she sighed, hoping he would stay well.

No one mentioned David again and Mimi was relieved. As she fed some pancake to Jennie, she decided that this was a topic best closed forever.

CHAPTER 52

Sharon was woken on Sunday morning by Mimi's weekly phone call.

"Guess what?"

"Mimi, I am half asleep. I can't guess anything."

Mike was asleep next to her. She picked up the phone and walked into the living room.

"I found a day home for Jennie. It is close to where we live and the woman who runs it is fantastic. Jennie charmed her."

"Jennie could charm anyone. That is great news. You were so worried."

"I can't believe that I am starting work in a few weeks. It is already August 15."

"I am starting school again soon."

"I am finally feeling like a strong independent woman."

"You have always been a strong independent woman Mimi. You just didn't know it yet."

Mimi sighed as she realized that as children she had shone and Sharon had flickered. Now they had reversed places. Sharon was the mature and wise one. She was living the life she really wanted and Mimi was faltering because of a stupid mistake named David.

"Is David still bothering you?"

"Yes, he is over all the time pledging his undying love and telling me how great we are together."

Her parents and Sharon had warned her. After she took him

back a second time, everyone was concerned except her. Well, no more wise, know it all Mimi. She was obviously not wise enough to make smart decisions when David was concerned. He was her Achilles heel, her fatal flaw. She had had a soft spot in her heart for him but no more. She knew women who fell into the pattern of constant break-ups and reconciliations with the same man. This would not be Mimi.

As Sharon and Mimi said goodbye, David decided that he would go to Mimi's again to try to talk some sense into her. He rang the bell and there was no answer. He walked to the back of the house and saw Mimi in her bedroom. He watched her through the open blinds. She was slowly undressing.

So, he went back to his car and drove home. Although he was angry, he was also quite aroused. He phoned Ellen, the perky blonde nurse he had been eyeing and asked to meet her for a drink that night.

After the drink, he asked her back to his place. As soon as they arrived, he started to kiss her roughly. He noticed that she looked scared but he didn't care.

He pulled her clothes off and took her roughly and forcefully. He scratched and bit her and mounted her with such force that she cried out.

After the sex, she lay on the bed looking like a discarded toy. She was red and bruised and she looked terrified.

"I'm sorry, was I too rough?" he asked her.

"No," she answered in a scared trembling voice.

"Please take me home," she told him.

David drove her home. He tried to make conversation but she didn't say a word. She ran into her house and quickly locked the door. David wondered for a moment if she would make any trouble for him but decided she probably wouldn't say a thing. It was just her word against his. He had enjoyed the rough sex.

Ellen never spoke to him again. She told every nurse what had happened to her. Many of them already disliked David. After that, there was not a nurse at the hospital that would ever go out on a date with him. The nurses went a step further. They were rude to him and would refuse to help him.

When David complained about some of them to the other doctors, someone would always answer,

“She is always helpful and friendly to me. I don’t know what her problem is with you.”

But the person did know. Everyone in the emergency department knew what David had done and even the doctors had little to say or do with him. David knew that he was a pariah at the hospital but he never had a clue as to why.

Martin Miller had heard about David’s exploits with the nurse. He wondered what he should do about it. Should he tell Sylvia? Should he tell Mimi? He really wasn’t sure. At the end, he decided not to tell anyone. It was gossip after all and gossip was often fictitious. He also felt sure that if Mimi knew she would never let him see Jennie again. David as a father was better than no father, or so he hoped.

David wondered if he should apply to work elsewhere. His talents were certainly being wasted here but he had been at this job a long time and he liked it. It fed his adrenaline just like rough sex did.

David sat cross-legged on his unmade bed. It still smelled of the sex he had had early that afternoon with Rosalie, his latest conquest. He was unshaven and wore only his pyjama pants. He was feeling very satisfied. Rosalie had been a willing participant in the rough ride he had given her.

David was wondering what he should do. He knew that Penny would soon be back at the hospital. There was not much he could do about that. He just hoped the bitch wouldn’t give him any trouble. He wondered if she would expect child support. Maybe he could say that the baby was not his. After all, the woman was a slut. The child could belong to anyone.

He decided that Penny would not pose a threat to him. He could easily handle her if she became a problem. That bitch was no match for him.

He decided to take a nap. Tomorrow he was working early. He had worn himself out and an afternoon snooze would do him good. He lay down on his bed and fell asleep with a smile on his face, satisfied with his life.

Martin and Sylvia were having a heated discussion. Martin told Sylvia all the rumours about David.

"There are rumours at the hospital that David raped one of the nurses," he told her as they sat reading the newspaper and drinking coffee.

Sylvia gasped. "I always knew that David was horrible. Shouldn't he be fired? Shouldn't he be in prison?"

"Well, there is no evidence to support this, Sylvia. It is just a rumour. The nurse in question has quit working there."

"What a shame. He still sees Jenny. Do you think we should tell Mimi to not let him see the baby anymore?"

"I don't know. He certainly seems to love Jenny. I don't think he would ever harm her."

"Did you think our former son-in-law was a rapist?"

"It is still only hearsay."

"Well, where there is smoke, there is fire. Would you like some more coffee Martin?"

"Yes please."

So Sylvia topped up both their cups and put a slice of warm apple crisp on each of their plates. They continued on with their leisurely Sunday but Sylvia was shaken. She felt that Mimi was unsafe but didn't know what to do about it. So she phoned Sharon. Maybe they could figure out what to do.

"Hi Sharon."

“Hi mom, is everything okay?” Sharon could detect a tremor in her mother’s voice.

“Your father told me that David is raping nurses at the hospital. He should not be allowed to see Jennie.”

“Is dad sure about this?”

She knew her mother could exaggerate.

“It is all rumours but he got it from reliable sources.”

“Don’t you think that if he was raping nurses they would press charges?”

“Maybe they are afraid to.”

“I don’t think that you should tell Mimi until you have proof. She has enough to worry about.”

“Are you sure?”

“No.”

“I will sleep on it and decide what to do later.”

“Good idea mom. Good night.”

“Good night Sharon.”

CHAPTER 53. SHARON

I used to be so in love with David. I thought that the world revolved around him. What a fool I was. He is the most despicable person in the world. He dumped my sister twice and now he is raping nurses. What is wrong with him? Why did Mimi and I both love him?

Mike seems like the perfect man. He is so kind and loving to me. Am I wrong about him too? Will he turn out to be another David? I am young and I don't think I see things very clearly when it comes to men. I look for the good in them even when it does not exist.

Mike has been asking me when we are going to get married. I am terrified to marry him. What if he turns out to be another David? He could also leave me when I am pregnant or worse. I can't see him doing that but who knows?

Not all men are terrible. My father is wonderful to everyone. He is a person with real integrity. He has put up with a crazy woman for years and been a wonderful father to me and Mimi.

I don't want to end my relationship with Mike but I am not ready to commit to him either. I am just too scared. I don't trust my own judgment anymore. What should I do?

I have been thinking about Penny, David's whore. I feel sorry for her. I know that she broke up Mimi's marriage but she was also in love with David and she also got dumped. Now she has a child to raise alone. It must be so hard for her. Mimi has such a hard time even though she has so many people to love her. What about Penny? Does she have anyone or is she all alone trying to raise a child all by herself?

I would like to talk to Penny. Maybe I could help her in some way. Maybe I am crazy to even consider this. She broke my sister's heart but she didn't do it alone. She is as much of a victim as Mimi is in many ways.

I know that Penny is back in Montreal. I would like to meet her when I am there. Perhaps I could help her in some way.

CHAPTER 54

Sharon was trying to work on an essay for one of her courses. She was in the library at university looking at research books and having difficulty staying focused on the task. She was feeling a bit off balance today. Last night, she and Mike had had a major argument The evening had started off innocently. They ate wonderful lasagna for dinner, compliments of his mother. Over dinner, they had chatted about their days and Sharon had made Mike laugh with an imitation of her professor, Dr Stone. After supper, they had some coffee. Still all was well.

Then Mike said, "I have something I want to show you at my apartment."

"I hope you are going to show me yourself with no clothes on," she told him. Normally, this would have made him smile but not tonight. When they walked in his living room, there was a beautiful wooden cradle standing in the middle of the room.

"Wow Mike, this is a work of art. Did you make it for your cousin?"

This was not an unfair question because Mike's cousin Maria was expecting a baby.

"No, I made it for us," he said with his heart sinking.

"What do you mean you made it for us?"

"For our baby."

"Mike, I love you but we are not even married yet. We are not about to have a baby. It will be old by the time we do that."

"I want to marry you now. I want to have a family with you now."

"Mike, I would love to marry you but not yet. I am in the middle of university. I have been derailed from getting my degree once and I need to do it."

"You could still go to school if you have a baby."

"It would be difficult, Mike. I am only 22 years old. What's the rush?"

"I love you and I am ready for a life together."

"We do have a life together. We are together all the time. I am just not ready for marriage and children."

"I can't wait forever for you."

"Mike you are being unreasonable."

"I think you are the unreasonable one. You don't love me enough to marry me."

"My mother guilted me for years. You are not going to guilt me into marrying you!"

Sharon felt like she was going to cry. She stormed out of Mike's apartment and slammed the door. She was surprised when he did not follow her. He didn't come back and she spent the night alone in her bed. She had not heard from him in two days and she was feeling terrible. She could not focus on anything. She wondered if they had broken up. Mike had been a gift and she did not want to lose him but she was not going to marry him until the time was right. What could she do to convince him to wait?

She looked at her watch. It was 5:45 pm. Mimi would be home from work. Maybe she would have an idea. Sharon gathered her books and walked back to her apartment. She was glad she had worn her winter jacket because the winds were already getting quite chilly. Even though it was mid-September, the chill in the air predicted what was to come. She arrived in her apartment with hope that she would have a note from Mike but there was nothing. She wondered what it would be like without him in her life and felt so sad. So she phoned Mimi.

"Hi sis, how's it going?"

"Not bad. I just finished feeding Jennie. I had a good day at work. I am tired. Mom is ranting about everything as usual. How about you? How is life in paradise?"

"I think Mike and I may have broken up." She felt a choke in her voice as she said this.

"I can't believe it. What happened?"

"He wants to get married and I am not ready. We had a big fight about it and I have not heard from him all day."

"And here I thought you had a serious problem. You have to remember that Mike is 29. You are just a 22-year-old punk. He is ready to settle down."

"But I'm not, Mimi. What should I do?"

"This one is too easy."

"It's not easy for me. I love him and I don't want to lose him."

"I think he is afraid to lose you. You should get engaged to him."

"Didn't you hear me? I said I don't feel ready for marriage."

"Who said anything about marriage? Get engaged. Tell him you will marry him when you finish university. That way he will know that you are committed to him."

"That is not a bad idea."

"It is a compromise. He will feel more secure and you will not feel rushed into a marriage."

"When did you get so smart?"

"I was born that way. I have to run. Jennie is destroying the house. I love you. Bye."

"Bye Mimi."

Sharon thought about it for a while. She ate supper alone at her table and she studied alone in her large armchair. She thought about it when she lay alone in her bed that night. She missed Mike's body warmth in the bed. After a sleepless night, she decided that she would talk to him about a compromise.

CHAPTER 55. SHARON

I don't know what I should do. I really love Mike but I don't want to give up my dreams for a man. I am finally in university after things kept getting derailed over and over again. My life is ideal right now. I have a wonderful relationship with someone I love and I am taking the courses that will propel me into the future that I want.

It's not as if I don't want to ever get married. I love Mike. He is a great boyfriend and he would be a great husband and father. I am just not ready.

Mimi's experiences with David have also scared me. He seemed so perfect for her but the man turned out to be a first class snake. To think that I had a crush on him. If I ever run into him on the street, I want to spit in his face.

Mimi's idea that I should get engaged to him seems to make sense. We would both know that we would eventually marry but it would give me some time. I don't want to marry Mike yet.

He says we could marry and I could continue school. That would work only if we did not have children. Once a child came into the picture, everything would change. I would have to leave school to raise our child or work hard at being a wife, mother, and student.

I look at Mimi. She is so tired she can hardly function. She has dark circles under her eyes. She looks older than her years. She rarely complains to me but I see the exhaustion and even hear it in her voice.

Whoever said that women can have it all was full of crap. Maybe if they are wealthy they can have it all but us regular folk can never have it all. Maybe Mimi was right. Would Mike settle for being engaged?

CHAPTER 56

Sharon spent the next 24 hours wondering what she should do. During this time, she missed Mike terribly and yet she didn't want to do the wrong thing. She had trouble concentrating on her classes and was even late for her favourite class. The following evening, she decided to approach him. Even though she had a key to his apartment, she knocked on his door.

"Come in," he said as if he had been expecting her.

He was sitting on his sofa watching television. He turned it off when she came in.

"I miss you, Mike," she said. She noticed that he looked sad. She also noticed that his handmade crib was no longer sitting in the living room.

"I miss you too Sharon," he said but he did not invite her to sit down.

"I have an idea," she told him. He did not respond. She was starting to get nervous. Maybe it was over between them. She decided to dive right in.

"How about if we get engaged now and married when I finish university?"

He looked at her thoughtfully and still didn't say anything.

"I love you Mike. I don't want to lose you. I want to marry you but just not right now."

"That might work. I need to think about it."

"I will leave you to think," she said and went back to her own apartment. She felt like all was lost but she had shown her hand. There was not much else to do but wait. About an hour later, as she was clearing her dinner dishes, Mike walked into her kitchen. He drew her into an embrace and kissed her so passionately that her head was spinning. Afterwards, he pulled out a small black velvet box.

"This is for you."

She opened the box. In it was a magnificent diamond ring surrounded by tiny rubies.

"Will you marry me?" he asked.

"Yes, yes, yes!"

He put the ring on her finger. It fit perfectly.

"How did you know my ring size?"

"Mimi told me."

"This ring is exquisite."

"It belonged to my grandmother. My mother wanted you to have it."

Tears started rolling down her face. She could not remember when she was last so happy.

"Yes, we can wait to get married until you finish university. I just don't want to lose you."

"There is no chance of that." He kissed her passionately. He couldn't stop. Soon he was kissing her neck and she was moaning. They went to the bedroom and undressed each other. They had wild sex and Sharon was left wearing only the ring and a huge smile.

It was impossible for Mimi to refuse to see her mother. When Sylvia got something in her head, "no" was not an option. She would be persistent until her victim gave in. This is how Mimi felt when she reluctantly agreed to have lunch with her mother. On Wednesdays, she had a free period so she and Sylvia could have some time to talk. Mimi did not feel like talking to her mother. She knew that this would not be a pleasant discussion. She just felt it inside.

Sylvia showed up at Mimi's school and they drove to Guido, Mimi's favourite Italian restaurant. Sylvia was looking quite fit in her jeans and blue silk shirt. Mimi felt that she must be quite the sight. She was tired and it showed. There were bags under her eyes and she was exhausted. She wondered how she would get through the school year as it was only October.

"How have you been?" Sylvia asked her.

"A little tired, Mom."

"I wish you would let me take Jennie sometimes. It would give you a rest. You do look a tad peaked."

"She is with David often mom. I get plenty of chances to rest." Mimi said defensively.

"What are you going to order?"

"I am going to have the pasta primavera and a green salad."

"Good choice Mimi. I will do the same."

So they ordered their lunches and coffees and Sylvia got right to the point.

"There are some rumours about David floating around at the hospital. They say he raped one of the nurses."

Mimi did not look surprised at all.

"I already heard about it."

"Do you think you should be letting him take your daughter?"

"Well, first of all, they are rumours. He has not been charged with anything. I have no grounds for not letting him see Jennie."

"Do you think he did it?"

"Mom, one time I would have said no way but he is not the person I knew and loved anymore so who knows?"

"Do you think that you should talk to a lawyer at least?"

"No it would not do anything. Let's change the subject." So they did.

The rest of the lunch was strained. When Sylvia dropped Mimi off back at work, they were both relieved it was over.

Mimi drove very slowly. She was so tired that she didn't trust her driving ability. She was also furious with her mother. Mimi knew that David had changed. She also wondered if he should see Jennie but it was not for Sylvia to decide. She had really been dragging all afternoon. She had an hour before picking up Jennie at day care. She would take a nap and then go get her little sweetie. Seeing Jennie would perk her up. She set her clock radio to wake her in 45 minutes and fell asleep on her bed still dressed in her jacket. She woke to her alarm music and felt a little better. She picked up Jennie who had a huge smile on her cherubic face. Mimi held her toddler and hugged and kissed her. With every passing moment she was feeling better.

Just after they entered the house, Mimi and Jennie had some apple slices and yogurt as an afternoon snack. Jennie was watching Sesame Street on television when the phone rang. Mimi was hesitant to pick it up. It was Sharon who was the only other person who could make Mimi smile.

"Hi Mimi girl."

"Hi pipsqueak, are you feeling better?"

"Yes, I am. By the way, you are a genius."

"Aw shucks. Well I knew that already. Did you and Mike make up?"

"Yes we did. I tried what you suggested and it worked like a charm. We are now engaged. He gave me his grandmother's ring. It is so beautiful."

Suddenly, tears sprang to Mimi's eyes as she felt a terrifying premonition that she would not be around for her sister's wedding.

"Congratulations pipsqueak. I am so happy it all worked out."

"You don't sound so great. Is everything okay?"

"I had lunch with mom today. She told me that there is a rumour that David raped a nurse."

"Mom already told me; do you believe it?"

"I don't know what to believe anymore."

"Did she think he should stop seeing Jennie?"

"Yes she did, even when I explained that it would be hard to accomplish."

"Poor you. You must be exhausted."

"I feel like I could sleep for a week."

"Well, I have some good news. Mike and I are coming to Montreal next weekend. He wants to ask dad if he can have my hand in marriage. It's kind of sappy but sweet."

"Where are you staying?"

"I think we should stay in a hotel. Mom will never approve of us sleeping in the same room."

"Nonsense. You will stay here with me and Jennie. I have that extra bedroom waiting for you. Jennie will be so excited to see you. Me too."

"Only if you are sure."

"More sure than about anything else. I have to go now. Bye pipsqueak."

"Bye sis."

Mimi was still exhausted but feeling so much better. In ten days, Sharon and Mike would be in Montreal with them. What could be better than this?

Sylvia was in a foul mood. Everything that had happened in the last few days had left her wondering. Mimi had become angry with her. When she told Martin about the altercation, he told Sylvia that she should have minded her own business. Then Sharon phoned and told her that she and her boyfriend Mike were coming to Montreal in two weeks.

"Why are you coming?" Sylvia implored.

Sharon did not want Sylvia to know before Mike even spoke to Martin.

"Do we need a reason?"

"No, it's just that the two of you don't usually come for a weekend."

"Well, maybe it will be the start of something new and wonderful."

"I'll prepare the guest room and your old bedroom for you."

This was the part Sharon dreaded.

"We are staying with Mimi. I really miss Jennie and I want to spend as much time with her as possible."

"Mimi's house is small. She has only one extra bedroom and we have two."

Sylvia obviously did not have a clue that Sharon and Mike were sharing a bedroom. Sharon did not want to disillusion her mother.

"Don't worry mom. We'll figure it out."

"Can I at least make dinner for all of us when you come?"

"That would be wonderful."

"What does Mike like to eat?"

"Everything."

"So I gather your relationship is going well."

"It's going very well. I couldn't be happier."

"Well, I am glad one of my daughters is doing well."

"Mimi is doing great, mom."

"I wish she could find a nice man. I have tried to introduce her but she doesn't seem interested."

"Mimi will find a man on her own mom."

"I hope you're right."

So they finished their conversation and Sylvia went back to her cleaning session. Every Monday she cleaned her house from top to bottom. Martin wanted her to get a cleaning lady but she would not hear of it. It was a matter of pride to her to clean her home until it sparkled. She cleaned fiercely today as she was upset with every member of her family. After the cleaning, she was exhausted and decided to take a rest and have a coffee before she went to the gym.

Sylvia remained in a foul mood for the rest of the day. When Martin came home with flowers, she smiled. They were an intoxicating arrangement of daisies, mums, roses, and lilies, all her favourite flowers. She couldn't help but smile.

"What is the occasion?" she asked.

"There is no reason except that I love you."

The truth was that he had phoned Mimi earlier in the day. They often had little telephone conversations when they were both at work. Martin called them stress relievers because talking to Mimi always made him feel better.

"Mom is on the warpath, dad," she made sure to tell him.

"What happened?"

"She warned me about David again and I did not heed her. Sharon and Mike are coming to town and staying with me instead of you. So, she is unhappy. You know mom. She wants to be loved and I don't think she feels that way right now."

"Thanks for letting me know."

Martin had had a very good day. Everything had gone smoothly at work so he decided to buy Sylvia flowers. The florist had her favourites so he had her mix them all into a huge bouquet. The reds, yellows, and pinks were stunning and bright. As Sylvia unwrapped them, Martin put his arms around her and gave her a loving kiss.

"How did you know that I had such an awful day?" she asked him.

"I didn't," he lied. They sat down to dinner. Martin complimented Sylvia on her new sweater and the delicious stir-fry. She smiled a lot during dinner as she told him about her day. He listened attentively not saying a word to interrupt. After dinner, they played a game of backgammon. As usual, Martin won. Later in bed, Sylvia actually reached out to Martin and initiated their lovemaking. As Martin dozed off, he was so happy and relieved that the evening had turned out so well. He didn't like lying to his wife but sometimes you just had to tell a little white lie.

David was busy. He had many emergency patients to attend to. David was still wondering what he could do to get Mimi back in his life. All of his conquests did not dull the ache that he still had for her. When he would come to pick up Jennie, Mimi did not even speak to him. She would bring Jennie and her backpack to the door and hand them to him without even saying hello.

He knew that there was probably no chance of getting her back but he still hoped. He knew that Penny was now working in the hospital but they had not run into each other. He had been eating his meals in the staff room instead of the cafeteria so he would not run into her. He knew that there might be a confrontation if he saw her and he was not up to it. He was afraid that she would make a scene and she had every right to. So, he took the cowardly way out and hid.

Penny was enjoying being back in Montreal and working at the hospital again. As she was working in the maternity ward, she never ran into David. One day, she was paged to a phone call at the nurses' station. She was surprised. No one ever phoned her at work. She became a little nervous. Had something happened to her wonderful daughter Linda?

She picked up the phone with shaking hands.

"Hi this is Sharon. I am Mimi's sister. I would like to meet you."

Sharon was not surprised that there was only a gasp on the line.

"Why?" Penny asked.

"I feel bad about what David did to you. He hurt you just as he hurt my sister. Your daughter is related to my niece. I just thought we might get to know each other."

"Okay," Penny said, hesitantly, as she felt nervous about meeting.

They decided to meet the following weekend at Mary's house where Penny and Linda were staying. That weekend Sharon and Mike would be in town so the timing was excellent.

Sharon hoped that Penny would not change her mind but would understand completely if she did. This was, after all, a strange request.

CHAPTER 57

Sharon was so excited and a little nervous about going to Montreal with Mike. She couldn't wait to see Mimi and Jennie but she was s little bit apprehensive about her parents. She wondered how her mom would behave and wondered about her father's reaction to Mike asking for her hand in marriage. Mike was also nervous. He wanted Sharon's family to like him. He didn't know them very well but he was most concerned about Sharon's mother. He knew that she had hated David from the moment she met him. It turned out she had been right but he was afraid that she would hate him as well. He wanted everything to go well. There was also the possibility that Sharon's father would not want Mike to marry Sharon. Mike believed that family was so important. He had grown up in a large and loving family. They had their fights but were always looking out for each other. He knew that family was important to Sharon. He wanted their children to have great families on both sides. He had gone to his mother for advice a few days before.

"Hi ma," he said letting himself into the house.

She was sitting knitting in the living room on their old sagging comfortable tweed sofa.

"Hi Mikey. I am so happy to see you."

This was what she always said when he came over.

"Are you hungry, Mikey?"

"No ma, I just ate an hour ago."

"Maybe a coffee then?"

He adored his mother.

"Sure, I'll make it for us both."

He filled the Italian espresso maker and put it on the stove to make the coffee. Then he put some biscuits on a plate. He brought both to his mother and placed them on her little TV table.

"Thank you baby."

"What are you knitting ma?"

"Baby socks."

"For who?"

"Who knows? Maybe for you and Sharon."

"We're going to Montreal this weekend."

"Be careful driving. Winter is here too soon."

"I am going to ask her father for her hand in marriage."

"That is wonderful Mikey. You two belong together."

His mother and entire family adored Sharon. Her warmth and kindness had won them over a long time ago.

"Do you think her father will say yes?"

"Of course he will. He knows how happy you make her. He also knows you will take good care of her."

"I hope so, ma. I am a bit nervous."

"Well you want to make a good impression. They will all love you. Remember they met you before."

"That doesn't count."

"Don't worry Mikey. It will go well."

She smiled at him and he saw all the memories of a lifetime in the creases of her face.

Sharon and Mike arrived at Mimi's house in mid-afternoon. They were both greeted with big hugs from Mimi and Jennie but Sharon noticed that he was not himself.

"Are you feeling alright Mike?"

"I am just fine."

Mike and Jennie settled down on the living room floor for a quick game of throw the blocks around and Sharon and Mimi went to the kitchen to have a coffee.

"Mike seems a little subdued today Sharon."

"He is nervous about seeing mom and dad. He knows about how mom has always hated David. He is afraid she will hate him."

"I can understand his nervousness. Mom is a tough customer to please."

"I don't care if mom likes him but he does."

Everyone was at the door. Sylvia wanted to cry as she looked at them. There they were: Mimi holding Jennie, Sharon, and Mike standing hand in hand looking like they belonged together. It was a beautiful sight. She took a snapshot in her mind to preserve it.

"Come in, come in," she told them. " You all look cold."

Mike handed her a bouquet of roses.

"Thank you, Mike."

Sylvia kissed him on the cheek.

"Let me take your coats," Martin said. He hung up the coats while Mimi took off Jennie's pink, fluffy fall jacket.

"Jennie has grown so much," Sylvia told her.

"You saw her last week. She is no different," was Mimi's answer.

"Come to grandma," Sylvia said and Jennie eagerly waddled over to her. Sylvia always had fresh cookies and they walked to the kitchen hand in hand to get some.

The others walked to the family room where the fireplace was lit and glowing and little canapés on trays sat waiting for them.

Everyone settled on the couch. Sylvia had prepared smoked salmon and cream cheese on crackers, tiny meatballs on toothpicks and spinach dip in a bread bowl.

"This is delicious," Mimi said.

"Do you think mom actually expects us to eat supper?" Sharon added.

Mike was quiet. He was nervous about asking Dr. Miller about marrying Sharon. He did not know him well and had no idea of what his reaction would be.

Martin was in a great mood. He poured wine for all the guests. He watched his two little girls that had both grown up into fine young women. He was so proud of both of them.

"How is life in the emergency ward, Dad?" Sharon asked him.

"Much the same. Your mom wants me to cut my hours so we can travel more."

"I think that would be a grand idea," Mimi told him.

"You work much too hard. You deserve a break," Sharon added.

"Dinner is served," was the next thing they heard. Sylvia came walking hand in hand with Jennie who had chocolate all over her face.

Everyone piled around the dinner table and stared in excitement at the feast before their eyes. There were numerous salads, breads and more canapés. Sharon couldn't believe that this was still leading up to the main course. She had to hand it to her mother. She really knew how to host a dinner.

As they tucked into the appetizers, Sylvia asked Mike,

"How is law school going?"

"I'm finished. I just have to take my bar exams and find a job."

"You must be excited," Mimi added.

"I am just glad it's almost over."

"Mike passed all his courses with flying colours," Sharon added beaming with joy.

"I had a good study partner," Mike added.

He honestly felt that Sharon was largely responsible for his doing so well in school and in life. She was always encouraging him and giving him hugs for luck. Well, it had worked.

The conversation flowed easily as everyone ate the main course of slow cooked lamb, roast lemon potatoes, Greek salad, green bean salad and couscous with raisins. Everyone sighed with delight as they ate the delicious food.

Soon dinner was over and Jennie was sleeping on the sofa. Sharon and Mimi were helping their mother clear the table and clean up after the meal.

Martin and Mike sat alone together in the family room with Jennie sleeping sweetly on the sofa between them.

They sat amiably sipping coffee. Mike decided to get right to the point.

"Dr Miller, I love Sharon very much. I would like to ask her to marry me. I would appreciate your blessing in his matter."

He realized that he sounded stiff and formal but he didn't care.

Martin looked surprised for a moment. Then his face broke into a broad grin.

"Will you always love her?" he asked.

"Every day of my life."

"Will you stay faithful to her?"

"Without question."

"Will you always accept her for who she is?"

"Yes, I love who she is."

"Will you always treat her with love and respect?"

"Yes I will."

"In that case, you have my blessing. When will you ask her?"

"We have already discussed it but I wanted to be sure that it was fine with you."

"It is more than fine."

"Thank you Dr. Miller. This means a great deal to me."

"Can I tell Sylvia?"

"I hope you don't mind waiting until we make it official."

"When will that be?"

"Tonight," said Mike with a chuckle in his voice.

He went to the kitchen where Sharon was laughing with Sylvia and Mimi.

"Let's go for a walk," he said.

"Not a bad idea. I have gained about 10 pounds eating this meal. Is it okay if we go out for a little while mom?"

"Sure, we are almost finished cleaning up. Dress warm. It is chilly out there."

Mike and Sharon bundled up and walked out into the bracing wind.

"My, it is windy and cold. What was the burning rush to get me alone?"

"I asked your father for your hand in marriage. He said yes! I want to tell your family. I want to tell them tonight."

Sharon knew how much Mike wanted to get married to her. She knew by his voice that this announcement was so important to him. So, she said the one thing she could say.

"Sure."

He pulled her into a strong embrace and kissed her with such passion that it took her breath away.

They walked quickly back to the house hand in hand.

When they came in, Sylvia and Mimi were just sitting down to coffee in the family room.

"You must be freezing," said Sylvia. "I'll make you some hot chocolate."

"Wait a minute, mom," Sharon told her. "We have something to tell you."

Everyone sat waiting and staring. Mimi saw that both Sharon and Mike looked excited.

"Mike and I are getting married!" Sharon blurted out.

A smile broke out on each face except for Jennie who was still fast asleep.

Mimi did not look surprised. Come to think of it, no one looked surprised.

"Congratulations!" Sylvia exclaimed.

"I have a bottle of champagne for this occasion," Martin said and went to get it.

Everyone toasted the newly engaged couple and asked a lot of questions. As they were speaking, Sharon realized that she really did want to marry Mike.

This was quite a revelation for her. Sharon had believed that marriage was a lifelong contract that was hard to break. Somehow, there would be time in the future for this type of commitment. She saw her parents' marriage and felt that its entire success was dependent on her father's ability to give in to her mother. She did not want this type of relationship. She wanted herself and her husband to be equal partners. She somehow felt that this would be the case with Mike.

Sharon had to admit to herself that she did not always trust the men in her life. Before Mike, her relationships with men had always ended badly. Then there was Mimi and David. He had betrayed her sister twice. Somehow she had a deep-seated mistrust of men but it was different with Mike yet again. She knew he would always love her and always be faithful to her. She felt as if she could trust him with anything.

She realized that Mimi had asked her the same question twice.

"Earth calling Sharon," Mimi said. "What world are you in?"

"Sorry, Mimi. I was just deep in thought."

Mimi gave Sharon a hug.

She whispered, "I am so happy for you. I love you pipsqueak."

Sharon felt tears welling up in her eyes.

"I love you too big sis," she whispered to Mimi.

After that everything was a blur. Sharon hardly remembered the rest of the evening. When she stumbled into bed with Mike, she was asleep before her head hit the pillow. She woke up late the next morning to the smell of fresh coffee and Mike's arm wrapped around her shoulder.

She peeled Mike's arm away. This normally woke him but he still slept. She got her bathrobe and tiptoed out of the bedroom. In the kitchen, Mimi was sitting at the table. Jennie sat in her high chair and ate a banana that was turning to mush in her fingers.

"Good morning pipsqueak," Mimi told her sister. "I think that last night went rather well, don't you?"

"It did. Even mom seemed fine with the news."

"It can't have been a surprise. You two have been tight as sardines for over a year."

"I realized last night that I really want to marry Mike."

"That is great. Want some coffee?"

"I thought you'd never ask."

Mimi poured Sharon some strong coffee and Sharon drank it eagerly. She was happy that Mike was still asleep. Moments alone with Mimi were rare. Sharon cooked some oatmeal and popped bread into the toaster. The two sat laughing and chatting while watching Jennie put on her banana show.

"Have I told you about David?" Mimi asked Sharon.

"Has he molested any new nurses?"

"He is thinking of leaving Montreal."

"That wouldn't be so bad. Where is he going?"

"There is a prestigious job as head of emergency in Toronto. He has applied for it."

"You will be well rid of that creep. Thinking about him makes my skin crawl."

"That is all well and fine but remember he is Jennie's dad. She loves him and she will miss him."

"Jennie is still young. She will forget about him soon enough, especially when you marry someone better."

"I wish I could just have sex at this point, sis. I have forgotten what it's like."

At that moment, a sleepy Mike stumbled into the kitchen., his curly hair falling in his eyes.

"What are you two laughing about?" he asked.

"Just some girl stuff," Sharon replied.

He sat down to breakfast with them and the conversation changed to wedding plans. Sharon and Mike wanted a small wedding but everyone else had other ideas. Sylvia wanted to invite a lot of people. Martin didn't really care. Mimi thought they should elope. That idea was sounding better and better all the time.

Sharon wondered if she should tell anyone about her phone conversation with Penny. She had mentioned it to Mike and it had confused him.

"Why would you want to meet Penny?"

"She is alone and she needs someone in her life."

Mike loved this about Sharon. She always wanted to help everyone. He was also concerned that her family would be unhappy.

She decided not to tell them yet. She was going out the next day very quietly to meet Penny and Linda. Only Mike knew about it and he would cover for her.

CHAPTER 58

On Sunday, both Sharon and Penny were nervous. Sharon would be coming over at 2:00 pm. She was on a tight schedule because she and Mike had to be back in Ottawa that evening. Penny was uncomfortable about Sharon's visit.

She brewed some coffee and prepared some lemon squares and wondered what to expect. The doorbell rang promptly at 2:00 pm.

Sharon stood at the door with a big smile on her face. This immediately put Penny at ease.

Sharon shocked Penny when she gave her a hug.

"I am so glad to meet you," she told her.

Penny visibly relaxed.

"Please come in," she said.

Linda was in the den playing with her Lego blocks. Sharon immediately beamed when she saw her. She didn't mention her resemblance to David.

"Your daughter is so beautiful."

"Thanks. Please come join us in the den for coffee and lemon squares."

Never one to mince words, Penny came right out with the question as soon as they were seated.

"What is the reason for your visit?"

"I just wanted to meet you. David really hurt my sister and I am sure he really hurt you."

"He did."

Sharon noticed that Penny's voice had a slight tremble.

"Your daughter and Mimi's daughter are half sisters. I feel like we are family."

This brought a smile to Penny face. She had not thought of this before. She realized that there was complete sincerity there.

"Would you like some coffee?"

"Yes please."

Just then Linda crawled up and sat on Sharon's lap. This made Penny sure that she liked Sharon. Linda was an excellent judge of character.

"I know you left Montreal for a while."

"Yes, I went back to Wolfville, Nova Scotia. That's where I am from. We stayed with my mother."

"That must have been wonderful. She got to know her granddaughter."

"Yes, my mother was thrilled to get to know Linda. Unfortunately, she died when I was there. After that I decided to come back to Montreal."

"Are you happy to be back here?"

"Yes, I love it. I was worried about running into David but I never do. I really love working in the maternity ward."

"When my sister first met David, I had such a crush on him. I can't believe I felt like that."

"Well, we all make mistakes. I am not sorry that I met David. Because of him, I have my beautiful daughter."

"I think my sister Mimi feels the same way."

"Tell me more about yourself Sharon."

"I am living in Ottawa. I am at Carleton University studying journalism. I came back for the weekend so my boyfriend could ask my father for my hand in marriage."

"How did it go?"

"Well, here is my engagement ring."

She spread out her hand.

"Congratulations. It's a beautiful ring."

"It belonged to his grandmother. I feel honoured to wear it."

"Tell me about your fiancé. What's he like?"

"His name is Mike. He is almost perfect. I am so lucky to have found him."

"Yes you are. I wish I could meet someone."

"You will when the time is right."

They sat in the den chatting like two old friends. Linda stayed on Sharon's lap cuddling with her as if they were best friends.

Both women calmed down as they realized they really liked each other.

Sharon could not get over Linda's sweetness. She hoped that someday Linda and Jennie could meet each other and maybe even be real sisters.

The visit went by quickly. Sharon had to get back to Ottawa. They parted like two old friends with a hug and a promise to get together the next time that Sharon was in town. Sharon was genuinely happy to have met Penny.

She wondered if she should tell Mimi. The two had no secrets from each other. She decided to wait to tell Mimi and her parents. Somehow it felt like the time was not right.

CHAPTER 59

Sharon and Mike were making wedding and honeymoon plans. She wanted a small wedding and he wanted a large one. She wanted a summer wedding and he wanted a winter wedding. She wanted a small intimate honeymoon and he wanted a lavish honeymoon in Italy.

They decided to give it a few days until they discussed this topic again. Sharon was relieved. She and Mike were arguing too much. Their relationship was normally as smooth as honey. She did not like the ripples this was causing. This was not to mention the suggestions that they were getting from friends and relatives. Of course, Sylvia and Martin wanted the wedding in Montreal and Mike's mother wanted it to be in Ottawa.

The weather was hot and beautiful. Sharon was finished with university for the year. She had made the honours list that term.

Mike was interning at a small law firm and finding too much drudgery in his duties. Sharon had to keep assuring him that it would get better.

It was a beautiful Sunday morning. Sharon and Mike were sitting at her kitchen table eating cereal with milk and drinking their first coffees of the day. They were both feeling a little grouchy from the stress of the wedding plans.

"How about it if we take a day off from talking about our wedding?" Sharon said. "I am exhausted by all of these arguments. Let's enjoy the summer before it's over."

"What do you have in mind?"

"Let's go for a picnic in the park by the Rideau Canal. We can pack some sandwiches and drinks and sit under a tall tree and just enjoy the warmth of the sun and each other's company."

"Good idea. Will we be done in time for dinner at my mom's?"

Sharon said, "sure," but she didn't feel that way.

She knew that when they went for dinner at his mother's house there would be more arguments about the wedding. She wanted to forgo dinner and whisk Mike somewhere far away where they could just escape from everyone and live happily ever after.

So Sharon made some tuna and some cheese sandwiches and cut up some celery and carrots for crunching. She added some apples and raspberry crumble and a few bottles of iced tea. They were ready.

"Mike," she called from the kitchen, "Let's go."

Where was he? He must have gone back to his own apartment. When she walked in, she heard him speaking on the phone.

"Yes, mom, I'll be there right away."

She didn't like the sound of that.

He told her, "My mother has a burst pipe in her laundry room. I have to go and fix it. Sorry. We'll go on a picnic soon."

Sharon was resentful. There were others who could help Mike's mother with her plumbing problems but Mike was always the one she asked.

He always said yes to his mother. She wondered if this would be a problem in their marriage.

He kissed her on the cheek and was gone.

She was thus left alone with sandwiches and no one to eat them with. She decided to go on the picnic by herself. Mike was not going not ruin her day.

She packed her picnic basket and drove down to the park. She spread out a blanket on the ground and sat down on the grass. She pulled out a novel and began to read. This was fine even without Mike. With a surprise, she realized that she preferred to be alone today.

As she was reading, she heard a voice behind her.

"Hi Sharon."

She looked up and saw a tall good-looking dark haired man. He looked familiar but she could not quite place him.

"I'm Todd. I was in your ethics of journalism class this winter. May I join you?"

"Sure, I was just about to eat. Would you like a sandwich?"

"Thanks. I would love one. I am starved."

So Sharon gave Todd one of the sandwiches and he wolfed it down so she gave him another. They talked easily like old friends.

They discussed university, courses, and Ottawa. Todd was also from Montreal. Sharon was so surprised that she had never noticed him. He was so tall and quite handsome. She especially liked the dimple in his cheek when he smiled.

"Can I let you in on a secret?" he asked.

"What is it?"

"I have had a crush on you for a year. I wanted to ask you out but someone told me that you had a serious boyfriend. Are you available?"

Sharon found herself saying yes because she was so annoyed with Mike.

After several hours of talk and laughter, Todd said he was going back to his apartment. Would Sharon like to come?

"Yes," she told him.

His apartment was a top level of a three floor walk up near the university campus. She was surprised by how beautiful it was. It had gleaming hardwood floors and plants everywhere. Everything shone.

"Would you like to have dinner here with me?" Todd asked her.

"Yes, I would."

She knew Mike would be back looking for her and she didn't care.

Todd barbecued some hamburgers on his hibachi on the balcony. She made a salad with vegetables from his fridge. They sat on his balcony in the early summer sunlight eating, and drinking cool beer.

After dinner, she was about to leave when Todd kissed her gently on the lips. She found herself kissing him back passionately.

Before long, they were in his bedroom and he was fumbling with the button on her blouse. When he saw her breasts, he sighed with so much pleasure.

Soon he was kissing them and the rest of her body. Sharon knew she shouldn't but gave in to the passion that Todd aroused in her. They lay on his bed perspiring from the heat and from their intense sex.

After the sex they lay together on his bed and Sharon felt like she was the worst person in the world. How could she have done this to Mike her fiancé? What would she do? What would she tell Mike? She could never get past this.

When Todd asked her, "Will you spend the night with me?" she said yes.

She was too embarrassed to go home and face Mike.

The next morning Sharon woke up confused and hung over. She didn't know where she was. As soon as she turned and saw Todd, she thought she was going to be sick. She realized that she had had sex and spent the night with him. She was beside herself. How would Mike ever forgive her? How would she forgive herself?

She knew that she had to get home as soon as possible. She quietly put on her clothes and sneaked out of the apartment. It was within easy driving distance to her own apartment. It was early. Maybe no one would notice her return.

When she walked into her apartment, to her dismay, Mike was sitting at her kitchen table drinking a cup of coffee. He looked haggard, pale and ill.

When he saw her, his face brightened up.

He ran over to her and swept her up in his arms.

"I was so worried about you. I thought you were dead. You disappeared for an entire day and night."

Sharon was terrified. She wondered if Mike would smell another man on her but he didn't seem to notice anything.

He just held her so tightly that she was beginning to feel smothered.

"What happened to you?" he asked her.

"I was angry at you so I left. I guess time just got away on me."

"Where did you sleep?"

"At Angela's."

She was Sharon's only friend in Ottawa. She hoped Mike hadn't phoned her. Come to think of it, he didn't know her number. Thank goodness for that.

"I already phoned the police. I was about to phone your family, Sharon. Please never do this again."

"I won't," she promised, relieved that he hadn't tried to get Angela's number.

Sharon was shocked when Mike started to cry. It made her feel even more ashamed.

She held him and then she had a shower. Sharon wanted to get the evidence of what she had done off her as soon as possible.

She was so relieved that Todd did not know where she lived. This was already too complicated. She wondered if she should tell Mike what she had done and quickly decided against it.

When she came out of the shower, Mike was gone. He had left her a note.

Sharon:

I had to go to work. I will phone later. I am so glad you are fine. I love you always.

Mike.

Sharon was in a real slump. She didn't know what to do. She felt guilty and she wondered if she should even marry Mike. If she could so easily fall into bed with another man, was she ready for a husband?

She went to bed and surprisingly fell asleep instantly. She woke up several hours later with the sun streaming into her room. She felt so much better. Had she dreamed this entire incident? No, it was true and she had a lot of thinking to do.

She decided that the best course of action in this case was to do nothing. She would go on with her life with Mike and marry him. There was really nothing to gain in letting him know. Still, the guilt was overwhelming. Could she live with it? In the past, she had never worried much about being faithful. No one was important enough to be faithful to. This had changed so much recently. Here she was about to get married and commit the rest of her life to Mike.

She needed to talk to someone about it. The first person who came to mind was Mimi but she would be busy with Jennie. Mimi was trying to do as much as possible with her daughter before summer ended and she had to return to work. The evening would have to do. Meanwhile, she could make herself busy by spending the day doing chores but she didn't have much to do. She decided to go for a walk.

Ottawa was beautiful in the summertime. The entire town was green. Trees were everywhere and flowers lined window boxes on the street. The bright colourful tulips were everywhere. It was still morning so the intense heat of the day had not yet set in. The air was sweet and dewy and clear and fresh with just a hint of coolness.

Sharon broke into run. She kept running for a long time. She ran like she was trying to outrun herself. She ran until all of her energy left her and then she slowly walked home. By the time she arrived home, she knew what she had to do. This was going to be the toughest day of her life.

That evening, Mike came over to Sharon's right after work. He had been concerned about her since she had disappeared and felt that something wasn't right. He just wanted to hold her and comfort her.

When he walked into her apartment, he noticed that she was sitting on the sofa staring into thin air. She looked very stressed. Her eyes were red and her lower lip trembled. The way she looked scared him.

"Sharon, is everything alright?" he asked her.

"Sit down Mike. I need to talk to you."

Her tone made him realize that this was serious.

"Mike, I need to tell you something very difficult. I did not spend the night with Angela. I spent it with Todd who is in my journalism class. I had sex with him, Mike."

Mike felt as if someone had punched him in the stomach. He just sat and stared at her.

"That isn't all Mike. I decided not to tell you. I thought that it would be better for our relationship. Then I realized that I wanted to sleep with Todd. It wasn't a mistake. I am only 22 years old. I am not ready for the commitment that you want. I'm sorry Mike but I have to break off our engagement."

Mike sat stunned on the sofa. Sharon walked over to him and placed her engagement ring in his hand.

"I am so sorry," she said. "I really do love you. If we had met when I was older and more mature, everything would be different. I still need to go out and enjoy my life. I am not ready for what you want."

Tears were streaming down her face. She watched Mike walk out the door looking as if he had lost everything. She knew that she had done the right thing but it didn't feel that way. He was a wonderful man and she had wounded him so deeply. How would she deal with it?

She decided that she needed to find another apartment. Running into Mike all the time would be a disaster for them both. The next day she would search. Right now she just wanted to lie down. She went to bed and cried herself to sleep.

Sharon woke to the phone ringing. She really did not want to speak to anyone. Thankfully, it was Mimi. It was almost like Mimi knew when something was wrong. Sharon had often felt that there was a psychic connection between the two of them since they were children.

"Hi pipsqueak," Mimi chirped in a happy voice.

"Oh Mimi," Sharon whimpered and started to cry.

"What's wrong? What happened?"

"Oh Mimi, I can't believe what I did. I was angry at Mike and I had sex with someone else. Then I told Mike and I broke up with him. I am not ready to get married. I am not ready for anything. I feel so terrible. Mike looked like I punched him in the face. I still love him. I don't know what to do."

"Come to Montreal to visit us. Jennie and I both want to see you. The extra bedroom is waiting for you. Don't even think about it. Pack your bags and leave."

"I don't know if I can do it," Sharon sobbed.

"Don't think about it. Just come right now."

"Okay," Sharon sobbed.

They hung up and Sharon went to pack her suitcase. In ten minutes she was out the door and on her way on the familiar highway. The summer day was beautiful. Even though it was late afternoon, the sun was bright and warm. Sharon rolled her window down and hummed as she drove. As she made her way to Montreal, she started to feel slightly better.

By the time she arrived at Mimi's door, three hours later, she was calm. She rang the bell and in an instant, Mimi was at the door with Jennie walking beside her. They both gave Sharon hug after hug and she felt so much better.

Mimi had made dinner and waited for Sharon. They sat at the kitchen table and ate some meatloaf, mashed potatoes and carrots. Jennie sat in her highchair eating and getting as much food on herself as in her body.

"This is delicious, Mimi. When did you learn to cook so well?"

"When I got married. Now I have to cook well for my little princess."

They both laughed as they looked at Jennie examining a carrot before she smashed it against the highchair tray.

Both sisters talked easily as they ate. After dinner, Mimi went to bathe Jennie and put her to bed. While she did this, Sharon sat on the sofa and relaxed. She still felt so horrible about what she had done to Mike. He deserved so much better.

Mimi returned and sat down in the wing back chair across from Sharon.

"Are you feeling better?" she asked Sharon.

"Yes, much better."

"Do you want to discuss it?"

"Not tonight. I am exhausted. What time do you go to work in the morning?"

"Sharon, it is August 5. I don't teach in the summer. Go to bed. We can talk in the morning."

Mimi came over to Sharon and gave her a hug and kiss.

"Good night pipsqueak," she told her younger sister who frankly looked worse for the wear.

Sharon went to the bedroom and brought her suitcase with her. She hadn't even unpacked yet. She did not bother to brush her teeth or even unpack. A sudden exhaustion came over her borne of her stress and sadness. She stripped down to her underwear and crawled under the covers. Within seconds, she was sleeping soundly.

Mimi went past Sharon's room to check on her and quietly opened the door. She saw her baby sister sleeping on her back and snoring soundly. She hoped she could help her. Sharon had done so much for her. She tucked the covers over Sharon's shoulders and opened the window so some air could come into the stuffy room.

Then she went to finally tuck herself in bed. Tomorrow would be a high energy day for her. She needed some deep sleep herself. She checked on Jennie on her way to bed and finally ended her own day.

CHAPTER 60

Mike was more angry than he had ever been. He still loved Sharon and still wanted to marry her despite the pain. He didn't feel that he could live without her. He had been stewing all day. At work, he had been distracted. When he finally arrived home, he didn't know if he should go to see Sharon or not. His pain was largely because she had ended their relationship. He was sure that they could get through this but she had obviously not felt the same way. He decided to leave her alone for now.

As he sat on his sofa drinking a beer, there was a pounding on his door. He was sure that it was Sharon having come to her senses. He ran to the door to answer it and there was a tall strange man standing outside.

"Excuse me, are you the superintendent of this building?"

"We have no apartments for rent at this time."

"I'm not looking for an apartment. I am looking for my classmate at university. Her name is Sharon Miller. I was told that she lives in this building. Would you please direct me to her apartment?"

So this was the man she had spent the night with. Mike wanted to smash his face in but he controlled himself.

"There is no one here by that name," he told Todd whose face instantly fell.

"Thanks for your trouble," Todd told him and walked away.

This made Mike even more angry. This man wanted to see Sharon again. This was not going to happen. Mike was not used to anger and this was threatening to destroy him.

Without thinking, he went to his basement workshop. There

stood the cradle that he had been building for Sharon. He took an axe and started chopping it to shreds. When he was finished, there was just a heap of shredded wood on the floor and he realized that he was crying. This had not had the cleansing effect that he had hoped for. He felt horrible that he had destroyed it. He also felt horrible that he had let Sharon end their relationship. He needed to forgive her and move on with their wedding plans but he wondered if she even wanted to marry him. She had been so unsure at first.

He would find her and talk to her. There had to be some type of solution. He went to her apartment and knocked on the door. There was no answer. Sharon was in Montreal visiting Mimi. Mike looked for her car outside and it wasn't there. He wondered if she had gone to see her sister. He knew Sharon very well and understood the closeness between her and Mimi. He somehow felt as if the two of them were twins. They could practically read each other's minds. He hoped that Sharon had gone to see Mimi. It would help her calm down and see that their relationship was still worth it, at least he hoped so.

CHAPTER 61. SHARON

I am the worst person in the world. I have a man who loves and treats me like a god. So what do I do? I go out and have sex with someone else. I don't even particularly like Todd. He was just available and I used him. I admit that I was terrified about how serious things were with Mike. So I went and ruined it. I don't blame him if he never wants to have anything to do with me again.

I don't know if this was a good thing. I am not ready to get married. I have so much to do. I feel like my dreams are always being put on hold. I spent so much time not knowing what I wanted and then I was finally on the right path. Then Mimi got sick and I couldn't possibly desert her and Jennie.

I am glad to be in Montreal with them right now. I can pretend my life is fine. Perhaps, if I pretend enough, it will actually be fine. Who am I kidding? I am a slut. Once upon a time, I would have had to wear a red letter on my shirt. Maybe I should still have to do this.

Still, there is something wonderful and therapeutic about spending time with my sister and niece. I forget myself and my stupid problems when I am with them. I focus on them rather than myself. This is always a good thing because my life is a disaster.

CHAPTER 62

Sharon and Mimi and Jennie were out at the park. Sharon had bought ice cream cones for everyone and they sat on a park bench eating them: Strawberry for Sharon, chocolate for Mimi and Neapolitan for Jennie. Jennie was getting ice cream all over herself. Mimi tried to wipe it off and spilled some on herself. Sharon giggled at them until she too spilled ice cream on her shirt.

The three of them were having a wonderful time. Sharon had made Mimi promise not to tell their parents that she was in town. Mimi had convinced Sharon to stay for a while. Mimi was not going back to work for several weeks and university was not starting yet.

"Let's have a vacation at my house," she told Sharon.

"What a great idea."

So every day, the three of them went out and had so much fun. One day it was the Granby Zoo. The next day it was the botanical gardens. Today they were in a city park spilling ice cream on themselves and laughing. Mimi and Sharon took turns pushing Jennie on the baby swings and then they went back to the house. After everyone was cleaned up, Jennie had a nap and Sharon and Mimi decided to make dinner.

"These last few days have been wonderful. I don't want to go back to Ottawa."

"Ottawa is your home now. You just don't want to face Mike."

"That's true but I am also having such a wonderful time."

"Mike phoned the other day," Mimi told her.

"Why didn't you tell me?"

"He said that he just wanted to check to see if you were okay. He suspected that you were here and he was concerned about you. That guy loves you so much. You're so lucky to have such a wonderful man."

"I know Mimi but I am just not sure what to do."

"He said he would like to speak to you but to take your time. He can wait, he said."

"That's good. I am not ready to speak to him yet."

"What do you want to have for dinner tonight?"

"I want to take you and Jennie out for pizza tonight. I don't think we got grubby enough this afternoon."

"It's a deal."

They both started to laugh.

As the week progressed, Sharon became calmer. She still did not know how to get past what she had done or deal with Mike but she was able to think. The week might have continued to go well if it wasn't for a surprise visit.

Mimi heard the doorbell ringing the next morning. She went to the door and there was Sylvia standing there with a large shopping bag in her hand.

"Hi Mimi. I'm sorry that I didn't call before I came over. I was shopping and I saw the most adorable dresses for Jennie."

"Come in mom."

Normally she would be happy for a visit from her mother but Sharon was here and she had sworn Mimi to silence.

Just then Sharon and Jennie came bouncing into the room.

"Hi mom," Sharon said.

"When did you arrive?" Sylvia asked her, looking suspicious.

"Just yesterday, mom. I was going to phone you this morning."

“Is there a special reason for this visit?”

“No mom. I just want to see my sister and niece and family.”

“Well, I am delighted to see you,” Sylvia said and gave Sharon a hug and kiss.

Sylvia had brought over some chocolate cake and everyone sat around the kitchen table eating it while Mimi brewed some coffee.

“How’s Mike?” Sylvia asked Sharon.

“He is just fine. He is very busy at work but things are going well.”

She hated to lie but she could not stand the interrogation that would ensue if she told the truth.

“When are all of you coming for dinner?” Sylvia asked.

“How about Sunday?” Mimi asked.

“Would you like to have a barbecue?”

“Yes, grandma!” Jennie blurted out.

“I guess it is settled then,” Sylvia said.

So Sunday it would be. Sylvia was already excited about what she would make for them.

CHAPTER 63. SHARON

I decided to visit Penny while I was in Montreal. I had really enjoyed meeting her and her daughter. Penny was so sweet and friendly. I felt terrible that I had called her "the whore" when I used to speak to Mimi. Yes, it was wrong of her to sleep with David but she was a victim as much as Mimi was. She had fallen in love with the wrong man and paid dearly for it.

I also really liked her daughter Linda. She was so cute and sweet. She and Jennie were just a few months apart in age. Penny must have gotten pregnant just after Mimi did. I wanted to tell Mimi about my new relationship with Penny but I wasn't sure how to approach it.

Then I decided to wait. Mimi had a lot on her plate already and she didn't need more. I didn't want to keep this a secret forever but I would for now.

"Hello, may I speak to Penny?"

"This is Penny. Hi Sharon, how are you?"

I was pleased that she remembered my voice.

"I am doing well," I lied.

"I am in Montreal for the rest of the week. Would you like to get together?"

"Yes, I would. I will be at work but we can find a time to get together."

I wanted to bring Jennie to meet Linda but decided that the time was not right. Besides, what would I tell Mimi?

We decided to meet at a park the next day.

"Where are you off to pipsqueak?"

"I am going to visit my friend Jackie."

"Have a good time. Give her my regards."

"I will."

I felt like a fugitive as I sneaked to the park to meet Penny and Linda.

The day was a glorious perfect mix of sun and breeze. I spotted them right away by the swings. Penny was pushing Linda on a baby swing and Linda was giggling.

"Hi Penny."

"Good to see you Sharon."

Penny looked happy and relaxed. She had lost some weight since I had seen her last.

"You look terrific."

"I have been working out."

"When do you find the time?"

"I am staying with my friend Mary as you know. She loves to look after Linda when I go to the gym."

"That's not all. You have a glow about you."

"Well, I started seeing someone. Mary introduced me to her nephew Tim. He is wonderful and he adores Linda."

"I am so happy for you."

"How are things going with your engagement?"

"We are going through a rough spot but we will get through it."

I wondered if this was true.

We sat on a bench with Linda and ate some apple and carrot slices that Penny had packed. I was so comfortable with her. I was so glad that I was getting to know her.

CHAPTER 64

Mimi was preparing for a very busy week. Tomorrow she was going back to work. Summer had been wonderful and her recent visit with Sharon had been a pleasant surprise. Now Sharon had returned to Ottawa and summer vacation was over. Mimi did not want to return to work. She loved teaching but it was hard to leave Jennie for entire days. Jennie loved the day care centre and her friends there but Mimi felt guilty about leaving her daughter. She assured herself that in a few years Jennie would be in school full time and it wouldn't be so bad.

Tomorrow Mimi would drop Jennie off at day care and go into school. She would spend the day in meetings with the administration of the school and do some lesson preparation. In a week she would be teaching again but for now she had to put up with all of this. It was her least favourite part of teaching. She resented going to work a week early so she could go to useless meetings and work on lesson preparation that she had already done.

She did look forward to seeing some of her colleagues again and for this she was grateful. She decided that she and Jennie would have a wonderful Sunday together so the next day she would be ready to work. She planned a picnic in the park for them. Afterwards, they would go out for ice cream together. This would be the perfect last day of summer vacation.

However, things did not go as planned. Just as Mimi was preparing the sandwiches for the picnic, her doorbell rang. She went to the peephole and saw David standing outside her door. For a moment, she wondered if it was his day with Jennie. So much had happened recently that she was confused. Then she realized that today was most definitely her time with her daughter and David was in her way.

She was tempted to just not answer the door but Jennie was singing loudly and David had probably heard her. So she opened the door to him and he stood there with a bouquet of roses in his hands.

“Hello David,” she said. She wondered why he would bring flowers. She was always suspicious of his motives.

“These are for you Mimi,” he said and handed her the flowers.

“Why, David?”

“May I come in?”

Jennie spied her father and ran into his arms. Mimi had to let him in now.

“Come in David. Thanks for the flowers.”

She did not want a long visit with him. She did not offer him coffee or a seat. He sat down on the sofa with Jennie still in his arms. He was tickling her and she was laughing with glee.

“Why are you here David?” Mimi asked him impatiently. She was in no mood for small talk.

“I have been offered a job as head of the emergency department in a hospital in Toronto. I don’t know what to do.”

“Will you take the job?”

“I don’t know. I don’t want to leave Jennie. I was hoping you could help.”

“You can still come to see her in Montreal when you have time off.”

“It won’t be the same.”

Mimi had to admit that David looked more like a lost little boy than the cocky arrogant man he had recently become.

“I still love you Mimi. I would like you and Jennie to come to Toronto with me. We could start over in a new place. It would be a new beginning for all of us."

"You have got to be kidding. I would not start over with you in any location. I can't believe that you are even thinking this. After all the times you hurt me, I will never trust you again. Not to mention what you did to Penny. You got her pregnant and left her."

He winced but decided to continue his plea.

"Please think about it Mimi. You wouldn't have to work. I could support us all. We could be so happy together."

She was furious.

"Please leave now David."

"But Mimi..."

"Get out!"

David put Jennie down on the sofa and walked slowly out the front door. Mimi slammed the door as soon as he left.

"Where da go?" Jennie asked her.

Mimi did not want to alarm her baby but she was having trouble calming down. She breathed deeply then answered.

"He had to go home. Let's go for our picnic."

She packed up the food and put Jennie in her stroller. Off to the park they went. As she walked, Mimi started to calm down. She was not going to let David ruin her last day of vacation. As they walked to the park, Mimi was so preoccupied with David's unexpected visit that she hardly noticed the warm breeze and the surrounding greenery. She hardly noticed the light changing. She stepped into the way of a fast-moving car. The stroller which was just in front missed the impact but Mimi was hit and sent flying into the air. She felt herself flying as if in slow motion then a searing pain as she hit the ground. Then blackness.

CHAPTER 65

Sharon had just returned from Montreal. After unpacking, she decided that it was time to talk to Mike. She had decided to discuss their relationship. They were sitting face to face on her sofa and Mike was asking her to give them a second chance. This struck Sharon as strange because she had been the one to cheat on him.

"I still love you," Mike told her. "I would do anything to make our relationship work."

Sharon said, "I still love you too. I am so sorry for what I did."

Mike held her as she started to cry. They were interrupted by the telephone ringing.

"I wonder who that could be," Sharon said.

She answered the phone to her father's shaky voice.

"Hi Sharon."

She could immediately sense that something was wrong.

"What happened dad?"

"Mimi is in the hospital. She was hit by a car when she was out with Jennie. Jennie is fine. The car missed her. Mimi is in critical condition. Please come to Montreal right away."

Sharon felt like she was going to be sick. Her head started spinning and she was nauseated. Her heart was pounding out of control.

"Okay dad, I'm on my way."

Mike looked worried.

She blurted out, "Mimi was hit by a car. She is not doing well. I have to go to Montreal right now!"

"You are in no shape to drive. I will take you. Let's leave now."

Mike grabbed his and Sharon's jackets and they ran to his car. In a minute, they were on their way to Montreal.

As they were driving, Mike remembered their last emergency trip to Montreal. Everything had turned out so well at the time. Maybe everything would be fine this time too. He certainly hoped so. He quite liked Mimi and he knew that losing her would completely destroy Sharon. He tried not to dwell on a negative outcome.

He looked over at Sharon. She was sitting quietly in the passenger seat with tears rolling down her face. He wanted to say something that would make her feel better but there were no words that could make a difference.

So, he kept his eyes on the road and turned up the heat in the car. When Sharon became stressed, she would always be freezing. He had reached out to hold her hand and it had felt like an ice cube.

Sharon's mind was a jumble of thoughts. She had seen Mimi yesterday. They were both laughing and having such a wonderful time. How could this have happened? Mimi was always so careful especially because of Jennie. How could she have been hit by a car? Maybe if she had stayed in Montreal with Mimi this would not have happened.

Sharon fell into an uneasy sleep full of nightmares. She woke up confused and asked Mike where they were.

"We are on our way to Montreal. Mimi was hit by a car. We are going to the hospital to see her."

"Please pull over Mike."

Mike pulled on to a shoulder on the road. Sharon stepped out and threw up in the ditch. She heaved again and again until she was empty. Mike looked at her and didn't know what to do. He put his arm around her and asked her if she would like to go back to the car.

"Yes, we need to get to Montreal, Mike."

She looked like a terrified child. Mike gently put her in the seat and put the seat belt around her. He put her jacket on her knees to help warm her and they were on their way again. Mike estimated that they should be there soon.

Of course, they wound up in traffic on the Champlain Bridge and were delayed an extra half hour. They arrived in Montreal at 11:00 pm. Sharon felt as if she would lose her mind. Finally they pulled into the hospital parking lot. Mike let Sharon out at the emergency entrance and went to find parking.

Sharon asked a nurse about Mimi and was directed to another wing. When Sharon arrived there, she saw her parents sitting in the waiting room. They both looked as if they had aged 20 years. They were haggard and crumpled like ancient people. Sylvia was crying and Martin was holding her. He had a hollow expression on his face like he had been drained of life.

Sharon ran up to them.

"What happened?" she asked them.

"How is Mimi?"

"Not good." Martin told her. "She has extensive injuries. She has some internal bleeding and her skull is fractured. She is holding on but we are not sure if she will make it."

Sharon felt the world spinning. Just then, Mike came into the room and caught her in his arms before she could fall.

Mike sat Sharon down on a chair. Martin repeated what he had told Sharon.

"How is Jennie?" Mike asked.

"We think she is fine. She is being held for observation but she appears to have no injuries."

Mike asked, "Has anyone phoned David?"

"No, we never thought of it," Sylvia answered.

"I will phone him for you," Mike said.

Mike went to the pay phone and dialed David's home number. The answering machine message said that David was not available. Mike left a message saying that Mimi and Jennie had been hurt in an accident and David should come to the hospital. He had no love for David but felt that David deserved to know. Jennie was his daughter and Mimi had once been his wife.

David was putting on his coat to drive to the hospital for an overnight shift when Mike left the message. He was in the waiting room in a very short time asking what had happened. He went to sit with Jennie and the others sat in the waiting room trying not to think about the worst case scenario. David was shaken to the core. He had a very bad memory of his encounter with Mimi earlier. He had hoped that she would somehow see the light and move to Toronto with Jennie to be with him.

David played with his daughter in her hospital room. The doctor on duty assured him that Jennie was just fine. The car had completely missed her stroller. They were keeping her in this hospital room just to make sure that she was fine.

The doctor on duty told David that he could take Jennie home with him. He said he would and went to cancel his rounds.

Then he went to the waiting room where Sylvia, Martin, Sharon, and Mike sat looking frightened and pale.

"Is there any news about Mimi?" he asked them.

"Nothing," Martin said.

He was sipping on a cup of coffee and suddenly looked old and haggard.

"I am going to take Jennie home with me. The doctors say that she is unhurt. It is better for her to be home than in this hospital."

David was surprised that no one argued with him.

Martin said, "Take good care of her."

David went back to Jennie's room and scooped her up in his arms.

"Where ma?" she asked him as they were leaving.

"Ma is at the doctor's. You are coming home with me. We can have pizza and play."

Jennie smiled at him and his heart melted. As they were driving back to his apartment, David felt ill at ease. He was worried about Mimi. He knew her injuries were severe and he prayed that she would be fine. She and Jennie had been the best things in his life. He hoped that Mimi would make a full recovery and would be fighting with him again in no time.

He wondered what would happen if Mimi didn't survive. He forced that thought out of his mind as he drove home with his precious daughter. He fed Jennie dinner and put her to bed after reading her a story. Then he phoned the hospital to see how Mimi was doing.

The doctor on duty told him, "She is hanging on but it is all touch and go from here. She has so many serious injuries that it is unsure what will happen."

"Thanks for the update," David told him. He hung up the phone and noticed that he had an answering machine message. The red light was blinking.

It was a message from Toronto asking him whether he was going to accept the job. It was the furthest thing from his mind. He made himself a grilled cheese sandwich and went to bed. He tossed and turned all night with worry about Mimi and her precarious state.

Sharon had gone to see Mimi in her room. She had been allowed in for just a short time. She had stared in shock at her sister. She couldn't believe that the vital woman she had seen just a day ago had been reduced to a motionless body covered with bandages. Mimi was so white that she looked like all of her blood had drained out of her body.

Sharon gently squeezed Mimi's hand. She couldn't speak. She knew she would start to cry.

She said, "I love you," and left.

She went back to the waiting room. A doctor appeared and told them to go home. He said that there had been no change in Mimi's condition for several hours and this was a good sign.

They should all go home and get some rest. Sharon decided that she and Mike would go to Mimi's house to sleep. She hugged her parents goodbye and she and Mike drove back to Mimi's house. It was filled with warmth and happiness. Mimi had made it so wonderful for her daughter. She looked at Jennie's art all over the fridge and wanted to cry again. Now what would happen, Sharon wondered.

She and Mike went into the guest room and fell asleep next to each other on the bed. They didn't even bother to take off their clothes or take the covers off the bed. They lay side by side in the usual fashion with Mike's arm wrapped around her shoulder and so exhausted that they were both asleep before they had turned out the lights.

Sharon woke in a confused state momentarily unsure of where she was. The phone was ringing and she wasn't sure if she could get to it in time. Mike bolted out of bed and rushed to answer the phone.

He shortly came back to bed and told her that it was someone trying to sell them a newspaper subscription. Sharon was relieved. She had been sure that t was bad news about Mimi. She got up slowly and dialed her parents' home number. There was no answer and Sharon again wondered what to do.

She phoned the hospital and asked for Doctor Martin Miller. Her father was on the phone right away.

"How is Mimi doing?" she asked him.

"She is the same as she was yesterday. She has not regained consciousness yet but she is holding her own."

He sounded like his voice would crack.

"I will be at the hospital right away, dad."

"There is no hurry. Have breakfast and take a shower first. You have plenty of time to spend here."

"Okay dad, I love you."

"I love you too, Sharon. Bye." and he hung up.

Mike had already brewed some coffee and was standing and watching her.

"How is Mimi?" he asked her.

"The same," she told him. She walked up to him and started to cry. He held her until she stopped.

"Take a shower and I'll make breakfast" he told her.

She showered and realized she hadn't brought any clothes with her. So she put on yesterday's clothes again. When she came out, Mike was stirring oatmeal. A cup of coffee stood waiting for her on the kitchen table.

Mike served her and they ate in silence. Sharon was so preoccupied with Mimi that she knew she would cry again if she tried to talk.

Mike cleared the dishes.

"Let's go back to the hospital," he said.

"You haven't showered yet."

"It can wait until later."

So they went back to the hospital. Everything was much the same but Sylvia looked worse than she had the day before. Her cheeks were hollow and she had dark circles under her eyes. She was staring into space as if she was in a trance.

Martin was sitting beside her drinking a coffee.

"Everything is exactly the same. I wish she would regain consciousness."

So they sat down and went back to waiting. Sharon offered Sylvia some food but Sylvia just shook her head. Sharon knew that this was her mother's protective mechanism and that she should leave things alone.

She heard Mike on the pay phone talking to his boss at work and explaining what had happened. She hoped this would not cause problems for him. He was always coming to her rescue. She did not deserve him.

Not much happened the following day. Mimi was just as she was before. Martin was concerned but he didn't share it with the family. Mimi should have woken up by now. Her injuries were all stable. She had received a huge crack on the head when it hit the pavement. The x-rays did not show any more damage but she still wasn't waking up. Martin knew that it was unlikely that she would ever wake up if she did not do so soon but he was hesitant to say anything.

He looked at the little group assembled in the waiting room. Sylvia looked so drawn that she seemed to have aged 20 years. Sharon looked exhausted and had a sadness to her that never seemed to lift. Sharon had convinced Mike to return to Ottawa later that day. He had been holding the group together and bringing them food and coffee. His was the only smile in the room.

Martin himself felt wretched. He had not showered or shaved in days. He had hardly slept at night. He was haunted by the idea that his beautiful daughter might not wake up. So everyone sat and played the waiting game.

Later that afternoon, their waiting game ended. Doctor Katz came to the waiting room to talk to them. They were all sitting together trying to have a conversation. Sharon sat with Martin who had his arm around Sylvia. They all looked and felt lost and exhausted.

As soon as Martin saw Doctor Katz, he knew that it had to be bad news. Dr Katz looked sad and resigned. Martin had seen this look before.

Everyone looked up at Dr. Katz.

"I'm sorry," he said, "but Mimi has died. She had a massive hemorrhage and there was nothing we could do to save her."

Sylvia felt like she was going to die. The world seemed to explode around her. Sharon was so shocked that she felt the earth moving. Martin was crying loudly. Sharon had never seen him cry before. They all sat in shock and disbelief. It was impossible to everyone that Mimi was gone.

"You can come to see her to say goodbye," Dr Katz told them.

They all walked into Mimi's room. She lay there looking just like herself but completely white and translucent. Sylvia went and kissed her. Then Martin and Sharon did the same. They all walked back to the waiting room, each one in their own private hell.

"Is there anything I can do?" Dr Katz asked them.

"You should phone David and let him know," Sharon told him.

At that moment, David was reading a book to Jennie who was curled up on his lap. He was enjoying all of this time with his daughter.

When he heard the phone ring, David had a bad feeling.

"Hi this is Dr Katz. I am phoning to let you know that Mimi died this afternoon." David felt like he had been kicked in the head. He looked at his beautiful young daughter and realized that she was now motherless. Mimi would never see Jennie grow up and become a young woman. She would never see the important dates of her daughter's life. He felt so sad and helpless. He sat on the sofa crying while cuddling Jennie. Well, he would have to step up and be both a mother and a father to Jennie. At that moment he realized that he would now have complete custody of his child. There would be no more asking anyone if he could see her. He could even take the job in Toronto and take Jennie with him. He would decide later. Right now he was too steeped in grief to know what he should do.

CHAPTER 66

Sharon was still staying at Mimi's house two day later when the funeral took place. David was still with Jennie. He had taken some time off work to be with her and help her through what was happening When she asked for Mimi, he did not know what to do. He told her that her mommy had gone away. How does a father explain death to his two-year-old?

Sylvia had completely shut down. She was so devoured by her grief that she did not know what was happening around her. Martin had to get her out of bed in the morning and make sure that she dressed. He had to feed her as she was not interested in any food. He had to make the funeral arrangements for his wonderful young daughter. He felt lost himself but he had to be strong for the rest of his family.

Sharon was in a haze. She was filled with disbelief and guilt. She felt that if she hadn't left Montreal this would not have happened. Mimi's death was her fault. None of them knew that Mimi had been very upset because of David's visit. As a result she was so preoccupied that she was not careful. If anyone was to blame it was David but he felt no guilt. He felt a deep sadness for himself and his daughter who would grow up with only one parent.

The funeral took place on a gloomy grey Tuesday. It was raining and it matched the mood of complete sadness and resignation of everyone who attended. Sharon looked around the room of the funeral chapel and saw hundreds of people. Mimi's students and their families were there. She swallowed as she realized how deeply her sister was loved by so many people. This would not bring her back. Nothing would bring her back.

Just then, David walked in holding Jennie's hand and they walked to the front row to sit with the family. Sylvia wanted to yell at David that he was no longer family but she was too overcome to say anything.

The rabbi said a beautiful eulogy for Mimi and then the immediate family went to the cemetery for the burial. Sylvia collapsed in Martin's arms as her daughter was being lowered into the ground. Sharon wanted to crawl in beside her sister who had been the most important person in her life.

That evening, there was the start of a seven-day shiva at Sylvia and Martin's house. Sharon stayed in Montreal. She was missing so much school but she didn't care anymore. People had sent all types of food for the shiva. There were hot trays of appetizers, casseroles, salads, sandwiches, and a multitude of desserts. Relatives and friends came to pay their respects to the family. Jennie ran around greeting everyone not really aware of what had just happened. Sylvia sat and watched her and wondered what would happen to her. She knew that David would get her but she didn't feel that this was right. She wondered if she and Martin could possibly get custody of Jennie. David might even agree. A young child would get in the way of his womanizing.

She looked at David who appeared to be quite sad. He was chatting with some cousins and looked wretched. Sylvia had no doubt that David had really loved Mimi but he had destroyed that love and she could never forgive him. She looked for Sharon who was sitting alone in a chair looking completely lost. It was as if the vital youthful side of her had flown away and all that was left was a shell. Sharon had not eaten in days and she looked thin and wan. There were dark circles under her eyes. Sylvia felt a pang of grief for her younger child then for herself. She didn't know how any of them would survive without Mimi to love. She ached so much that her own body was just a well of pain. She didn't think that she would ever emerge from the well. Instead she would drown in her grief.

That evening, Jennie went to stay with her grandparents. David had to go back to work the next day. Sylvia and Martin loved Jennie. Her visit with them was giving them a reason to go on living.

After Jennie was fed and tucked into bed, Sylvia asked Martin, "Where will Jennie live?"

"With David."

"He doesn't deserve her! Should we try to get custody?"

"I don't think we would be able to. David is her father. He is a good father to her. We would have no grounds."

"What about his disgusting behaviour to women?"

"These are all just rumours. He has the right to have custody of his daughter. The problem is that he might take her away."

Sylvia gasped. "What do you mean?" she asked.

"Well, there is a rumour that David has a job offer in Toronto. If he accepts it, he will take Jennie there with him."

"We have to stop him, Martin. Jennie is all that we have left of Mimi now."

"We can't do anything to stop him if he decides to take the position. Let's just hope that he says no."

Sylvia was sick with grief as well as exhausted. Martin had given her a tranquilizer to help her sleep but she was still unable to drift into sleep. She kept wondering how she could possibly survive with the loss of her daughter and granddaughter.

Meanwhile, Martin was experiencing his own personal hell. Thoughts kept swirling around in his mind. Why had he been unable to save his own daughter? How would he survive without Mimi's smile? How would he survive at all? He took a sedative but he still could not sleep. He wondered if he would ever sleep again.

David was also in a quandary. He felt horrible about Mimi's death. He wanted to accept the job in Toronto so desperately. His work in Montreal was not making him happy. He felt like an outcast at the hospital. No one wanted to have anything to do with him. He could not get any of the nurses to even smile at him. He desperately needed a fresh start.

He could have this fresh start with his daughter but Jennie might find it difficult to adjust. She had to learn how to live without her mother and now he would be taking her to an entirely new place with strangers. Who would take care of her while he was at work? He had the money to hire a nanny but he did not feel comfortable about it. He wanted his daughter to have a real mother.

He was also having trouble sleeping with the confusion and chaos. He knew that he soon had to give an answer about his new job but he still did not know what the answer should be. He felt that staying in Montreal or moving to Toronto were both fraught with difficulties.

Then he started thinking about Sharon. He had always found her very beautiful and sexy. She had grown into a mature and smart woman. She would do anything for Jennie. Was there some way that he could convince Sharon to help him? The seeds of an idea started taking shape in his mind. Sharon would be the key to resolving his problems. He was becoming more and more sure about this.

As for Sharon, she felt like she was drowning. She was still staying at Mimi's house. She was missing school and unwilling to talk to Mike about their relationship or even when she would return. She felt unable to move. She spent her days sleeping and waking up to the realization that she would never see Mimi again. She lost her appetite and wore the same clothes day after day. She refused to answer the phone. She knew it would either be Mike checking in on her or her parents asking her to come for dinner.

One morning when Sharon looked at herself in the mirror, the sight of the pale unkempt skeleton with the wild hair made her do a double take. She decided to take a shower and get dressed, although her desire was to go back to bed.

Instead of showering, she sat and cried. She cried for the loss of her sister and for her niece who would grow up without her loving mother. She cried for her parents who had lost their daughter. She cried for herself. She had lost her best friend. After exhausting herself crying, she went back to bed and fell into a deep sleep.

Sharon was woken up by the doorbell ringing. She was so groggy that she decided to just ignore it. But it would not stop. She eventually stumbled out of the bed and went to answer the door. She had expected maybe her parents but was shocked to see David standing there looking calm and collected. He had on a suit and she wondered what in the world was going on.

When David looked at Sharon, he almost changed his mind about what he was going to do. The bright and beautiful woman he knew had been replaced by a haggard pale woman with messy dirty hair and a haunted look.

Sharon was about to close the door in his face when he started to talk.

"How are you holding up?" he asked her looking quite sincere.

"How do you think?" she asked him with hatred burning in her eyes.

"I know you and Mimi were close and it must be very difficult for you. I hope the pain will subside over time."

Sharon stood staring at him through tears as he let himself in the door.

He walked to the kitchen and put the kettle on the stove. When he returned, Sharon was sitting in a crumpled little ball on the sofa. She looked like she had shrunk.

"I am making us a cup of tea," he said.

"What do you want David?"

She was aware that he always had a motive.

"I have an idea that will help us both," he told her.

"How could you possibly help me?"

"I have always liked and admired you. You are wonderful to Jennie and she adores you. It will be difficult for her to grow up without a mother. I am hoping you and I can raise her together."

"Do you mean that we would each have her part of the week? Don't you remember that I live in Ottawa?"

"No I mean that I would marry you. Together we can raise her and love her. I think that is what Mimi would have wanted."

Sharon stared at him as if he was insane. She didn't say anything and he chose that moment to go to the kitchen and make them each a cup of steaming tea.

When he returned, Sharon was still looking as if she was in shock. He put the mug of tea in front of her.

"Aren't you moving to Toronto?" she asked him.

This was going better than he had expected. He had believed that she would scream, hit him and throw him out.

"No. I think it is best for Jennie for me to stay here. She will have people she loves around her. What do you think Sharon?"

"Okay. I will marry you," she said.

Her voice was flat and devoid of emotion.

David was shocked. He didn't know whether he should hug her but he just decided to leave things alone for now.

"I will come back tomorrow and we can make some firm plans."

"Okay," she said.

When he left, she finished her tea and went back to bed for another long sleep, barely registering what had just happened.

Sharon woke up several hours later in a drugged haze. She couldn't believe the dream she had just had. David had asked her to marry him and she had said yes. Her dreams were becoming more and more bizarre. What would she dream next?

She decided that it was time to shower and dress. The hot water felt good as it beaded down her body. She washed her hair and stepped out of the shower. She looked terrible in the mirror. At least she now looked clean. She decided that she owed it to Mimi to make sure that Jennie was well. She had thought only of herself but that was over now. She had her niece to consider. How about her parents too? They had lost their daughter. Sharon had been so submerged in her own grief that no one else existed for her.

Now she would get back into her life. She looked at the answering machine. It was blinking wildly at her with its menacing little red light. She clicked on check messages and there were 10 messages for her. Three were from Mike. Four were from her parents. The other three were from the university. Mike and her parents had left loving messages asking her how she was. The university wanted to know when she was returning to school.

She made herself a coffee and wondered if she might be ready to return to Ottawa and to Mike and her studies. After a few slices of toast with jam, she realized that she was actually hungry. The wall clock read 8:45 pm. It was too late to do very much tonight but tomorrow morning she would start to get her life back on track. She was still devastated about Mimi's death. However, Mimi would be the first to tell her that lying in bed all day was a waste of a life.

She would also return the phone calls tomorrow. She wanted one more night of solitude until she reentered the world.

The next morning, Sharon woke up to the phone ringing. She struggled into a sitting position and said,

"Hello."

"Hi Sharon, it's David. I have Jennie with me and she would love to see her aunt. Would you like me to bring her over?"

Sharon smiled for the first time in weeks. She was always so happy to see Jennie.

"Sure, what time?"

"How about an hour from now. I will pick up some fresh bagels and we can talk about our plans. Bye Sharon."

She was really confused. What plans did she and David have? Did it have to do with Jennie? She honestly did not have a clue.

She took a quick shower and got dressed. She started the coffee brewing and before she knew it, the doorbell rang.

David was standing there with Jennie beside him. She immediately ran into Sharon's arms.

"Hi Auntie Shawan!" she yelled.

Sharon loved this little girl so much that is broke her in two.

David stood by the door holding a bag of warm fresh bagels. Sharon had to admit to herself that they smelled wonderful. He walked in and placed them on the table with a tub of cream cheese.

"Hi Sharon," he said. "I thought you might like some bagels."

"Thank you, David. I brewed some coffee. Would you like some?"

"Sure," he told her looking so happy. She wondered why.

The three of them sat at the table eating while Jennie got her bagel and cream cheese all over herself.

After they were finished, Jennie was tired and Sharon put her on her crib for a nap. She expected David to leave but he sat down on the sofa.

"We need to talk," he said.

"About what? I appreciate you bringing Jennie over. You can pick her up later this morning or she can stay here overnight. What else is there to discuss?"

"Us."

"What about us, David?"

"I asked you to marry me and be a mother to Jennie. You said yes."

Sharon felt the breath rush out of her. She sat down hard on the sofa.

"I don't remember any of this David."

"You did seem out of things at the time but the offer is still there. I want us to get married and raise Jennie together."

"Why?"

"Because we both love her and that would be the best arrangement for her."

"What about us? We don't love each other."

"I like you very much. I always have. I could grow to love you easily. I can't think of a better person to be with Jennie and with me."

Sharon was flabbergasted. She sat on the sofa wondering if this was all a bad dream.

She wondered if she could ever learn to even like him. All she could feel for him right now was hatred and mistrust.

"David, you like being with a lot of women. This is not what I want."

"I am ready to stop seeing all these women. I am serious about this marriage. I want it to work. I will be faithful to you."

"What about your move to Toronto?"

"I will not accept the job. I will stay here with you and Jennie."

"Okay," she said reluctantly, "I will marry you." All the while, she felt her spirits sinking lower and lower and her dreams floating away.

They talked for a long time. They decided that they would get married as soon as possible and move into David's apartment temporarily. Jennie was already settled there and this would be the best solution. Sharon would drop out of university and return to Montreal. David wanted her to continue her studies but they both decided that this would happen in the future.

After David left, Sharon realized that she had to tell Mike and her parents that she was marrying David. She knew that the responses to her news would not be very happy. First, she phoned her parents. Her father answered on the first ring.

"Hello."

"Hi dad, how are you and mom doing?"

"As well as can be expected but I am worried about your mother. She has stopped eating and she hardly says a word. I don't know how long she can go on like this."

Sharon felt a pang of guilt. She had been so preoccupied in her own sorrow that she had forgotten that her parents were mourning the loss of their daughter.

"How about if I come over to say hello?" she asked Martin.

"That would be great. It might even bring your mom out of her shell."

"I'll see you after lunch, dad."

Sharon could not eat another bite. The bagels had really filled her up and she was nervous.

When she arrived at her parents' house and came in the door, she was shocked by the mess. Sylvia was normally so fastidious. They were piles of newspapers, cards and take out containers all over the living room. A layer of dust coated every surface. Sylvia sat on the sofa in a bathrobe looking like she was in a daze. Her eyes were wide open and she stared straight ahead.

Martin had been sitting with his arm around her and he got up to hug Sharon.

"Hi dad, how about if I make us all a cup of coffee?"

"Good idea, Sharon. You know where everything is."

The kitchen was also in complete disarray but Sharon found some coffee cups and other supplies. She came back to the living room with three piping hot coffees and some chocolate chip cookies on a tray.

Martin stirred some sugar and cream into his coffee and made a coffee for Sylvia who just stared at it.

Sharon sipped on her coffee and looked at her mother. Sylvia had retreated into herself. It was as if her spirit was gone and only her body remained.

"Dad do you think that maybe mom needs to see a doctor?" she asked Martin.

"She has seen a doctor. He says she will slowly start to come back when the time is right."

Sharon walked over to her mother and squeezed her hand. It was limp and icy.

"Mom, do you want some coffee?"

No response.

"I have some news for you. David came over with Jennie today. He is taking very good care of her. He suggested that he and I should get married and raise Jennie together. We both agreed to it. I will be returning to Montreal and marrying David. We will stay in Montreal."

Her father looked shocked.

"What about Mike? What about your education? You can hardly stand to be in the same room as David. How will you marry him?"

"I think it is best for everyone."

"I will respect any decision you make but please think this one over."

"I did think it over and it is the right thing to do."

"Then you have my support. What do you think Sylvia?"

Sylvia did not utter a word. Tears started rolling down her face.

When Sharon left, her father walked her to the door. Her mom still had not said a word but the tears were still falling.

"I love you, dad."

“I love you too Sharon. Please think about your decision to marry David.”

Then she was off back to Mimi’s house. She thought about phoning Mike but she would have to do this in person no matter how much it hurt.

After talking to David and deciding on a wedding date, Sharon drove back to Ottawa. When she arrived, the first thing she did was go to the university and withdraw from all of her courses.

CHAPTER 67

Sharon went straight to her apartment and started sorting out her belongings. Aside from her plants and clothes, everything else would have to go. She phoned some charities and arranged pick up of her furniture.

Then she went down a floor and knocked on Mike's door. He answered right away. He looked so wonderful to her. He was so happy to see her that she could tell her wanted to hold her but was keeping his feelings to himself.

He was wearing pyjamas and she realized it was already evening.

"Hi Mike," she said rather quietly.

"Hi Sharon. It's great to have you back here. Do you want to come in?"

"Yes but only for a short while."

He looked so happy to see her that it was breaking her heart. She decided to get right to the point.

"I am here for just a few days. I am dropping out of university to move back to Montreal."

He looked sad but understanding.

"Your family must really need you right now."

"I am moving back to Montreal to marry David. He and I are going to raise Jennie together."

Mike looked like he'd been punched in the stomach. She expected screaming and anger but all he said was,

"You have to do what you think is right."

Then he shuffled her out of his apartment saying he was very tired.

When she left, he sat down on his bed and cried tears of anger and frustration. He still loved her but he knew that there was no swaying her. She had made up her mind and he would have to live with that.

Sharon went back to her apartment and started packing up whatever she wanted to take to Montreal.

The next morning, she slipped her tenancy notice under Mike's door along with instructions to let a charity in to remove her furniture. She mentioned that he could take what he wanted.

She left that morning to return to Montreal. She had decided the night before that it was definitely time to put her life in Ottawa behind her.

She drove in her T-shirt and jeans feeling the late summer breeze on her arms. She wondered if she would ever return to Ottawa or to her schooling. Somehow she doubted it. Her life would be different from what she had believed. The question was whether it would be a happy life. She knew that raising Jennie was the right thing to do but had she made a pact with the devil to do this? She pushed her fears aside and headed towards Montreal and her new life.

When she returned to Mimi's house, the red button on the answering machine was flashing. There were five messages. Three were from friends wanting to know how she was holding up. One was from her father asking her to make sure that she was doing the right thing. One was from David telling her that he wanted to make plans for their wedding.

Sharon phoned him and they arranged a wedding with a justice of the peace for the following week. The wedding was attended by Sharon, David, Jennie, Martin and Sylvia, and David's parents Lois and Saul. Jennie wore a lacy pink dress and looked sweet. Sharon had managed to find a pretty silk beige sheath dress in her closet. She was surprised that it was loose on her. Jennie was confused about why Auntie Shawan was marrying her father.

Afterwards they all went out to an Italian restaurant to celebrate and ordered a meal. Sharon picked at her Caesar salad and chicken Parmesan. She noticed that her mother still looked like a scarecrow but at least she was eating a little.

David was solicitous and loving toward Sharon. He made a toast to his beautiful bride. After this, Jennie went home with Sylvia and Martin for the night and Sharon and David went to a swanky hotel room for their wedding night.

Sharon was surprised when David immediately started kissing and undressing her. She was startled. Somehow she had not expected sex to be part of this. To her, it had been a business arrangement. Obviously, it was more than that to David. He had been looking forward all day to having sex with Sharon.

After he unbuttoned her blouse, his hands slipped down to the her skirt zipper. In a moment her skirt was on the floor. He smiled with excitement at her standing in her bra and panties. She felt very unready and awkward. She wanted to protest but not a word came out of her lips.

Soon, he was unhooking her bra and kissing her breasts hungrily. He carried her to the bed and started to devour her entire body. When he thrust himself inside her, he was insane with desire. Sharon felt like a victim. She felt no joy, only pain and disgust. She had really enjoyed sex in the past and this man on top of her was making her sick.

When it was over, David lay holding her and asked her if she was satisfied.

"Yes," she whispered and pretended to fall asleep.

The next morning they had sex again, ordered room service breakfast and went back to pick up Jennie. Later that day they moved into David's apartment. They were a family now.

CHAPTER 68

Did Sharon and David live happily ever after? Well, they lived in a mostly happy marriage. David had decided to grow up and stop cheating. He and Sharon sold Mimi's house and bought a large house quite close to her parents' house and had two more daughters. Sharon never went back to university to finish her journalism degree but she got a job working at a community newspaper when all three of the children were in school.

David was very much in love with Sharon. He felt lucky every day to have her as a wife. He adored their children and tried to be a good father to them. He was a caring and kind husband except in bed. He still wanted wild unruly sex and Sharon obliged him whenever she could. She sometimes wound up with bruises and bite marks on her body but she learned to live with it.

Despite David's strong objections, Sharon became close friends with Penny. Sharon and Penny see each other often. They bring Jennie and Linda and their other children and have a wonderful time together. Jennie and Linda especially adore each other. Penny is now happily married but she still does not want to see David. David does not want to see her either. He wants that phase of his life to be completely over.

This is a real bone of contention in Sharon and David's marriage. Sharon cannot believe that he does not want to see his own child. David wants to be with his family and does not want to see Penny or "Her child" ever again. This is a continuing issue in their relationship. Sharon thinks it will never be resolved.

Sylvia slowly became her previous self but never got over the death of Mimi. She still blames it on David. When Sharon and David come over with their brood, she is thrilled to see Sharon and the children but wishes David would disappear. She still hates him – even more than she did before. She is civil to him; after all, he is her son-in-law again, something she finds most distasteful. She wishes that someone would kill David but then Sharon and the children would be alone.

Martin is as happy as he can be considering he lost his daughter. He has retired and he and Sylvia travel a great deal. He still misses Mimi every day but has learned to live with it. He adores his three grandchildren and dotes on them shamelessly.

Mike was broken for a long time. He couldn't believe what had happened to him. He had done everything right and still lost the love of his life. After two years of sadness and mourning, he agreed to meet a friend of his sister's. Laura was a sweet and beautiful young widow with no children. They dated for a long time and eventually married and had two children together. Mike loves Laura but not in the same way he loved Sharon.

Mike became a successful lawyer. One day, while on his way to Montreal to do a deposition, he had just landed at Dorval Airport and was waiting for his luggage. He decided to go buy a coffee. As he was passing a boarding gate, he saw Sharon sitting on a bench waiting to board a flight. She looked as beautiful as ever and very pregnant. He realized at that moment that he still loved her as much as he ever had. The sight of her was enough to make him want to cry. She looked like she was about six months pregnant. Her wild hair was cut short and lay in ringlets around her face. She was holding hands with Jennie who was sitting next to her. Jennie had grown so much. She must have been six years old. She was the spitting image of Mimi with her long chestnut hair and slim small boned face. On the other side was David reading a newspaper. They looked like a happy and content little family.

He felt a jolt of anger surge through his body. How dare Sharon be married to David! How dare Sharon have sex with David! How dare Sharon be pregnant with David's baby! He wanted to rush over to them and start to scream. He wanted to hold Sharon and tell he that he still loved her and punch David in the head.

He then thought of his own wife Laura and decided not to do anything.

He knew Sharon very well. She was smiling at Jennie and looking at her with great love but the smile never reached her eyes. She was sitting in a slightly slouched position and looked sad. He wondered if he should say hello but decided instead to buy his coffee and get his suitcase. He walked away into the afternoon light.

Printed in Great Britain
by Amazon

43655101R00187